NURSE'S ORDERS

'Nappies, bottle, cream, powder, pins ... you are well prepared. I suppose you expect me to soothe your bottom after your caning?'

'Yes, please ... Nanny.'

'Nurse, please.'

'Please, Nurse Poppy. I am sore.'

She nodded, trying to hide a smile as she picked up the tube of cream. 'Over my lap, I think,' she said. 'Come along.'

Why not visit Penny's website at
www.pennybirch.com

By the same author:

THE INDIGNITIES OF ISABELLE
(*writing as Cruella*)
PENNY IN HARNESS
A TASTE OF AMBER
BAD PENNY
BRAT
IN FOR A PENNY
PLAYTHING
TIGHT WHITE COTTON
TIE AND TEASE
PENNY PIECES
TEMPER TANTRUMS
REGIME
DIRTY LAUNDRY
UNIFORM DOLL

NURSE'S ORDERS

Penny Birch

Nexus

This book is a work of fiction.
In real life, make sure you practise safe sex.

First published in 2002 by
Nexus
Thames Wharf Studios
Rainville Road
London W6 9HA

www.nexus-books.co.uk

Typeset by TW Typesetting, Plymouth, Devon

Printed and bound by Clays Ltd, St Ives PLC

ISBN 0 352 33739 7

One

'Time to show off the chocolate starfish, Gabby.'

'Yes, Monty.'

'Then spread those pretty arse-cheeks.'

I reached back to pull the cheeks of my bottom wide, stretching my anus open for his inspection. Beneath my hands, my skin felt sensitive and oddly hard, the result of a spanking. It was a sensation I was getting to know only too well.

Monty – fat Monty Hartle – had held me across his knee for the best part of half an hour, spanking me, groping me, fingering me. Twice he had brought me to orgasm with one fat, soft finger rubbing against my open sex, until I had come from simple friction. Four times he had reduced me to tears, applying mercilessly hard smacks to my bare bottom until I broke down. Between each session he had soothed me, nursing my spanked bottom and teasing my sex and anus until I had become excited again. Now, with my face streaked with tears, I kneeled on a chair, nude, my red bottom pushed out for his amusement, my cheeks held wide. He was masturbating, his erect cock slapping in his hand, his pig-like eyes fixed on my body, and specifically on my anus.

It was typical Monty – perverse. He knew I was anally virgin, just as he knew I hate to be spanked. So that was what he chose to come over – my beaten

1

bottom and the tight hole in which he was so eager to sink his penis. Deeper in his dirty mind, there would be his knowledge of my feelings, my memory of the pain of spanking and my frightened anticipation of the pain of sodomy. Had I enjoyed spanking and the penetration of my anus, he would have chosen something else.

He was getting frantic, close to orgasm, with his fat belly held up so that he could get at his cock properly. Ripples spread through his pasty flesh as he jerked at himself. His face was red, as red as the bloated cock-head that protruded from his hand, and nearly as shiny. It was an obscene sight, all of it, and the knowledge that I was naked and at his command made it a great deal more so.

'I'm coming,' he grunted. 'I'm coming over your dirty little arsehole, Gabrielle, I'm . . .'

He finished with a choking cry and sperm erupted from the tip of his cock into the air, to splash down on his taut ball-sack. More came, bubbling up over his hand and his belly, leaving blobs and trailers of thick, yellow-white fluid in such abundance that I knew he must have been saving it up for me.

The orgasm left him puffing, his chest heaving, until at length he recovered his breath and a happy grin spread slowly over his fat face. Not bothering to speak, he pointed to the mess on his belly and genitals. I got down on to my knees, crawling quickly to where he sat on the bed. Poking my tongue into a thick wad of sperm caught up in the hair of his balls, I began to clean him up.

He waited patiently, stroking my hair as I licked his sperm up, sucked his cock and kissed the smaller blobs from his belly and hand. I didn't swallow but let it collect in my mouth, until by the time he was clean I could show him the pool of slimy, salty sperm I had collected on my tongue.

'Good girl,' he said, patting my head. 'You may swallow.'

2

I obeyed, wincing as the slimy mess went down my throat and fighting back the urge to gag. He watched, grinning more broadly than ever at the expression of disgust that must have shown on my face.

'That's about fair, yeah?' he asked.

I nodded dumbly. It was fair. For hours I'd been his sex toy, submissive and obedient, allowing him to use my body as he pleased, save only for the sanctity of my anus. He had enjoyed me thoroughly and slowly. It had started with dinner, which I'd prepared and cooked with my skirt tucked up at the back to show my panties, into which he'd dropped a handful of baby new potatoes in a typically childish piece of erotic humour. I had been ordered to perform a striptease as the pasta cooked, which I managed well enough, despite his choice of heavy metal to dance to. I'd served naked, eaten my share from a dog bowl on the floor and washed up in just a pinny while he sipped beer and admired my bare bottom. Afterwards he had made me pose for him, adopting a series of exposed and lewd postures as he stroked his cock through his trousers. Once it was hard I'd been made to suck it, while he explained to me how much he was going to enjoy my coming punishment.

The exposure, the supposed humiliations, I had enjoyed, happy to go bare, with none of the embarrassment or sense of indignity he imagined. All my blushes and shame-filled looks had been for his benefit, a pose to allow him his pleasure in degrading women, right up to the moment he announced that I was to be spanked. After that, it was real. He'd seen the fear in my eyes and the sulky, doubtful look on my face, and laughed. Then had come the beating, to leave me in tears of pain that were in no way an act.

It had been worth it. Sometimes a girl has to compromise to get what she wants.

The price of my evening as a sex slave had been his acceptance of my own fantasy, not submission, but very definitely control. All afternoon he had been my nanny, undressing me when I arrived, bathing me, drying me, putting me in my nappy and the pink pyjamas I had brought. He had read me a story as I sucked my thumb, curled up on the bed and sinking slowly into that blissful sense of absolute freedom, complete relaxation that comes no other way. I'd wet myself when I needed it, neither forcing it nor holding back. It had felt so good I'd masturbated, then and there, on my back with one hand down my soggy nappy and Monty watching. As soon as I'd finished he had changed me, chiding me gently as he peeled off the wet nappy, wiping me, applying powder and cream to my sex and bottom, completely intimate but never sexual. At least, not overtly. By the time he'd finished with me and put me down for an afternoon nap he'd been fit to explode, the consequences of which I had just swallowed down.

'Going to stay over?' he asked. 'I'll put you in the other nappy for bed if you like?'

'Thank you, but I have a client at nine in the morning,' I answered. 'I had better be getting back.'

'Get up with me; you'll be there in plenty of time.'

'No, really, I need to consult my notes first.'

I didn't want to point out that sharing a bed with him was unbearable. Not only did his bulk leave me very little room, but he snored and could be guaranteed to wake me by prodding his erection in between my bottom-cheeks. I also did have a client coming to see me, one of my most difficult, Jocasta Warren, a woman who was able to find problems in her life under even the most felicitous of circumstances.

'I'll walk you to the station anyway,' he offered. 'Maybe even come in to Victoria with you. The trains can be pretty lonely this time of night. I'd drive you, only I'm sure I'm over the limit.'

'That would be considerate,' I answered as I began to sort myself out.

'I'd didn't say I'd do it for nothing,' he said.

'As you will,' I answered.

I left him to retrieve my clothes from the living room floor. Sex with Monty was frequently messy, and I'd packed fresh underwear and a change of clothes, just in case. My bag also contained the last of the three nappies I'd brought down, and the memory of what we had done put a smile on my face as I packed it away.

A brief shower, a little cream for my bottom, a touch of make-up for my face, my clothes, and I was ready. Whatever Monty might want, I was not going to get frozen stiff for him, and I put on thick tights under my skirt and a jumper – hardly elegant, but practical for a November night.

Monty was still in his bedroom, but dressed. As usual, he hadn't bothered to clean up properly, apparently content with the services of my tongue. I didn't mind – or, at least, I didn't feel it was my place to criticise him. After all, our relationship was no more than a mutual convenience and, if he was far from perfect, he was at least sufficiently intelligent, open-minded and, frankly, perverse to provide what I asked. That was rare.

My need to be nursed was not strictly speaking a regressive fantasy. Looking back, I can think of one or two experiences which must at least have added detail to my needs, but no more. One of my earliest boyfriends had liked to watch me pee, especially through my panties, but I had seen it only as a higher level of the exhibitionism I was already starting to enjoy. Then there had been Thereze, a girl in the lesbian society at college. She had been big – fat, really – and had liked to suckle me at her breasts. I had enjoyed it, but never understood it as more than an affectionate eccentricity. Mainly, it was something which had evolved in parallel with my career. At college my sexuality had been relatively straightforward, centred on the need for openness and understanding. From early relationships with boys I had come to believe I was lesbian, and later to accept my bisexuality. While evolving my ideas on therapy I had held to the idea that any properly balanced person should be entirely at ease with their sexuality, also open about it. Only when I began to practise did I realise that this was not always the case.

The problem was my clients. After a day of helping others to achieve mental and physical well-being I would be exhausted. Relaxation proved difficult, especially as whatever technique I used I would be constantly analysing its effects. I realised quickly that what I needed to do was surrender control and when, after a particularly harrowing day, I found myself sucking my thumb, I realised how.

It worked wonderfully. Within a month I had transformed one of the rooms in my flat into a nursery. After a bad day I would lock my door and strip naked. I'd wash and curl up on my bed with my thumb in my mouth, letting it all slip away. It felt blissful and intensely sexual. The first time I'd found the courage to wet my bed I had masturbated until I was sore, coming so often I lost count. After that I began to enhance the fantasy, buying myself girlish pink clothes, especially nighties, cuddly toys, baby bottles, powder, cream and finally nappies.

The nappies were the final, perfect touch. They were big and pink and soft, fitting snugly around my hips and over my bottom to create a sensation so good it made me dizzy. They were also expensive, coming from a discreet mail-order company somewhere in the Midlands, made to measure and for sexual pleasure, not incontinence. It was worth it.

Being in a nappy transformed me from Ms Gabrielle Salinger, inventor of Whole-Being Therapy and professional shoulder-to-cry-on, to Miss Gabby, a grown-up baby girl without even enough self-control to hold in her pee. It was glorious, and it helped me relax so well that the extra work I could take on more than paid for it. Glorious, but not perfect. To be perfect, I needed a nanny, my *bobonne*, to cuddle me, to change me, to spank me when I needed it, however much I hated the pain.

I couldn't tell anybody else. Much of my success relied on appearing absolutely in control, and none of my clients would have understood, let alone been able to take on the role of nanny. None were right; all too insecure, or self-obsessed, and generally simply too repressed. Only when Jo Warren rang me from the south of France in a state of high emotional crisis did I dare to think I might have found a partner.

She had been on holiday with her boyfriend and another friend, Natasha Linnet. Natasha had been to see me once, and had struck me as tough, unyielding and secretive. At the time I'd put this down to insecurity and low self-esteem. From Jo's account she was a sort of female de Sade, with a touch of Dr Crippen thrown in. What she'd actually done was suggest that Jo might like to have sex with her, including spanking sex. Reading between the lines, it was clear that Natasha needed something special sexually, something she was not prepared to be open about. She was also beautiful. I had to try.

I succeeded. Natasha was cruel. She spanked me and gave me a milk enema with my baby bottle, making me cry. She also gave me some of the best orgasms of my life. Unfortunately, she would have preferred to have been on the receiving end and was obsessed with her own humiliation. She was a good playmate, but not my *bobonne*.

She also introduced me to Monty Hartle. He was anything but beautiful, and certainly no nurse. On the other hand, he was intelligent, open-minded and, unlike Natasha, he would do what I wanted him to. He would also do a lot more, but I was prepared to put up with that. So it was a compromise, my fantasy for his, nursing for allowing myself to be objectified and, frankly, abused.

As we walked to the station, I was fully expecting to be put through my paces on the train. If we were alone in a compartment I would probably be made to open my blouse, allowing him to fondle my breasts so that we risked being seen by people in other trains. He had done that before and enjoyed it, if slightly disappointed by my lack of embarrassment. To me, nudity is freedom. Still, it had been good – good enough to come over, and good enough to have my sense of erotic anticipation rising strongly as we walked.

We were lucky at the station, arriving just as a Victoria-bound train was pulling into the platform. We made a dash for the front carriage and, sure enough, it was empty.

'Non-stop,' Monty panted as he caught up with me. 'East Croydon to Victoria, that's twenty-two minutes. Enough.'

'Enough for what?'

'Oh, I don't know. Maybe a nice, leisurely blow-job.'

'What about ticket inspectors?'

'A four per cent chance. I can cover my cock with my coat if I have to.'

'If you like, then.'

'Doesn't anything embarrass you, Gabby? Think about it. You'll be down on my cock. People will see in the windows.'

'Why should it embarrass me if it does not embarrass you?'

'Because you're a girl!'

'You are so English, Monty!'

I laughed, sitting down as the train shuddered into motion. Monty sat on the bench opposite, fat thighs well apart to show off the bulge in his trousers, or at least as much as showed beneath the overhang of his belly.

'Could you come again so soon?' I asked.

'In your mouth? In twenty minutes? Yes. In fact, I think I'll spunk in your face just as we come into Victoria, all over your glasses. That should make you colour up.'

'No, don't. I'm not completely immune to embarrassment, Monty, and it doesn't excite me.'

'It excites me. I'd love to make you walk through Victoria Station with your face covered in my spunk. Just the thought's making me hard.'

'Well, it's not going to happen, but I will suck you. Pull out your cock.'

'Dirty bitch,' he answered, and began to fumble for his fly.

We were still drawing out of the station but he didn't seem to care, pulling out his cock and balls to leave them hanging out of his open fly, as obscene as ever. He slid forwards, pulling his belly up to get at them. It was warm enough in the carriage, although it had been cold outside, and I opened my coat, assuming he would want me at least partly bare.

'Shall I?' I asked, putting my fingers to the hem of my jumper.

'Yeah, why not? I reckon a girl should always take her tits out to give a blow-job, and you all seem to like it.'

'So we don't soil our clothes.'

'Sure. You just like to have your knockers showing while you suck.'

He was right, in a way. I do like to stroke my breasts while I suck a man's cock – but then, I like to stroke my breasts during sex anyway. I had pulled up my jumper and opened the top button of my blouse as we spoke, and followed with the second and third, slowly, to tease him. His cock was already growing, and I could see his wristwatch showing that we had nineteen minutes left.

I opened the rest of my buttons, wondering how to best display my breasts without looking too much of a

9

ragamuffin and deciding that I'd have to take my jumper right off.

'No, leave it,' Monty said as I began to pull it higher. 'I love that look – you know, dishevelled, like you've been interfered with, you know, your clothes disarranged and your tits pulled out.'

It was certainly making his cock swell, so I left the jumper and pulled my bra up, leaving my breasts bare to him in a mess of clothing. He grinned and began to pull harder at his cock, which was close to erection. I took my breasts in my hands and began to stroke them, bringing my nipples out.

'Nice,' he said. 'Not as big as Natasha's, but nice.'

'It is best not to compare one girl's breasts with those of another,' I told him, 'or any part of her body, but yes, Natasha's breasts are lovely.'

'I like perky,' he went on. 'I like the way your nipples point up. There are internet sites devoted to girls with tits like yours. Puppy-dogs, they're called.'

'I think I had better suck,' I told him, nodding to his now fully erect cock.

'No,' he answered. 'I want to see a bit more of you. Pull up your skirt.'

I nodded, glancing at the connecting door even as I took hold of the hem of the knee-length, woollen skirt I'd chosen. I stood to pull it up, enjoying the feeling of exposure as I sat down with just my tights between me and the fabric of the seat.

'Tights down,' he said, 'all the way.'

'Wouldn't it look better if I took them right off? An inspector might come.'

'Not likely. I want you dishevelled. I want you sucking with your little bare arse stuck out behind. Now do it, tights first, then turn round to take down your panties.'

'I would be bare anyway . . .'

'Shut up. Get those tights down.'

10

I complied, rolling them down off my hips and pushing them low to my ankles. It was risky, but not very, and it did feel delicious, with my breasts bare and just my panties to cover me from waist to ankles. He was grinning, enjoying the view and wanking hard. I waited, expecting the final order, to be told to pull down my panties and go down on his cock. I was going to enjoy it, and I was going to masturbate too, with an easy fifteen minutes remaining.

'Drop 'em,' he panted. 'Like I ordered, arse stuck right out and peel them down real slow. Pull your cheeks open too; I love to see that tight pink arsehole and your little shaved cunt. You always shave, don't you?'

'Yes.'

'Then show me it. Sod it, sit on my cock. I'm going to fuck you . . .'

He stopped abruptly as the train came to a halt. I peered from the window, where an embankment led down to a terrace of suburban houses much like Monty's own. Several windows were lit, a few with the curtains open. I closed my coat.

'Hey, what are you doing?' Monty demanded.

'What if an inspector comes, perhaps to explain why we've stopped?'

'Fat chance. This is Britain, Gabby. It just means we get more time. I can give you a proper fucking now, on your knees on the seat. Maybe someone'll see from those houses if you're lucky.'

I glanced at the houses again. Nobody was visible, but anyone looking out of a window would be able to see into our carriage. If they couldn't see everything, they'd get a pretty good idea of what we were doing.

'Anyhow,' Monty went on, 'if we do get caught you can offer him a blow-job. Take him in his cabin and suck his cock. You'd love that, I bet. Actually they come round in pairs, so you'd have to go two up, one in the mouth, one up the cunt.'

He was fantasising, and wanking so hard I thought he'd come in his hand. I let my coat open and put my hand to my panties, checking I was damp enough to take his cock. I was.

'I'd tell them you'd been drinking,' he went on, 'that you're anybody's after a few lagers. No, I'd tell them you were desperate, that you'd been going to piss yourself. Now that would have you blushing, wouldn't it? Yes, you're to do it, Gabby. Piss your knickers, right now.'

'No,' I managed, but it was weak. The suggestion was too close to my favourite fantasy, and he knew it.

'Since when can Miss Gabby hold it in?' he demanded. 'Come on, if you need pee-pee, just do it.'

He had pushed my button. I decided to do it.

'Through my panties?' I asked. 'Or do I pull them down, to squat between the seats, maybe? You could see my puddle . . .'

'No, I want you sitting in it,' he said. 'Then I'm going to fuck you doggy, with your pissy knickers pulled aside.'

I just nodded. I knew I could do it, a little anyway, enough to show. It wasn't the way I usually like to wet myself, but it was good, too good to resist. I opened my legs, showing him the clean white crotch of my panties as I tensed my bladder. His grin grew broader still.

'Here it comes,' I gasped, and pushed.

Pee spurted out into my panty gusset and through it, in a little yellow fountain, soaking into the cotton and trickling down on to the seat. I looked down, watching as I peed myself, the wet patch growing with the damp cotton tight to my sex, showing everything.

'Fucking nice!' Monty exclaimed.

I moved forwards a little, pressing my bottom into the wet patch and pushing harder. Pee sprayed out through my panties to splash on the floor. Some had gone in my tights, but I didn't care. It felt so nice, showing off, half-dressed and wet with my own piddle, out of control.

My hand went to my panty gusset, squeezing the warm, wet cotton to my sex. The pee was still coming, wetting my fingers, and running back to moisten my vagina and seep in between my buttocks to my anus. There was time to masturbate, and I was going to do it, when Monty pulled me up short.

'Not that, you dirty bitch,' he said. 'Not yet, and what about me? What happens to girls who wet their knickers?'

'They get put in nappies?' I asked hopefully.

He nodded and patted the bench beside him. I came quickly, knowing we didn't have much time. My panties were soaking, pee dribbling down my legs as I stood up to leave a big wet patch on the seat. Monty stood to retrieve my bag and rummage inside it for my nappy as I levered off the wet panties, taking my tights with them. My shoes came too, leaving me bare from the waist down and feeling more exposed than if I'd been stark naked.

Monty knew what he was doing, having had plenty of practice. As soon as I lay down he had me by the ankles, rolling me up to lift my bottom from the seat. He had the cream and squirted it out on to my bare pussy as he held me. I felt the cool touch, then the texture as he quickly rubbed it into my sex and anus, unnecessarily pushing one joint of his finger a little way into my ring. I managed a mew of protest but no more. My eyes were shut, my thumb in my mouth, and I was concentrating on the feelings of my lower body, my bare legs, my moist sex, then the soft nappy material as it was slid under my bottom.

With swift, certain motions my legs were pulled wide, the nappy pushed up between them and pressed to my belly, the tabs pulled up, one side then the other, and fastened into place. It was done, my hips, bottom and belly encased in soft, pink, material, bulging above bare legs, the way a grown-up baby girl should be, only in a painfully risky place.

I had to do it anyway. My hand went down the front of my nappy, straight down, to find the creamy, slimy folds of my sex. I began to rub, one finger on my clitoris, desperate to come before anything went wrong. I was too far gone to really care what Monty did, but gave no resistance as he took me by the thighs, pulling me around so that he could get at my sex. His hand took hold of my nappy, pulling it wide to expose me, and an instant later the bulbous head of his cock pushed up into my body. He fucked me as I masturbated, grunting and blowing, his great fat belly splaying my legs wide and smacking on my flesh. I was starting to come even as the train once more jerked into motion, rubbing frantically as I thought of how I was, near naked, in my soft pink nappy, with Monty's fat penis working in and out of my hole ...

I heard my own scream as I came, in a long moment of blinding, beautiful ecstasy. It was truly wonderful, and so nice of him to make me pee myself, nicer still to put me in a nappy to fuck me. As I pulled myself quickly upright my overwhelming emotion was gratitude.

'Thank you, Monty,' I told him. 'Thank you.'

'Don't,' he panted, and pulled his cock out.

I was taken by the head, his fat fingers locking in my hair. He moved round, sitting, to tug me after him. I went down, kneeling right in the little puddle of pee I'd made on the floor. Before I could move his cock had been stuffed into my mouth. He began to fuck my head urgently, although he was panting with the effort of what he'd done and his cock was beginning to lose its stiffness. I sucked harder and stuck my bottom out, showing off the rear of my nappy to him. It was half down, the way he'd pulled it, with a little of my bottom crease showing at the top, a sight I was sure would get to him.

It did, but slowly. I sucked anyway, as best I could with him holding me by the hair. Gradually he grew properly stiff, and ever more urgent, until it was all I could do to make my mouth a comfortable slide as he jammed his cock in and out, faster and faster . . .

Too late I remembered his threat to come over my glasses. He did it, jerking his cock from my mouth at the last possible moment, to snatch my head back and empty himself in my face. My cry of shock and denial was ignored, my head held firmly in place as gout after gout of sperm was emptied out into my mouth, over my nose, across one lens as I closed my eyes by reflex. Something pressed to my other lens, and I realised he'd wiped the last of his come off on to it.

'I said not that, Monty!' I exclaimed.

'Sorry,' he puffed. 'I just love it too much!'

'I can hardly see!'

I'd opened my eyes to find both lenses smeared with come, enough to leave much of my vision a blur of off-white. I pulled my glasses off, groping for my bag, with my anger rising in the face of Monty's helpless laughter.

'Here,' he said, and put something into my hand, my discarded panties.

There was no time to fuss and I quickly used what little of the seat was still dry to get the worst of the sperm off my glasses, all the while demanding that Monty help me. He was laughing too hard, and struggling even to get his cock back into his trousers. I pulled my jumper down over my breasts and tried to use the panties to clean up my face, but only succeeded in making the mess worse, and in the end was forced to use the tail of my blouse. When I at last managed to get my glasses back on Monty was still laughing.

'You have no idea what you looked like!' he boomed. 'Sorry, but the expression on your face, it was just so funny!'

15

'Can you help me, do you think?' I demanded. 'We will be in Victoria in minutes!'

I glanced from the window, to find yellow lights reflecting on water, the Thames.

'Quick, help me change!' I urged him. 'There are some spare panties in my bag.'

'Just pull your skirt down and put your shoes on. I'll stick your wet things in the bag.'

'No. There is time, just. Quick, my panties!'

He finally responded, searching in the bag futilely. I pulled it away but we were already slowing down. I stood, rummaging frantically and providing a train going the other way with a view of my nappy-clad bottom and bare legs. I couldn't find the spare panties and we were pulling in, the lights of Victoria Station visible outside the windows. Abandoning the idea of fresh panties, I snatched up my tights, only to discover that they had gone in the pool of pee on the floor and were soaked. Monty laughed and I threw the wet tights at him.

There was no time to do anything but get out of my nappy and pull down my skirt. I grappled for the tabs, stopping as a thud sounded from the end of the carriage. I looked up to find a man pushing at the door between the carriages. In a second he would see me. I snatched my coat shut even as I sat down, right in my own puddle. The man came in, the huge rucksack on his back jamming in the door just long enough to allow me to retrieve my panties and tights. I stuffed them into the bag. The man passed, throwing me a puzzled look as the train finally came to a halt.

Monty was in stitches, clutching his fat sides and shaking with laughter, his expression close to pain.

'Will you help?' I demanded as the man left the carriage.

'Sorry, I can't,' he answered, shaking his head, his face still red with laughter.

There was really nothing he could do. I was left to cover my nappy with my skirt and put my shoes back on. That was all I dared, with several people milling around on the platform outside the window, including two in railway uniforms. Outside, I was very glad indeed for my coat. I might have been decent underneath, technically, but it would have been very obvious I had a nappy on under my skirt. It bulged horribly at the front and sides, while I wasn't at all sure my rear view wouldn't look peculiar even with the coat.

There was nothing I could do, only endure Monty's crude laughter as I hurried down the platform in the vain hope of avoiding attention. There were quite a few people about, station officials, a drinking school, a few stragglers from parties, people making for the Gatwick Express. Some saw a few gave me odd looks, but nothing more.

I hurried anyway. This was Victoria, and I had altogether too many friends who used the station and, worse, clients. Even bare legs beneath a coat look pretty strange, and I knew my hair and face would be a mess, despite my efforts to clean up. I was cursing Monty all the way as I crossed the concourse, and seriously considering telling him where to go. I didn't, knowing full well that my need for what he could give would prove too strong, and that it would only end with me crawling back, for which he would exact a heavy price. I was also cursing myself for getting so easily carried away, and for trusting him. He had completely betrayed me, yet I had known that when it came to attempting to humiliate me sexually he was not to be trusted. To him it was simply a game.

The station was mercifully clear of anyone I knew, but walking down the Buckingham Palace Road seemed altogether too risky. I turned right instead, looping around the back of the station and into quieter roads, with Monty tagging along behind. I was walking fast

17

and he was having trouble keeping up, puffing and calling out for me to slow down. I ignored him until a pair of seedy-looking men stepped out unexpectedly in front of me, one making a remark about the shape of my breasts as they passed. I paused, allowing Monty to waddle up beside me.

'What's the hurry?' he demanded.

'The hurry is,' I snapped, 'that I am in a nappy under my skirt, and it shows!'

'Only from the back. Anyway, you love that stuff!'

'Not here! For goodness' sake, Monty, have you no sense at all?'

'I thought you'd like it. I thought you'd get off on it.'

He was whining and I drew my breath in to try and calm down.

'Come on, Gabby,' he went on. 'It's gone midnight. Who's going to see you? It doesn't show that much, anyway.'

'It doesn't show? Look at it!' I hissed, and turned to show him.

I put my hand to my bottom, touching the bulge of the nappy. My coat was damp with pee.

'Yeah,' he said, 'but who's going to know it's a nappy? It just looks like you've got a disproportionately fat bum . . . and you've wet yourself.'

I opened my mouth, but he had raised his hands in a gesture of defence.

'Not really,' he said quickly, 'more like you sat on a wet bench.'

'I suppose you're right,' I admitted. 'Still, I want to get back quickly. For one thing, it's cold. Now come on.'

He came, still not as fast as I'd have liked, and making annoying little snickering noises as he went. I ignored him, walking a little way ahead, even though I knew he was enjoying my discomfort immensely and that his eyes would be fixed on the rear of my coat. We reached my street, which was deserted.

'Can I come up?' Monty demanded as we reached the door of my flats. Again there was that whining note in his voice.

'No,' I insisted. 'Sorry, but you know you'll end up missing the last train and staying over.'

'I won't, I promise – or if I do, I don't mind going in the ordinary bedroom. I'll even tuck you in. A story maybe?'

'Shh! I do have neighbours, Monty.'

'Sorry. Come on, Gabby, you know you want it.'

'I do not. I'm tired.'

'Oh, come on. Just a coffee, then. I did come back to make sure you were safe.'

'Yes, so that you could abuse me on the train! In all honesty, Monty . . . oh, very well, a coffee, no more.'

'Thanks, Gabby.'

We were already in the hallway of my flats and I knew he would have just followed me upstairs anyway, or made a scene on the landing. For all my convictions on not judging people by their physical appearance, I was conscious that not everybody shared my view, in particular my clients. Some had been known to visit me late at night.

One had – Jo Warren, who was standing outside my door.

There were worse people it could have been, but very few. Everything about Monty was anathema to Jo, but especially his weight. To her, being fat represented a level of social undesirability on a par with being a peeping Tom or a panty thief. Monty was two of those things, and quite possibly all three, but fortunately for me only the fat was evident.

'Hi,' she greeted me, throwing an uncertain glance at him, as if she couldn't quite believe it, but otherwise ignoring him.

'Jocasta, hello,' I responded, searching frantically for the best line to take. 'You need to see me?'

'Urgently,' she answered. 'Sorry, it just couldn't wait. I've found the most wonderful way to dispel all the tensions, everything . . .'

'A moment, please.' I interrupted her and turned to Monty, who was standing behind me, looking sulky.

He was no fool, and I knew he would have immediately sensed her distaste. To her, he was someone she would not even want to acknowledge, nor even expect to resent her attitude. He was familiar with the response and tended to get pretty annoyed about it. I could only hope he wouldn't want to take his anger out on me.

'Thank you, Monty,' I addressed him. 'That was considerate of you. I imagine you will want your usual appointment in the week?'

'Yes,' he answered, 'but I really feel I need a little more, in the circumstances.'

I knew exactly what he meant. The next time I saw him it was going to hurt.

'Of course,' I said. 'Call me tomorrow. We will discuss it.'

He nodded and started back down the stairs. I let my breath out slowly, thanking him silently for his compliance in my lie. I also felt guilty, as in a sense my behaviour was no better than Jo's. Then again, I would be punished for it; she would not.

'Who was that?' she breathed as he disappeared around the corner of the stairs.

'A client,' I answered.

'He's so fat! How does he cope? I mean, if I was that fat . . . half that fat, I'd just kill myself!'

'It is a serious problem, Jocasta.'

'I'm sorry. I realise you must have to put up with people like that in your work. But . . . but he's just so fat! He smelled of pee, too, I'm sure of it. You're so caring, Gabrielle.'

'There is a great deal of pleasure in helping people, Jo. Besides, I have my professional responsibilities.'

20

'Of course . . . but, I mean, how can he live like that? Why doesn't he just lose some weight?'

'It is not so simple,' I addressed her, talking fast to keep her attention from the shape of my coat as I opened the door to my flat. 'He is in severe denial, imagining his problem to be physiological, when it is in fact entirely psychological. He imagines himself to be unable to lose weight, and so becomes depressed. To allay his depression, he eats, telling himself that it will make no difference. Thus the cycle of depression and weight gain becomes self-perpetuating. His depression is verging on the suicidal, so when he called this afternoon I had little choice but to go and see him. Once he was calm, he offered to escort me home.'

It was an outright lie, but it was what she wanted to hear. She nodded, and allowed me to usher her through the door and into the clinic, all the time with my back away from her. Having claimed that I had seen Monty as a client I could hardly refuse her, besides which, as she knew full well, she would be paying double time.

'So how are you treating him?' she asked, settling herself into the usual chair.

'I am not at liberty to say, as you know. Client confidentiality.'

'Yes, but not the physical treatments, surely, not with . . . with that?'

'He is a human being, Jo, like you and I. But no. I take on very few male clients, and I do not offer them the full range of therapies. It is too easy for them to form inappropriate attachments.'

'Of course. Anyway, I've got to tell you . . .'

'A moment.'

I'd stopped in the door and retreated hastily. She had already thrown one or two odd looks at my bare legs, and I was sure the outline of my nappy would show if I wasn't careful. I needed to change, and quickly. In my ordinary bedroom I tugged up my skirt, pulled my tabs

21

free and wriggled quickly out of my nappy, kicking it under the bed. Nothing else mattered nearly as much. I washed and changed as quickly as I could before returning to the clinic. Jo had not moved.

'I apologise,' I addressed her. 'You were saying?'

'Yes,' she said. 'My idea. Remember how you said I needed to face my tensions and bring them out into the open?'

'Yes.'

'Well, I know how to do it. I'm going to put it all down, everything that's happened to me, and my feelings . . .'

'A good idea.'

'Yes, in a novel.'

'A novel?'

'Yes. That way I can express myself to so many people. Everyone'll understand how I feel. It'll be the most wonderful thing!'

'I see.'

'You don't sound too enthusiastic.'

'Not at all,' I lied. 'I am simply considering the implications of such a public catharsis. You will include everything? The traumatic incidents with Natasha Linnet?'

'Those most of all. Everyone'll understand how I feel.'

'You had told me you were concerned to keep that private. She has somewhat embarrassing photographs, I believe you said.'

'But that's the clever thing! It'll all be fictional. The characters will be different and, of course, I won't use Natasha's name, or anyone else's, or places. But my emotions will be there for all to see. I'll know that thousands and thousands of people will know what I've been through.'

'Somewhat vicariously.'

'It will work, Gabrielle. I know it will.'

22

I paused, steepling my fingers in thought so that she would give me time to bring my brain into gear. There was no doubt that the idea would achieve the drastic catharsis she intended. As a journalist, there was every chance her novel would get published. It might not sell as well as she seemed to anticipate, but that didn't matter. Natasha Linnet would buy a copy, along with their mutual friends. The change of names and places would fool nobody. Natasha would be furious and take the most vindictive revenge she could, pinning up the photographs on the notice board at Jo's workplace. They showed her expelling an enema, in detail.

It would traumatise Jocasta, without question. Not only that, but the fact that Natasha had had sex with Jo's boyfriend was likely to come out. The situation could only escalate, resulting in the full exposure of Natasha's sexual habits, and very possibly my own. Natasha, after all, knew everything, and might well blame me.

'It will be dedicated to you,' Jo announced.

That set the seal on it. Natasha would definitely blame me.

'Thank you,' I answered her. 'You are prepared, then, to risk having these photographs made public?"

'She wouldn't do that. She wouldn't dare, not with everyone on my side.'

'I suspect otherwise. For her, the damage would already have been done. She can be vindictive.'

'That's for sure! You really think she'd do it?'

'I do.'

'Oh.'

'I think you underestimate the risks. I also think you underestimate your own sensitivity.'

'Yes, I am sensitive. But I have to get these feelings out, Gabrielle, I have to!'

'Yes, absolutely – but while your novel is an excellent idea in itself, I fear the consequences are likely to outweigh the benefits.'

'So what can I do?'

'Find a new focus. Continue with your regime of physical therapies ... Do you wish to discuss your progress now, incidentally, or tomorrow?'

'Now, if you don't mind. I'd rather put off tomorrow. My boss isn't too happy about me taking so much time off work for therapy. He just doesn't understand. A typical man. How do you mean, a new focus?'

'Something that will take your mind away from the situation with Natasha. You must face your tensions, yes, but what you must face is their root cause.'

'Natasha.'

'No. She may have triggered your specific feelings of insecurity concerning your sexuality, but the root cause remains latent guilt.'

'I still say I've every right to feel guilty. It's awful what she wanted me to do to her, and it excited me. I can't be like that! You have to stop it.'

'As I have explained, Jo, that is not necessarily the answer. You must come to terms with your sexuality.'

'That is not part of my sexuality! I don't like girls, and I certainly don't like ... like hitting their bottoms. It's awful!'

'Again, we return to your latent guilt. If you have sexual feelings for other women, you should acknowledge them.'

'I don't! I swear it!'

'And yet you say you wanted to punish Natasha, and that you found the idea exciting.'

'I wanted to punish her, yes. She was so ... so impudent. I mean, imagine asking Hugh to smack her bottom, right in front of me, and for me to do it too! I wanted to do it to her, to teach her how it felt, to hit her! I don't even know why it had to be on her bottom, and ... and I was so wet. It's not me, Gabrielle. I'm not a violent person! I don't do violent! I'm not a lesbian, either! I don't understand, Gabrielle!'

'And how do you feel about her now?'

24

'I hate her. What she did . . . and she's so smug . . . and so confident . . . and so slim! I still want to smack her bottom.'

'So we return to your weight. You are slim, Jocasta, by any normal standards. Monty Hartle, who you saw just now, is fat. You are slim.'

'Monty Hartle's how I feel I look! I'm fat next to you, Gabrielle, and Natasha, and Ami, and . . . and . . .'

She burst into tears. I leaned forwards to take her hand, showing concern but keeping my opinions firmly to myself and considering her figure. She was athletic, with a lot of muscle on a middling frame, but not an ounce of surplus fat. Still she saw herself as fat. It was a problem we had wrestled with repeatedly, and had been her major concern before the issue with Natasha had arisen. An idea occurred to me.

'Possibly,' I suggested, 'your need to punish Natasha is not a sexual thing at all but a response to your feelings about her being slim, with her suggestion that you should spank her merely providing a trigger, a way of expressing a need.'

'I was wet.' She snivelled. 'Soaking.'

'Because of Natasha? Are you certain of that? Could you not be confusing cause and effect? You were with Hugh also, were you not?'

'Hugh never makes me wet, not like that.'

'The physiological responses that cause secretion by the vulva are not simple, Jocasta. A woman may become physically aroused without any mental stimulus of which she is consciously aware. Very possibly your physical reaction was the result of something entirely separate, which you subsequently linked to your desire to punish Natasha.'

'I don't know. Maybe you're right. Yes, you are, it makes sense. So it's all because I'm fat.'

'No, no,' I said hastily as her tears started again. 'It is because you see yourself as fat. It is entirely a mental image, with no relation to the physical reality.'

'You say that, but . . .'

'It is true. Consider; do you see me as irresponsible?'

'No, of course not, never!'

'If I was, I would recommend a stricter diet, thus pandering to your need to feel you should be slimmer. I am not, and therefore I do not. If you trust me, this in itself should be proof that you do not need to lose weight.'

She considered, gave one heavy sniff and looked up at me, smiling. I gave her hand a squeeze, let go and sat back.

'We will explore the idea in depth at a later session,' I promised. 'I think the novel idea is good. It will provide a positive focus for your energies. I just don't think it sensible to make it such an exact reflection of your recent experiences. Perhaps you should consider another plot, one that allows a less overt expression of your feelings?'

She nodded and pulled a tissue from the box on the table.

'You were going to tell me how you have been getting on with your physical therapies.'

'OK. Well, the aromatherapy works as long as I'm not too tense, and you were right to say I should put more of the cypress oil into the blend. When I'm bad, it just doesn't seem to make any difference.'

'I see. And have you begun to irrigate again?'

'Yes, only it's not the same, not since . . . Especially when I expel.'

'I understand. And masturbation?'

'In private, yes, but I still feel guilty about self-sex. I know I shouldn't, but I can't face asking Hugh to do it. He'd just snigger.'

'I see. Again, we come back to your latent guilt. I can not stress it enough, Jocasta, masturbation is entirely harmless and also therapeutic. It is an act of freedom. To feel guilty is to accept the patriarchal suppression of female sexuality.'

'I know, Gabrielle, I just have trouble getting my head around it. It feels so much better when you do it.'

'That is because you are displacing your guilt . . .'

'Yes, I know, but . . . please?'

'You want me to masturbate you, now?'

'Yes. It's the only thing that'll make me feel better. I'm just so tense!'

I was already tired and still in a sexually submissive state, very far from the clinical detachment I needed to masturbate her. I knew what it was going to do to me. What I wanted to do was tell her to either go home and do it herself, or come to bed with me. What I said was very different.

'If you feel you need to come, yes.'

'Thank you.'

She got on to the couch, composing herself, with her arms above her head. I got up, glancing at the clock to discover that it was very nearly one a.m. Keeping my face carefully neutral, I went to the medical cupboard, to take out the box of gloves. Jo watched as I pulled them on, her face set in a shy smile.

'You will have to take your jeans and panties down,' I pointed out.

She nodded and put her hands to the button, tweaking it open. Her zip came down to the gentle pressure of her tummy and her thumbs as she stuck them into her waistband. Lifting her bottom, she pushed jeans and panties down as one to her ankles, revealing the low swell of her tummy, bare, golden legs and a puff of dark blonde hair on her pubic mound.

'Shall I show my breasts?' she asked.

'If you normally do so.'

She responded by pulling up her jumper, revealing a big white sports bra. It followed, the cups raised to spill out two large breasts, only a touch paler than the skin of her legs and stomach. Her legs came up and open,

27

displaying her sex. As she closed her eyes I put a finger to her sex to see it she would need lubricant. She didn't.

Her back arched to my touch, pushing out her sex. I began to masturbate her carefully, stroking her sex and trying to keep my mind on something else. She opened quickly, her vulva growing rapidly moist and puffy under my hand. Her breathing grew faster; her hands went to her breasts, cupping them and stroking her nipples. I began to rub harder, watching as her tummy began to twitch and the red flush spread out across her breasts. She sighed; her mouth came open; she gave a little cry and tensed, her thighs coming up to squeeze tight on my hand as she came. I waited until her contractions had died down before speaking.

'Better?'

'Yes. That was beautiful. I feel so much better.'

She might have felt better. I didn't. I was desperately aroused from the sight of her naked body and the smell of her sex. I could understand exactly why Natasha had wanted to have sex with her. Unlike Natasha, I had the self-control not to do anything about it when it was obviously inappropriate.

As I peeled off my gloves and dropped them into the bin she got up, swinging her legs off the couch and standing to pull up her jeans and panties. I was given a last glorious view of her bottom as she bent, knock-kneed, her cheeks wide enough apart to show her sex and hint at her anus. The pose also left her large breasts hanging from her chest for a moment, making me think of being suckled, something I hadn't enjoyed since having sex with Natasha. It had felt wonderful and Jo would have been better still, physically as tall as me, with her heavy breasts and big, dark nipples . . .

I shook my head, ridding myself of the image of her as my nurse.

'You are so good at that, Gabrielle,' she said, pulling her bra back over her magnificent breasts. 'With anyone else it wouldn't feel right, but you, you're just so detached.'

What she meant was 'emotionless', the image I always try to project to my clients; sympathetic, calm, a rock they can lean on. I drew in my breath and glanced once more at the clock. Her time was nearly up.

'Do you wish to reschedule your appointments?' I asked. 'You said you were having trouble at work.'

'Well, yes, if you don't mind. I'll call, yes?'

'As you please. Do you feel we have made any advance?'

'Yes, absolutely. I feel completely relaxed. We've resolved a lot, I think, and all that tension's just gone. You're wonderful.'

I managed a smile. We had in fact resolved very little, and the drain in tension was entirely the result of her orgasm, something I badly needed myself.

It took me another ten minutes to get rid of her. By then I was exhausted, too exhausted to manage anything elaborate. I didn't need it. I was still thinking of her breasts and how good it would have felt to suckle her, and I knew that was what I had to come over. I stripped in my ordinary bedroom, stark naked, and retrieved my nappy from under the bed. As I fastened it around my hips I could already feel the tension draining away and my arousal pushing up over my tiredness.

In my special bedroom I curled up on the rug, my thumb in my mouth. My hand went down the front of my nappy to find the smooth lips of my sex and the moist crevice between. I began to rub and to think of Jo, with her big, golden-skinned breasts pulled out of her sports bra, hanging down beneath her chest, the nipples hard, for me to suckle on as she stroked my hair, soothing me, whispering gently to me as I masturbated . . .

A sense of annoyance came over me. She was what I needed physically: a full-breasted, sturdy young woman, healthy and beautiful, the perfect nurse. Mentally she was hopeless; neurotic, insecure, self-obsessed, no more capable of being my nurse than of becoming the elfin waif she saw as the ideal of femininity. Masturbating over her was simply not going to be fully satisfying.

I tried again, thinking of the way Monty handled me so easily, lifting me by my ankles to change my nappy, his fat fingers patting the powder on to my bare bottom or rubbing cream over my sex, slipping into the hole, loitering on my anus ...

It was no good. I wanted to think about being suckled, and that was one thing Monty could never do, despite having as much fat on his chest as Jo and I put together. He was too openly sexual about it as well, so that however closely he followed my instructions I always felt I was being molested rather than taken care of.

I tried to think of Thereze but it was simply too long ago, and it was impossible to get a clear image of her face, which is crucial to me. Natasha was better, smaller than me but with fuller breasts, full enough to play nursemaid. She had suckled me and it had been nice. It had been after a spanking too, with my bottom hot and red and the tears still wet on my cheeks. True, it had been lovely to be soothed after punishment, as she'd assured me it would. She was just so cruel, always determined to hurt me and humiliate me before giving me what I wanted – really not so very different from Monty, just prettier.

She was the best, though, between them: cruel, yes, but understanding. It had been worth the spanking just to get my mouth open around her soft, full breasts, with her nipple hard in my mouth. I'd had my nappy pulled down at the back for the spanking, but it had still been on, around my thighs, one tab tickling my hot bottom. She had done it for me too, her hand curled around my thighs, her fingers busy with my sex, her thumb tickling the crease of my bottom ...

It was good enough. She was good enough. I slid my hand further down my nappy to push a finger into the wet cavity of my vagina, then a second, probing myself as I tried to rationalise Natasha's cruelty with my fantasy. I'd always known that getting spanked was likely to be an element of relinquishing control to another and I even felt I deserved it, sometimes. It made me wet, too, but it just hurt so much. I'd told her but she'd done it anyway, telling me I needed to be punished, and laughing as my bottom bounced and jiggled under her hand and the tears streamed down my face, so cruel . . .

Cruel maybe, but she had comforted me, and perhaps it wouldn't have been so good without the spanking. Perhaps I had needed it. She certainly had, so that she could hold me, shivering and contrite in her arms, red-bottomed and sobbing, feeding at her chest as she masturbated me, just as I was now masturbating myself, nappied, spanked and masturbated . . .

I came, thinking of how it had felt to feel my mouth open around Natasha's nipples as the orgasm hit me, how soothing it had been with my bottom hot behind me, the pain of my punishment past, giving way to the abandoned bliss of suckling at another woman's breast. It held, for a long time, focussed on Natasha, only to break at the memory of how she'd laughed at my tears and the way I'd grovelled on the floor after my punishment. My *bobonne* might have spanked me, but it would have been with regret.

Two

I woke in the morning to what was becoming an increasingly familiar sense of dissatisfaction. When I'd had nobody to share my fantasy with I had imagined that any partner would be better than none. Now that I had two playmates, as Natasha called herself, I should have been spoiled for choice. Unfortunately, neither was perfect, and if anything I felt more frustrated than before.

I'd put myself to bed in my nappy and a pink pyjama top. I was wet in the morning, as I'd done it just before sleep, the time at which I achieve the deepest level of abandonment and irresponsibility short of the moment before orgasm. With Jo Warren dealt with, I had no appointments until midday. I changed myself, going through the familiar and comforting routine of cleaning my sex and bottom-crease – wash, dry, powder and cream – before putting on a fresh nappy. All the while I was wishing I had someone else to do it for me and, not for the first time, I began to visualise my ideal.

She – there was no question my nanny had to be female – would be a little older than me, ideally in her early thirties. She would be quite big, certainly heavy-breasted and broad at the hips, but firm, with plenty of muscle, padded by just enough fat at belly and waist to make it comfortable as she held me. Her arms would be strong yet soft, so that I would feel both cradled and controlled. Her nipples would be large – very large in fact, the areolae wide and dark, the teats broad and long, big enough to suck on properly. Her hands would also be large and, again, soft yet strong, ideal to hold me, masturbate me – even to spank me if she had to.

She would spank me but it would be gentle, with no cruelty in it, simply a necessary and occasional admonition. It would be done when I was naughty or difficult, and always on my bare bottom. As much as anything it would be done to reinforce her control over me and my reliance on her. I wouldn't need to be hurt, just put firmly in my place with a gentle but absolutely inescapable spanking. It would reflect her character, firm yet gentle, loving yet strictly no-nonsense, very practical. Inevitably she would want to take her pleasure of me, but again it would be done without cruelty, with none of the need to try and humiliate me that characterised both Monty and Natasha. She would stay clothed too, or at least partially clothed, exposing her breasts or sex as necessary, but seldom if ever naked.

I knew it was a lot to ask, especially as I would need to be changed properly, yet I was sure that somebody, somewhere would be close. In fact, rationally, there would be many people. As I know from my work, variation in human character is extraordinary, and anybody who uses such phrases as 'all women do this' or 'all men think that' are fools. Even somebody as determined to fit into what she saw as social normality as Jocasta Warren was a complex and highly individual being. Natasha fitted the city-girl stereotype still less well. Somewhere, my nurse would exist.

Having run over the ideal in my head, it was impossible not to take a moment for self-analysis. One thing I could be sure of was that it was not the image of my mother. Like me, she was tall and thin, with slender hips and small breasts. In personality she was warm enough, but detached and with a fastidious dislike of mess that I remember from earliest childhood. Many analysts would have argued that my nurse image in fact represented those female traits lacking in my mother. It was a theory that could not be easily dismissed, despite my not having developed the fantasy until my early twenties.

Those same analysts might have regarded it as a problem, something to be explored then got rid of. To my way of thinking, nothing is more important than feeling right about oneself. There was nothing I enjoyed more, therefore it was not a problem to me. The only problem was realising the full potential.

For the rest of the morning I indulged in the luxury of wandering around the flat barefoot and bare-legged, in just my clean nappy and pyjama top. It felt good, as it always did, just to be like that as I made coffee, read the news on the Net and went over the notes for my noon appointment.

At eleven I stripped naked, put everything related to my baby-girl persona into my special bedroom and locked the door. Twenty minutes later I was in a grey wool two-piece, a plain white blouse, tights, sensible shoes – and frilly pink panties, just to keep an edge.

My client was one of those who took therapy as a piece of conspicuous consumption rather than because she had any need for it. What she did need was for me to listen to her woes, which were frankly trivial, and to sympathise with her. As she was under no obligation whatever to come to me I was happy to do this. At the end I recommended increasing the frequency of her shiatsu sessions and changing the blend of her aromatherapy oil, simply because I knew she would not be content unless I made some sort of change. She left happy, which was what mattered.

There were two more appointments that afternoon, neither particularly taxing. The last was not really a client at all, Amy McRae, an old friend and the editor of *Metropolitan*, to whose recommendations I owed much of my success. She had been at college with me in Paris, and to bed, being an out and proud lesbian. That had been before I'd begun to develop my baby-girl fantasies, about which she knew nothing. Nor was she going to.

We had supper together, sharing a bottle of wine, which left me pleasantly relaxed when I returned to my flat. Lying on the sofa with my shoes kicked off, I began to muse on the problem of securing a good nanny once more.

What I could not do was trawl London's lesbian and fetish clubs for a suitable partner. It might have worked in the short term, but in the long run was sure to lead to my preferences becoming common knowledge. I needed somebody entirely detached from my own social group, and preferably from my environment altogether.

One option was to put my details on one of the Net's fetish dating sites with a suitable smokescreen to protect my identity. I'd tried before unsuccessfully, attracting plenty of fakes but nobody remotely suitable. It was also a passive technique and I prefer to take the initiative.

I'd looked for suitable adverts before, with no success. This time was no exception. After three frustrating hours I gave up and posted my own advert, with some trepidation and no great hope. That done, I retired to my ordinary bedroom.

The rest of the week passed without anything unusual happening. There were only two responses to my advert, both from males and utterly inappropriate. I had not forgotten about Monty, but if he was going to do something horrible to me I was not going to be the one to call. It was Saturday afternoon before he did.

As always, he expected me to be free, asking me to meet him in a pub in Croydon within a couple of hours.

He also made it clear that he wanted to punish me, and promised to make up for it. I agreed cautiously.

I had been to the pub before, the Green Dragon, a favourite haunt of his and, I suspected, also of his work mates. I was sure his motive was to show me off, as on the previous occasion he had twice exchanged knowing looks with other men, but for some reason had not introduced me. He had also asked me to dress in revealing clothing, which I knew meant in the type of outfit typically worn by the girls in the cheap pornographic magazines he favoured. That was not something I was willing to do, if only for aesthetic reasons, but I was prepared to compromise. He also wanted me without panties.

It had grown colder still over the week, and bare legs were out of the question. Jeans would have been sensible, but I settled on thick tights and a woollen skirt short enough to risk showing the tuck of my bottom if I bent over, under my coat naturally. A bra with plenty of support and a thick but tight jumper finished my look, very far from what he wanted, but enough to provide me with a pleasantly light sense of showing off.

He was there before me, his enormous buttocks spread across over half the width of a padded bench, in jeans, a faded sweatshirt advertising the tour dates of a rock group, and a blue anorak. In his hand was a pint glass of dark beer, with another glass beside it, empty but for foam.

He looked up as I approached, his grin growing wider as I shrugged off my coat and laid it across the back of a chair.

'Nice skirt,' he stated, his eyes travelling slowly up my legs, from ankles to hips. 'Turn around and bend down, yeah?'

'Not here,' I answered, 'but yes, my bottom shows.'

'No knickers?'

'I am afraid not. I find it uncomfortable bare under tights.'

'I did say. Maybe I ought to spank you.'

'If you really must. I agree that I owe you something, and if you wish to punish me you may, but please could it not be so hard this time?'

'It's no fun if I don't do it hard. You make such a fuss, and I just love the way you kick your legs about. You know your cunt and arsehole show when I do it, don't you?'

'Monty!'

A man at a nearby table had looked around as he had spoken. He looked quickly away as I met his eyes to whisper something to a friend, who sniggered, as did Monty.

'I bet they'd love to watch,' Monty went on. 'Maybe I should do it now, right here, in front of everyone. I bet that would get to you.'

'We would be thrown out.'

'Yeah, shame. Maybe another time. Don't think I wouldn't dare. I did it to Tasha.'

'I know. She told me.'

'Nice. She hated it, but she was so wet I could have stuck a cucumber up her and she'd never have noticed. Want a pint? This is 3B. They've got Broadside on, too.'

'Ricard, please, or absinthe if they have it.'

'Whoa! You want to watch that stuff.'

'If you intend to torture me, it seems advisable to be at least a little drunk.'

'I'm not going to torture you. I'm going to bugger you.'

He was on his feet and already walking towards the bar. The two men were staring again too, open-mouthed this time, one with his drink frozen halfway to his lips. I knew Monty was trying to embarrass me, and even wondered if the men were workmates. That was not what worried me, but his return to the topic of anal sex. Since I met him he had wanted to sodomise me, and when I had told him that I was anally virgin and too

37

tight to take his cock, he had simply grown more eager. Evidently he was going to use my sense of obligation to try and persuade me once more.

When he brought the drinks back he was grinning, but there was a familiar trace of petulance in his voice as he put the inevitable question.

'Well? How about it?'

I leaned forwards, replying in a whisper.

'I have told you, Monty, I simply do not have the physical capacity.'

'Bullshit. All girls can take it up the arse if they have to.'

'Not me. And, before you start, it is not a moral or hygienic issue. As you know, I take an irrigation nozzle frequently, and you may use a finger so long as you are gentle. Your penis is simply too large.'

'It would fit.'

'It would hurt!'

He made a sulky face. I sighed and took a sip of absinthe.

'It just that you've got such a pretty arsehole, Gabrielle,' he whined, with no attempt at all to keep his voice down, 'and you're virgin. I've never had a virgin arsehole. I just have to bugger you . . . please?'

'No.'

'At least let me try. I'll grease you up properly, with that cream you use.'

'No, Monty.'

'Ah, come. I'll be gentle, I promise. I'll do your thing too. You can even fill your nappy . . .'

'No!'

He went back into his sulk, moodily sipping at his beer. I was simply not going to give in, but the last thing I wanted was him in a foul mood.

'Cheer up, Monty,' I whispered. 'You can spank me with your hairbrush, all right?'

For a moment his mouth twitched up into the familiar sloppy grin. I winced, thinking of the pain and

38

the inevitable tears. The hairbrush I meant was a huge wooden thing he'd had since school. It stung crazily and left bruises, as I'd discovered when he'd used it before briefly, applying three agonising swats before I'd managed to call out my stop word. He didn't reply, but took another swallow of beer.

'Nude,' I offered, 'or dressed up any way you like. Come on, Monty. I will serve your dinner too, like last time.'

'I was thinking of a curry. I could just do with one.'

'I would rather not, but don't let that stop you. Have a takeaway and I will serve for you. Don't worry about me, because you can bottle feed me later. You can use me as a footstool while you eat, if you like, but you will put me in nappies later, yes?'

'Yeah, sure. I just want the better half of the deal this time.'

'Is not using me as a footstool good enough? It's very degrading.'

'No. I've got a better idea. That's what I'm going to do. I'm going to have my tea off your bare arse, then fuck you in the mess. You can clean up afterwards. How's that?'

I nodded dumbly, accepting my fate and reflecting that it wasn't nearly as bad as being spanked with his hairbrush. He was grinning again, and when he put his beer glass to his mouth it was to tip at least half the contents down in one go. Another swallow finished it and he immediately picked up the pint he had bought when he had fetched my own drink. A minute later he was finished, and my eyes were watering from swallowing my absinthe too fast.

It hit me quickly, too, so that I was feeling distinctly unsteady by the time we got to the Indian takeaway he favoured. I was beginning to feel aroused as well, with the thought of my coming exposure and what I would receive in return for my surrender to his perverse scheme. Unfortunately he had miscalculated. In his urgency to get started, he hadn't realised that it was over an hour until the takeaway opened. I could only laugh at his frustration, which got my bottom smacked in the street. I skipped away, still laughing, and simply made a face when he threatened to drag me down over the bonnet of a car. He knew I could outrun him with ease, and was forced to content himself with wagging one fat finger in my direction.

There was a minimarket next to the takeaway, and he disappeared inside, emerging a moment later with a bag. I was still wary of his threat to spank me in the street and kept my distance, walking ahead of him as we made our way back to his house. Only indoors did I let my guard down and was rewarded by having him grip me hard by the ear and force me down on to my knees, squeaking in pain. He laughed and pulled my head in to his crotch, then rubbed my face over the bulge of his cock and balls.

'Strip,' he ordered as he let go.

I nodded. The order had put me in role, and the only thing to do was obey, just as I expected him to follow my instructions exactly when it was my turn to have my fantasy played out.

I did it in the hallway under his watchful eyes, stripping stark naked as he squeezed his crotch and let his eyes linger on my body. Nor was it simply a matter of undressing. As soon as my coat was off I was made to turn round and bend over, showing him how my skirt lifted to show off the tuck of my bottom-cheeks. With me touching my toes, he took a leisurely feel of my bottom, then moved forwards to rub the now considerable bulge of his cock between my cheeks.

'I've saved it for you,' he told me. 'I haven't wanked for four days.'

I felt my throat tighten instinctively at the news, thinking of the extraordinary volume of sperm he always seemed to produce, presumably the result of eating so much.

'I might even do it over your tights,' he said, rubbing more firmly. 'That feels good.'

'No, please. I have only one spare pair.'

'Don't tempt me, Gabrielle. No, that would be a waste, but it is tempting.'

His cock was now fully hard, a rigid bar pressing in between my buttocks. He had me by the hips and was rutting freely with his belly resting on my upturned bottom, making me struggle to keep my balance. When he finally stopped it was so that he could pull his cock out. I stayed down, wondering if he was going to come over the seat of my tights after all. My skirt had ridden up with his pushes and the whole of my bottom was showing, tightly encased in blue wool, a sight I knew would appeal to him.

'Get on with it, then,' he ordered, and took his cock in hand. 'Stick your arse out and peel 'em down, nice and slow. Tights only.'

I obeyed, pushing out my bottom in a thoroughly lewd pose as I eased my tights down to show off the seat of my panties. Although I'd declined to go without, I had chosen tarty red ones, the sort he liked best, and he smacked his fat lips as they came on show.

'That'll do,' he instructed as my tights reached the level of my thighs. 'Tits out now.'

I stood and turned. I knew what he wanted exactly, a display of my breasts at once lewd yet coy, ideally with my cheeks flushed red with embarrassment as I showed myself to him. I did my best, pouting as I unfastened my bra and pulled it off down my sleeve, then raising my jumper to show him my bare breasts.

'Cute,' he remarked. 'I like you like that. Skirt off.'

He was pulling on his cock, quite hard, as I quickly undid my skirt and dropped it to the ground. Bending, I pulled it free of my ankles in such a way that I let him see my breasts loll forwards.

'Tights off,' he ordered. 'And do that again.'

I repeated the manoeuvre, taking my boots with my tights to leave myself in panties and the raised jumper. Monty was wanking harder than ever, his face already starting to turn red. As I stood up once more I turned to let him see the full effect.

'Now the jumper.'

I nodded and pulled it quickly up over my head. Again he licked his lips.

'Knickers,' he said, 'and stick it out as you pull them down, right out.'

I obeyed, or began to. He had started to puff and was jerking at his cock so hard that I was sure he'd come at any moment. As I stuck my bottom out and pushed my thumb into the waistband of the tarty red panties, he moved close, the head of his cock touching the material. I had already begun to lower them, showing the top of my crease, but I stopped, wondering if he wanted to rut between my buttocks again.

'Hold them out,' he grunted. 'Show your bum.'

He was really hammering at his cock, and I realised what he was going to do even as I pulled out the rear pouch of my panties to let him look down them. An instant later it happened, sperm erupting from his cock to splash across my lower back and between my buttocks. The second gout went down my panties, the third over the seat. Then he had taken me by the hips and pushed himself against me, rubbing in my crease, to smear the sperm between my buttocks and over his cock. I almost fell but held my place, letting him finish off over my soggy panty seat. When he finally finished I was left soiled and sticky, with the panties pushed into my cleft and sperm smeared from the small of my back to my anus, into which a piece had trickled as he rutted on me.

'Shit!' he swore. 'I meant to make you eat that. Still . . .'

He took hold of my panties and jerked them down. A finger was inserted between my cheeks to touch my anus and pulled slowly up, collecting the sperm from my crease. I couldn't help but screw my face up as I realised what he intended to make me do, but I opened my mouth obediently enough when the dirty finger was put to my face, slimy with sperm. He pushed it in and I sucked, tasting him and my own bottom, which really brought home the urgency of my sex. I began to suck eagerly, mouthing on his finger to get as much in as possible, until he finally pulled it free.

'Dirty bitch,' he remarked. 'Right, get those dirty knickers off and into the kitchen with you.'

I completed my strip, dropping the now thoroughly soiled panties and kicking them aside. Nude, and with my bottom-crease still slimy with sperm, I walked into the kitchen. The pinny was behind the door and I put it on without having to be told. He sat down, his cock and balls still hanging from his trousers, and began to unpack the bag of groceries he'd bought in the minimarket. There was a can of beans and another of meatballs, margarine, a loaf of bread and that was all.

'Get going, then,' he instructed, nodding to the little pile.

'I will stick to my bottle, I think,' I told him.

'Good, all the more for me.'

I began to cook or, rather, heat, as all it involved was pouring the contents of the two cans together in a grubby saucepan and putting them on the hob. I spread the margarine on to the bread as the rest heated up, all the while acutely conscious of my bare, messy bottom and of Monty playing with his cock behind me. By the time I'd prepared six slices of bread the beans had begun to bubble. I turned the gas off, not wanting to risk getting scalded, and turned Monty a questioning glance.

'How do you want me?' I asked.

'Well, you can go and wash your arse for a start,' he replied. 'You may eat spunk. I don't.'

I nodded and made for the bathroom to wash my bottom and inspect myself in the miserable little mirror he used for shaving. I'd shaved my sex and bottom that morning and my crease was pink and smooth, as was my pussy, although my vagina was already leaking fluid.

Back in the kitchen, Monty had spread the table with newspaper and placed his bread bin in the centre. It was big and made of tin, with a curved top, actually rather a good thing for bending a girl over – for punishment. The thought put a lump in my throat and my fear must have showed in my eyes, because Monty's lit up immediately.

'Of course, I owe you a spanking!' he crowed. 'I'd forgotten. You said I could use the hairbrush, didn't you?'

'Yes,' I admittedly sullenly, 'but not hard, please, Monty?'

'We'll see,' he promised. 'Get in position.'

He left the room as I crawled up on to the table, thinking miserable thoughts and cursing myself for allowing my face to betray my emotions. The bread bin was cold and made my tummy twitch as I laid myself across it, positioning myself so that my bottom was pointing straight up in the air, with my anus showing at the centre. It was hardly a comfortable position, but a girl doesn't need to be in a comfortable position to have her bottom smacked, not when it hurts so much, just a vulnerable one.

Monty came back almost immediately, holding not the hairbrush but a huge wooden spoon with the words 'The World's Biggest Stirrer' painted on the handle. It was enormous, the bowl just about big enough to cup one of my bottom-cheeks, and I could only stare in horror.

'This was what I first spanked Tasha with,' he announced proudly. 'You should blame her, really, if you don't like it. She was the one who got me into spanking, and I love it!'

With the last word he brought the horrible thing around hard, full on to my bottom. I heard the smack of the impact, mingled with my scream of shock and pain as it hit. It was worse than the hairbrush, far worse, agony. I'd jumped, but he grabbed me by the scruff of my neck and pushed my face down on to the table, even as a second swat caught me full across my cheeks to set my legs kicking and wring another scream from my lips. Monty just laughed and set to work, holding me down by my neck as he beat me, smack after smack until I was crazy with pain, kicking and screaming and wriggling my agonised bottom about in a futile attempt to escape the blows.

It was so sudden, so fast, that I didn't actually think to use my stop word. Nor did I burst into tears until it had finished, when I made up for it with a vengeance. He stopped as suddenly as he'd begun, to leave my bottom throbbing furiously, the muscles of my legs and stomach jumping, my sex contracting on empty air. It hurt so much, and as a great stab of self-pity hit me I just exploded into uncontrollable sobs, gasping and blubbering out my feelings into the newspaper under my face. It showed a picture of some dignitary, perhaps a mayor, smiling benignly as he bent to cut a ribbon, an image that stuck in my head and somehow made me feel yet more sorry for myself.

Monty had gone silent and let go of my neck. I knew he was wondering if he'd overdone it, and he had – but then, he always did. I was really blubbering, with my whole body shaking to my sobs, and I simply couldn't speak or I would have told him exactly what I thought. Then he began to stroke my hair, and my response was immediately turned in on itself. I turned to manage a weak smile.

'Too hard, yes?' he asked.

I nodded feebly. I was shivering and blind with tears. There was mucus running from my nose on to the picture of the mayor, along with the spittle from my open mouth.

'It's got to be done, you know, Gabby,' he said. 'I'll show you why.'

Even as he finished speaking, one fat finger found my sex and pushed in, up my vagina in one easy motion, to make me gasp again, only not with pain.

'No girl's ever so wet as when she's been spanked,' he said, 'or you're not anyway, nor's Tasha.'

I didn't answer, but slumped back down, laying my cheek into the little pool of my own wet on the newspaper. I could see Monty, just about, still with his cock and balls hanging out of his trousers. Whatever the spanking might have done to me, it had certainly affected him. His cock was already half hard, pushing up against the overhang of his belly, with the red tip half out of the foreskin.

'Tea time,' he declared happily, and turned to the stove.

He picked up the saucepan, dipped a finger in, sucked it and nodded in satisfaction. I braced myself, confident it wouldn't be scalding, but sure it would be hot. It was. He brought it up over my bottom and tipped gently. I gasped as the sauce touched my skin full between my cheeks, and again as the first trickle reached my anus, a third time as my vagina began to fill. Monty just chuckled and poured faster, slopping the beans out into my crease. They landed as a mass, filling my cleft and spilling out across my buttocks and the small of my back, also down over my sex and on to the tops of my thighs. The meatballs came with them, the last of them plopping down between my buttocks to leave my whole rear soggy, with the mess trickling slowly down over my skin. I could feel the weight of it too, a not unfamiliar sensation that drew an involuntary sigh of pleasure from me.

Still looking back, I watched Monty replace the saucepan on the stove. He picked up the plate of bread

46

and margarine I had prepared for him and put it down behind me out of sight. I was still clutching the table, the way I had been when my spanking finished, and moved to rest my cheek on my hands as he took a knife and fork from a drawer, then a spoon.

I was wondering why he needed three implements, and tried to look back over my shoulder as he came beside me and bent over the pile of food on my bottom. He had the knife and fork in one hand, the spoon in the other, his fat face beaming as he lowered it to touch my sex.

My mouth came wide as my vagina was levered open. My hole immediately filled with baked beans, trickling in along with the sauce until a meatball blocked my passage. Monty gave a cluck of amusement, took the knife and pushed it in.

'Must you?' I managed as I felt it squash in my hole.

'Yes,' he answered decisively, and tugged down on the spoon.

It hurt, and I gave a hiss of pain as my vagina was stretched wide. More beans went in, and another meatball, which Monty pressed in after the first. A third followed, and a fourth, Monty chuckling in childish glee as he stuffed my vagina. When he eventually pulled the spoon out I was so full I could feel the wad of food inside me, again a not completely unfamiliar feeling.

My bottom still hurt but I was back in control, more or less, and starting to enjoy what was being done to me, if only because the feelings were so similar to one of the nicest things of all. Monty seemed happy stuffing me, and I let him get on with it, even purring a little as more and more of the mess was caked into my vagina.

Finally he tired of the game, put the spoon down and began to eat, using the knife and fork to scrape up beans and sauce from my bottom. I relaxed into it, actually quite enjoying the rough, smacked feeling of my bottom-flesh, as well as the slowly cooling food. I closed my eyes, imagining a different situation, with not Monty but my *bobonne* standing over me, scraping mess off my bottom as she chided me gently for getting into such a state. It was a nice fantasy, and had me purring properly before Monty had finished with my bottom-cheeks and began to eat what was between them.

I knew he was getting excited when he put the knife down and began to tug at his cock. Hoping he'd lick me, I lifted my bottom, only to have the fork jab into my flesh, right down in my crease.

'Ow!' I complained. 'Careful!'

Monty nodded and put the fork down. A moment later I got my wish. He didn't hesitate but just buried his face between my upturned buttocks, indifferent to the mess. I felt the beans squash out over my bottom again and into my crease, against my anus. He began to lick, and to kiss, taking individual beans up off my roughened bottom-skin with his lips, and lapping at the sauce left behind. It was getting good, very good indeed, and I was hoping he'd make a proper job of my sex and make me come.

It got better when he began to clean up my crease, with his tongue right on my bottom-hole, a sensation I enjoy second only to having my clitoris licked. He made a thorough job of it too, lapping and probing until my hole was pulsing and urgent. It was also vulnerable, and I was terrified he would try and sodomise me as I was so obviously ready for penetration.

He didn't try anything, despite his cock being rock hard once more, but licked until my crease was clean and wet, with my anus moist and a little open at the centre. Only then did he turn his attention to my sex, mouthing at my vagina to suck out a mouthful of meatballs and beans. Most of it came out in one, and I gasped again as I was unplugged, to leave my sex gaping and ready. I was wondering if he would have the decency to make me come or just fuck me, and I was going to ask – only for him to forestall the question. He had begun to suck up the sauce from my pussy, and when his lips found my clitoris I could only stick my bottom up for more as a long sigh escaped my lips.

For a moment he stopped to move round to the end of the table. I groaned in disappointment, thinking he was going to mount me without making me come, and I was going to speak again when he took me firmly by the legs, pulled them wide and buried his face in my bottom. He kissed my anus, sucking at the little ring, lapped at the little bar of flesh between my holes, probed my vagina briefly, kissed my sex-lips and suddenly, sucked my clitoris into his mouth, hard. I screamed at an unbearable sensation combining ecstasy, a stabbing pain and the worst tickling sensation imaginable.

'No, too much!' I gasped. 'Ow! Monty!'

He just ignored me, holding my clitoris between his blubbery lips and licking the end. It was truly unbearable, but he'd got me by the thighs and was pulling me into himself, with his nose stuck up my pussy and the bristles of his face rubbing on my sex. I screamed again, utterly out of control as my muscles went into spasm, buttocks and thighs squeezing in his face, my sex twitching and jumping. I was coming, my vagina in frantic contraction, my anus pulsing, my muscles jerking, then rigid as his teeth closed on my clitoris.

I really screamed with the full force of my lungs, and jerked frantically to one side with all my force. Monty held on but let go of my clitoris. I lashed out frantically behind me, struggling to hit him even as I babbled for mercy. All I succeeded in doing was slapping my own bottom, but he stopped to pull back, with his fat, grinning face smeared with baked-bean juice, and blurred because my glasses had fallen off.

'Nice,' he said. 'Don't you just love it?'

All I could do was collapse, unable to speak, unable to think straight. My head was spinning, my vision blurred. My sex felt red raw, adding to the pain in my bottom, and I could feel what remained of the mess he'd put up me dribbling slowly down over my pubic mound and between my thighs.

'Hang on a minute, and I'll fuck you,' Monty remarked casually.

Something touched my bottom, wiping at one sauce-smeared cheek. I managed to turn my head, wondering what he was doing, to find him stuffing a piece of bread into his mouth, left handed, while he tugged at his cock with the right.

I lay still as he ate the bread, slowly recovering. Each piece he used to wipe sauce up from my bottom, and in doing so smeared me with margarine. By the time he'd finished, my bottom was a greasy, shiny ball, my reddened cheeks glistening in the light as I craned back again to see. He'd stood up, his face still crammed with bread, and was swinging one huge leg up on to the table.

'Cunt time, Gabby,' he announced as he swallowed. 'God, I just love the way skinny girls show from the rear. Cunt on show, arsehole on show.'

The table groaned as Monty climbed on behind me. He straddled my thighs, his fat legs squashing them together, although my position still left my sex vulnerable. Also my anus, as he'd pointed out to me.

His cock came down in the cleft of my cheeks, hot and hard, his balls squashing between them to the rear of my sex. He began to rub.

'You're squashing me, Monty,' I protested.

'I adore your arse, Gabrielle,' he sighed, ignoring me completely. 'You're so small and round and girly, and your arsehole shows nearly all the time, so pink and tight. You need to be buggered, so badly.'

'Monty, no.'

'Maybe I should just do it. Maybe I should just tie you up good and tight, grease you well and stick my cock up that dirty little hole. You'd soon get to love it.'

'Monty!'

'Oh, all right. I don't see why you have to make such a fuss, though.'

'Because it would hurt! You might even tear my anus.'

He gave a sceptical grunt and went back to rubbing his cock in my bottom-crease. I was helpless under his weight, so that if he wanted to sodomise me he could. It was terrifying, knowing he wanted to do it, and that his excitement would be telling him to, and as he took hold of his cock and pushed into down into my cleft I was bracing myself to be forced.

I'd have screamed and struggled, maybe managed to stop him. More likely I'd have been sodomised. Fortunately he had enough decency left not to try, but contented himself with rubbing his cock-head on my anus before putting it to my vagina, and up.

It was impossible not to sigh as I filled with cock, but there was relief as well as pleasure. He began to fuck me, grunting and panting as always, his belly slapping on my upturned bottom. I was sure there were still meatballs up my vagina, because there was an odd, squashy feeling inside me.

He didn't seem to care in any case, humping away happily on my bottom, and pulling out occasionally to rub himself in the slimy valley of my bottom-crease. I knew it would take a while, or that he might not even find the energy to come a second time, and tried to relax, despite the feeling of being crushed. When he was well in the hairs on his balls would tickle my clitoris, which was nice, but never enough to bring me off. Before long I was beginning to want to come properly, but with the bread bin in the way I had no way of masturbating. I could only be patient, enduring my fucking with the knowledge that my orgasm would be nicer still once I was full of sperm.

As his panting became more urgent I pushed my bottom up to meet him, hoping some lewd behaviour would take him over the edge. He pushed harder in response, and faster, until I was panting and clutching at the table in reaction, only for him to stop suddenly, wheezing and gasping for a moment before he spoke.

'I can't,' he puffed. 'You're too sloppy. Let me use your arsehole, Gabby, please?'

'No, I am sorry, but no,' I managed. 'Wait a bit, Monty, then finish. That was nice.'

'I can't. I really can't. Not up your cunt. You're so fucking sloppy. Come on, Gabby, I can see you're ready. Your arsehole's greasy and loose. I know I could get my cock up. God, you need buggering, so badly.'

'Monty!'

'Oh, all right!'

He began to climb off, silent as his cock pulled out of my hole. I wasn't going to let him sulk, and waited until he had sat down before getting up myself. My whole body ached, but I went down anyway, kneeling between his thighs with my mouth open in invitation. He resisted for a second, then slid forwards on the chair and lifted his belly, offering me his cock and balls.

I nuzzled my face in, licking his balls, which were dirty with juice. When I took his cock in it tasted of processed meat, but I sucked anyway, quickly bringing him back to full erection. If he was messy, I was worse, with fluid dripping from my sex now that I was the right way up. I knew there'd be a puddle under me, and wondered if I dared pee on the floor before masturbating. He was going to make me clean the mess up anyway.

I let go, putting my hand to my sex as the piddle spurted out, hot and wet on my fingers, pooling in my palm and splashing out to run down my thighs. Monty was watching me suck his cock, and if he noticed he gave no sign, just grinning down at me as I mouthed eagerly on his penis and my puddle spread out beneath me. I let it come, as much as I could, until I was kneeling in it, with my sex and the tuck of my bottom wet and warm. I'd have done more if I'd been able to, but it was enough. I shut my eyes, concentrating on the delicious thought that I'd just peed on the floor as I began to masturbate.

Monty had begun to grunt and to push his cock up into my mouth. A phone rang somewhere in the background but he ignored it, taking me by the head to control the motion of my sucking. He was going to come, and I rubbed harder, eager to reach orgasm as I got my mouth filled.

I didn't make it. His cock jerked; I felt the sperm erupt into the back of my throat and my mouth filled with the salty, male taste. He grabbed his cock, pulling my head back to try and spunk in my face, but managed no more than a dribble, which he wiped on to my nose. I was close and squatted down, sitting my bottom in the pee-puddle. My mouth came open, letting him see the pool of come and saliva inside, which began to run out as my jaw went slack. Some fell between my breasts and I slapped it over them, rubbing yet harder.

He was watching me, amused by my urgency, grinning out of his dirty, red face. I thought of my nudity, the way I was completely on display to him, naked, while all he was showing were his cock and balls, and that so they could be used in me. It was glorious, utterly abandoned, naked, fucked, wriggling my bottom in a puddle of my own pee, masturbating furiously as I smeared his sperm over my breasts. I started to come, gasping as my thighs locked on my hand, my muscles twitching, my bottom splashing in the piddle as I squirmed and jiggled, until I hit my peak, long and high and so, so good.

'Dirty bitch,' Monty remarked as I finally slumped down.

I nodded in acknowledgement and gave him a smile. I was still high and eager for my turn, which I had undoubtedly earned. It was going to take time, though, and the first thing I was going to make him do was spend a good half-hour creaming my bottom. Both cheeks felt bruised and tender, while my sex was more than a little sore. It was definitely time for play, and not for conventional sex.

Monty was still recovering his breath, with one hand on his chest, a gesture I always found worrying. I let him take his time and stayed squatted down in my rapidly cooling pee-puddle, not wanting to break the game. Only when he began to wipe the baked-bean juice off his face did I speak.

'I am afraid I have piddled on your floor. I think I need to be put in nappies.'

'OK, but you can clean your mess up first, while I see who that was on the phone.'

'Monty!' I protested. 'Never mind that. Do you not want to watch me clean the floor?'

'Hang on.'

He left the room, waddling out as he stuffed his cock and balls back into his trousers. I sat still for a moment, cursing him, then got up, reasoning that it wouldn't take long, and that I could start on the floor. In fact, the whole kitchen needing doing, and not only the mess we'd just made. Monty was an absolute slob and there wasn't even any kitchen towel, only an unopened packet of disposable dish-cloths stuck behind a tap, where it looked as if it had been for months.

I do actually enjoy cleaning up, especially in the nude, so I retrieved my glasses and set to work, opening the packet and wetting a cloth. I did myself first, or at least the worst of it. I was sweaty and plastered with various kinds of muck from my lower back down to behind my knees – also my sex, belly and breasts. I was going in the pee-puddle anyway, and the floor was filthy, so there was no point in more than a quick rub down, which I managed.

Monty was talking to somebody on the phone, patiently at first, but with ever greater irritation. I wanted him to watch me mop up the pee, so started on the table and bread bin. He went on talking, with my sense of sexual submission gradually fading to be replaced by irritation. He was talking about computers, so it was obviously something to do with his work. Finally he put the phone down, to re-enter the kitchen looking peevish.

'I've got to go in,' he told me.

'What, now?'

'The whole system's crashed.'

'It's Saturday, Monty, nearly six o'clock.'

'Our servers are down, everything.'

'Is there not somebody else to sort it out?'

'No. I'm the man.'

'How long are you going to be?'

'Depends.'

As he had spoken he had picked up his anorak and pulled it on. I just stood there, the dripping dish-cloth in my hand, feeling incredibly frustrated and not a little angry.

'Ring back, say you're busy,' I suggested.

'No can do.'

'You're ill? The car has broken down?'

'Look, I've got to go, Gabby. Wait, yeah? I'll be as quick as I can.'

I opened my mouth, intending to say something stinging. What came out was truly pathetic.

'Don't be late, please?'

'Climb in bed if I am.'

His last remark was made from the hallway. A moment later the door shut behind him and I was left, absolutely seething. I was not going to get my baby-girl session, not soon anyway. At best I could stay over, which was never comfortable, and wait for the morning. It was hardly ideal.

I dropped the dish-cloth into the sink and sat down, forcing myself to think sensibly. Monty had to get to Reigate, sort out the problem and get back. It was unlikely to take him less than a couple of hours, very likely more. If he returned at nine, or even ten, there would be time for some play, if nothing elaborate. In any case it was likely to be a poor recompense for what he'd done to me. After all, my bottom was bruised, making it quite obvious I'd been spanked, so I wouldn't even be able to visit the Haven, or at least not to go naked. If he was very late, he would be too tired to look after me properly, and would grow sulky if I pushed him.

It had also broken my mood, so I quickly dealt with my puddle and went up to the bathroom to wash properly and inspect my bottom. I was a mess, with curved, deep red marks on both cheeks where the end of the spoon had caught me, along with a general flush of rich pink. The bruises were already starting to rise. There was no question that anybody who saw my bottom would know I had received physical discipline. It was going to be at least a week before I could visit Haven or do anything else that involved being bare-bottomed in polite company.

Not surprisingly there was nothing to douche with, so I did the best I could with Monty's shower hose. I calmed down as I washed, reasoning that it was unfair to blame Monty. After all, had I received an urgent call from a client during an elaborate sex session I would certainly have done the same, and expected my partner to understand my choice of priorities. It was still irksome, but the only sensible thing to do was clearly to try and make the best of a bad situation.

Even in Monty's absence I could play a game with myself, building up slowly until his return, when he could take over. In many ways it was ideal, as it would allow me to become thoroughly aroused before he became involved. That avoided the problem of his becoming excited long before I was ready for actual sex. Not that I particularly minded being put on his cock in the middle of a feeding session, or being fucked while having my nappy changed, but it was not the ideal.

By the time I'd finished my shower I knew what I was going to do. I dried myself and went to fetch my bag, lying on his bed to powder my pussy and bottom-hole before I began to cream myself. I took my time, lying face down with a mirror adjusted so that I could see my bottom and the rear view of my sex as I rubbed cream into my smacked cheeks. It felt as soothing as ever, more so for having been spanked so hard. By the time my whole bottom was a smooth, glossy ball I was feeling properly relaxed and also aroused. My anus showed in the mirror and I began to tickle the powdery little hole with a nail. It was tempting to apply more cream and put a finger in, even two, which was about as much as I could take. It would have been too early and I held back, contenting myself with teasing and thinking arousing thoughts.

His central heating was full on, making the house pleasantly warm – warm enough to stay nude, or at least semi-nude. Once I was satisfied with creaming my bottom I selected a nappy and put myself in it, lying down as if I was being changed. Even before the tabs were fastened it had started to work, making me want to squirm and wriggle on the bed, with my bottom stuck out to display the fat pink bulge behind, or my legs rolled up to show off the way it covered my pussy.

I could see in the mirror too, my body naked but for around my hips; my feet bare, my legs, my chest, everything, but for the puffy pink nappy around my middle. I'd been letting my hair grow out, long enough to make a short pony-tail or even little spiky bunches. I'd been going to wait a little longer then do it with pink ribbons, just as a treat for myself. Now seemed as good a time, assuming Monty owned anything girlish enough to work.

I couldn't see him owning any ribbons, and pink was not his colour. Cloth would do, at a pinch. He was pretty obsessed with girls' panties, and I had a sneaking suspicion he collected them. He'd kept a pair of mine from the first time we'd met in any case. On another occasion he'd had me wank him off with the pair I'd been wearing wrapped around his cock, then pocketed them so I had to go back with nothing on under my skirt.

I felt a little guilty going through his drawers, but decided that having to search through his own under-clothes was punishment enough for the breach of courtesy. His chest of drawers drew a blank, also his wardrobe and the drawers under his bed.

There were no panties, but there was plenty of porn, unfortunately all too tacky to excite me. Judging from his collection his ideal woman was about eighteen, with uncomfortably large breasts, a big bottom and extreme-ly cheap taste in clothes. Two were devoted to spanking girls, both recent issues, another to bondage, but none to girls peeing, let alone grown-up baby girls. I quickly gave up and returned to my panty hunt, which had now become a need in its own right, regardless of my desire for ribbons in my hair.

Despite my not having found them anywhere obvi-ous, it seemed safe to assume they were in his bedroom, given his dirty habits. For the same reason it seemed likely that they were somewhere easy to get at, or at least fairly easy. I tried the top of the wardrobe but found only dust. There were various boxes, none of which proved fruitful, although there were more porn magazines and also videos.

Failure only made me more determined. He had two pairs of mine and I hadn't found them. Therefore I wasn't looking in the right place. Clearly they were hidden, although it seemed odd that he would hide his collection of panties more carefully than his magazines or videos. I started to consider less orthodox spaces and struck lucky with my first try. They were in the space beneath the lowest of his drawers, a gap six inches high, accessible simply by pulling the drawer completely out.

One glance and it was obvious why they were carefully hidden. There were hundreds or pairs, far more than he could possibly have been given by girlfriends. The realisation put a catch in my throat, and for a moment I wondered exactly who I was dealing with. Only when I had examined a few pairs did my qualms recede, partially at least. They were all clean, except for mine and one other pair, so he had evidently stolen them from washing lines rather than actually removed them by force. Having said that, if anybody had forcibly divested women of the number of pairs of panties in his collection there would have been a major outcry, even if it had been done over several years.

They were also labelled, every single pair, with a neatly printed card pinned to each, recording a place, a date and sometimes a name. I picked mine out, one pair and then the other, and read the legends – 'Gabrielle Salinger, nappy freak. War Down Man, Hampshire' and 'Gabrielle Salinger, girlfriend. Home'. The dates they had been removed followed.

I wasn't entirely happy about being referred to as a 'nappy freak', although as he freely described himself as a 'panty freak' I didn't imagine it to be intended as an insult. Nor was I sure about 'girlfriend' – but there was a much greater concern, which was that he was a panty thief. It didn't altogether surprise me, but it was hardly socially acceptable behaviour.

In my position of intimacy, the responsible thing to do was clearly to try and talk him out of it. Unfortunately that meant admitting I'd searched through the room for his collection. I was going to have to do that anyway if I wanted pink cloth to make hair ornaments. I decided against that, both because they'd been so carefully concealed and because it seemed wrong to spoil a pair when he had taken such obsessive care over the collection.

My discovery had broken the mood in any case, much to my annoyance. I began to look through the collection, very carefully, fascinated despite my moral reservations. The collection, along with Monty, could probably have produced enough information for a doctrinal thesis, certainly a spectacular case-study. Not that he was likely to co-operate.

The collection reflected his tastes and was certainly not random. There were no huge granny pants and nothing suspiciously small, only pretty briefs and thongs, mainly scarlet or black, along with white, pastels and the odd bright primary. He also seemed to have a taste for nylon.

Only when I began to worry about him coming back did I start to put them back. I was careful, replacing each pair exactly as it had been, every bit as methodical as Monty himself. My own had been on the top, along with a white silk pair belonging to Natasha, making me wonder if he had given up his dirty little hobby since he had been having sex with us. It seemed entirely possible and added a new dimension to my moral dilemma.

With the panties safely away, I lay on the bed, thinking and trying to get back in the mood for baby-girl sex. It was not easy, with images of Monty sneaking through darkened alleyways and into people's gardens to steal girls' panties constantly intruding on my thoughts. I also kept expecting him to come back.

Eventually I gave up and went to make myself a coffee. Oddly enough that worked where all my deliberate efforts had failed. Being in just my nappy as I walked about downstairs gave me a thrill I had been unable to achieve in the bedroom. Pleased with myself,

I swallowed the coffee and followed it with two pints of water. After that I knew what would happen, and I could feel my sense of erotic tension building slowly as I waited, simply reading one of Monty's books on military history to help pass the time.

I was hoping he'd come back before I was ready, but there was still no sign of him by the time my bladder had begun to feel tense. I fought the urge down, letting it build with my arousal. Very slowly it began to get painful, but still I held back, wanting Monty to watch. Before long I was on my knees in the centre of the living-room carpet, holding my tummy, with my sex clenched tight to keep it in. Only when my eyes had begun to water with the pain did I give in, letting go to fill my nappy with pee and my head with a glorious, unmatchable sense of relief.

With my nappy hanging soggy and heavy between my thighs it was more than I could resist not to masturbate, Monty or no Monty. I did it with my eyes closed, one hand down my wet nappy, the other in my mouth, to bite on my fingers and suck on my thumb as my orgasm hit me in a wave of ecstasy that faded all too quickly to disappointment.

Three

Monty returned sometime after three in the morning. By then I was fast asleep, curled up in his bed with my thumb in my mouth, by instinct rather than for the sake of sexual arousal. He woke me, hoping for sex, and got turned down. It was the same in the morning, and he went into such a sulk that I ended up going home.

I was seriously wondering if it wasn't time to call an end to our relationship, or agreement, which was a better description of the way we worked. It was not good. I'd let him use me exactly as he'd pleased, and been left to masturbate for my own pleasure. When he had finally come back what he had expected was a quick blow-job, with no consideration whatsoever for my needs.

With every meeting he seemed less suitable. On the other hand, there was the fact that without me he would probably go back to being a peeping-Tom, a panty thief and whatever else he got up to. To cut him dead was clearly irresponsible, and went very much against my personal ethics. I would have to be tactful at the least. I also felt obliged to speak to him about the panties.

It seemed sensible to discuss the matter with Natasha, and that was not the only reason I needed to speak to her. Following my conversations with Monty, I was beginning to wonder about her motives in introducing me to him. Certainly the two of them seemed more compatible than he and I, considering her love of physical punishment and her ability to be aroused by humiliation. At the time I had accepted her assertion that he would make a good playmate for me. Since then it had come to seem increasingly likely that she had found him more than she could handle, and had simply wished to get rid of him safely by foisting him on to me. She was also the only person I could talk to about my need for a proper nanny, so I had no intention of risking bad feeling between us. I called and she agreed to meet me for lunch on Monday, at a favourite haunt of ours, the Café Eperney in Covent Garden.

I arrived early, ordered a glass of the Sylvaner they do and went to sit in my favourite alcove, well away from where we might be overheard. Inevitably there were several people I knew there, including clients, but all of them respected my obvious need for privacy except for Jocasta Warren. After throwing a few hopeful glances in my direction, she left her table and came over to mine.

'Gabrielle, hi. Have you got a moment?'

'Certainly. Although I think I should warn you that I'm lunching with Natasha Linnet.'

'You are?'

'Yes.'

'Oh. Well, anyway, I've been thinking over what you said about my novel, and I think you're right. I've got this great plot, original, but right up with the times.'

'Good.'

'This is it. My heroine is a woman, thirty-something, independent, professional, attractive, very strong . . .'

'Essentially how you see yourself, only in ideal terms?'

'No, no. She'll be totally different. Much slimmer, a natural ash blonde, totally confident in her appearance and ability. I want my readers to sympathise with her. She's not in journalism either. She's in films.'

She paused to take a swallow of her water. I held my peace, both amused and interested by the subtlety of those distinctions she saw as making her character 'totally different' to herself. To a truly detached observer they would have been barely distinguishable. Essentially the plot was a piece of personal wish fulfilment. I could see that it would benefit her, or at least distract her. She went on.

'The plot is that she's made her first film, writing the script and directing. There's this critic and he really slates the film, so badly it flops. Now the clever thing is that he's an ex-boyfriend, or maybe someone she's turned down, but she doesn't know that. Anyway, she's really down and only keeps going because all her friends are telling her how her work is really great. The only trouble is, she can't get finance any more, so it looks like she's finished – only she meets this other guy and falls in love with him, and it turns out he's really rich. So he finances her new film and it's a smash. Great, yeah?'

'I'm not an expert, Jo, yet does it not rely a little heavily on coincidence? Also, if the first man successfully slates the first film, why not the second?'

'Yeah, I've got to get rid of him somehow, haven't I? You don't sound as if you like it.'

'As I say, I am no expert. I note that it does not relate to your problems with Natasha, which can only be positive.'

'Yeah, I decided that was the wrong thing to do.'

'Wise.'

'So anyway, let me tell you about . . .'

'Natasha is here.'

'Oh.'

Jo turned, looking distinctly worried, as if expecting a confrontation. Natasha was in the doorway and bounced over to the table, smiling happily, to greet us both.

'Hi, Gabby. Hi, Jo. How's the therapy?'

'Progressing,' Jo answered, managing to put a considerable weight of accusation into the single word.

'Not hitting the Prozac, then?'

'No, Gabrielle advised against it . . .'

'I was joking, Jo. Lighten up.'

'I'd better be getting back to my friends,' Jo finished, and left. Natasha laughed, kissed me and sat down.

'Sylvaner?' I offered. 'A spritzer?'

'Not on a day like this. It's freezing. Australian Shiraz. I'll get it.'

She turned to signal the waiter, allowing me a moment to consider her and see if she had made an effort to project any particular signals. It was a habit, but in her case only practice, as I could simply ask.

Her hair was freshly done, the loose brown curls arranged with artless simplicity to accentuate the delicacy of her face. She had made up carefully to enhance the brilliance of her eyes and the shape of her slightly full mouth, but in understated tones. Her manner was vivacious, playful, careless; a reflection of her true character rather than a contrived mood. With her full-length leather coat on it was hard to tell how she was dressed, except that her blouse was a brilliant orange silk, and had at least two buttons undone at the neck. The image was neither stern nor exceptionally girlish, which brought me an instinctive touch of disappointment.

'No sex today,' she said casually. 'I'm flooded. Third day.'

'You're good at reading expressions, Natasha.'

'No, I just thought I'd let you know. Otherwise I'd have been up for it. After all, we haven't seen each other properly for, what, two months?'

'Slightly more.'

'Must be. So what's this with Monty Hartle? How are you getting on?'

'Not so well. He isn't ideal for me, while his own tastes are frankly abusive. He beat me with a spoon, among other things. I'm quite badly bruised.'

'I know the feeling.'

'So he tells me.'

'Did he make you roll the big dice, to see how many swats you got?'

'No, he just beat me, then ate a revolting mixture of beans and meatballs from my bottom.'

'That sounds like Monty.'

'Yes. There is another thing. Did you know he was a panty thief?'

'Yes, he told me.'

'I discovered his collection. Over a hundred pairs. All but a few stolen from washing lines.'

She laughed.

'It is not funny, Natasha.'

'Oh, it is! It's hilarious.'

'What of the victims?'

'Having a pair of panties stolen hardly makes you a victim. Sure, I suppose having Monty creeping around in your back garden could be pretty alarming, but he's harmless really.'

'I know. Still, such behaviour can have serious effects. I have had clients require months of treatment to get over far less.'

'Well, yes, but they're your clients, aren't they?'

'I beg your pardon?'

'Oh, come on, Gabby. Half your clients are neurotic. The other half only go to you because they need somebody who'll listen to them wittering on about their boring lives, and to show off how much they can afford to spend on luxuries.'

'That is not entirely how I see my work, Natasha.'

'Sorry. You know what I mean, though. Look at Jo Warren.'

'You've added a whole new dimension to Jocasta's psychological imbalance.'

'Well, she's a silly cow, then. She should have spanked me when I gave her the chance.'

'Perhaps, but we were discussing Monty Hartle. There is another thing, Natasha, and please don't take this as an aggressive statement. When you introduced me to Monty, were your motives entirely altruistic?'

'Yes, completely.'

'I suspect you felt his behaviour, and perhaps his appearance, to be unacceptable, a liability?'

'No way! You know how it was. You can handle exposure so much better than me, and I knew he'd do your nappy thing for you. OK, so I only ever really got off because he's so gross he brings out my feelings of humiliation, but he still does. Sorry, but it's not my fault he's too rough for you. Still, you can spank me if you want, when my period's finished, maybe cane me.'

'I was not intending to punish you. I simply wanted to know.'

'Shame. Seriously, maybe he is a bit freaky for me, but I did think you two might get on as well, honestly. I mean, body image doesn't seem to bother you.'

'Something you didn't know until after you had arranged the meeting, and which is not entirely true, although my preferences for body image are admittedly unconventional. Did your reasons include his being a panty thief?'

'No. Like I said, it doesn't bother me all that much. He does have some morals. He won't touch or deliberately scare a woman. At least that's what he says.'

'I am sure of it. So far as actual interaction is concerned, he likes to know what is going on inside a woman's head, for her feelings to be strongly sexual. Fear and revulsion don't appeal to him, although he enjoys loss of control.'

'That sounds about right. So what are you going to do, dump him?'

'Possibly. I'm concerned that if I do he might go back to panty stealing, peeping and so forth.'

'Oh, I wouldn't worry about that.'

'I would.'

'Yes, you would, I suppose. You can't take the whole world's problems on your shoulders, you know.'

'This problem relates directly to me. I would feel responsible. Besides, he isn't all bad, and entirely tolerant, although very far from my ideal nurse.'

'No?'

'No. I need a woman, Natasha, a woman who enjoys being in charge of me, yet isn't cruel.'

'Unlike me?'

'Unlike you, as I think you would agree.'

'Yes, although I hope it's not going to stop us playing together. I like what we do.'

'No. I like it too. I just wish that if you have to spank me, you would be less rough.'

She smiled, then giggled as she realised that the waiter was standing directly behind her in the act of uncorking a bottle. I waited as she went through the ritual of tasting, accepted the wine and allowed him to pour her a glass. Lifting it, she spent a moment admiring the deep red-purple colour against the weak winter sunlight, took a sip, then spoke.

'I'll tell you who probably could help, if you want a decent nurse, and that's Percy.'

'Percy Ottershaw? Your spanking playmate?'

'Yes. He knows lots of people, and he's discreet. He might well be able to introduce you to somebody. He'd expect to spank you, of course, but that's only fair.'

'Why do they always want to spank me?'

'Because you've got a cute bum? No, seriously, if you want to find somebody who enjoys your submission, especially with what you're into, you can pretty well guarantee they'll want to punish you. Count yourself lucky it's not tight bondage and hot wax. '

'You are saying the desire to spank me is a corollary to the dominant counterpart of my baby-girl fantasy?'

'Yes. In my experience.'

'*Merde.*'

'Exactly, and you can hardly blame them. Still, I'll tell Percy you want somebody gentle, and we'll see.'

If the Internet was proving slow, then the same could not be said for Natasha and Percy Ottershaw. She called on the Friday night, drunk and giggling, with a recommendation, a woman called Anna Vale.

It sounded good. Anna was apparently in her early forties, a misandrist lesbian with an obsession for the fashions of the middle twentieth century. She lived in north London with her long-term girlfriend, Poppy, a relationship which apparently included domination on a twenty-four hours a day, seven days a week basis. I would fit in, Natasha assured me, and both were apparently looking forward to nursing me on Sunday. I accepted without hesitation.

It meant putting Monty off, but my bottom was still bruised and I wasn't entirely happy with him, so that was no great hardship. He sulked a bit when I told him I wasn't coming down, but he had little choice but to accept my decision. I didn't tell him what I was doing.

I wasn't entirely sure about the retrospective part of the fantasy but, as always, if she was prepared to accommodate me, it was only fair that I reciprocate. It was also fun buying towelling and big old-fashioned nappy pins, which took me most of Saturday afternoon to find, and provided a delicious thrill of anticipation in the process.

By the time I got back, I was eager to explore the fantasy but held back, contenting myself with spending the evening sewing my towelling into large squares, cut to fit my hips. I made four, which I was sure would be enough. Once finished, I experimented a bit, learning how to fold them and put them on, naked, as seemed appropriate. They felt heavier than my modern nappies, and more comfortable, soft and snug around my bottom and sex, albeit less safe. It took all my willpower not to go in one, but I managed and contented myself with sleeping in my special room, nude and masturbating myself to sleep.

Sunday morning was clear and cold, with frost on the trees outside my window. I dressed appropriately, with a woollen body stocking over my underwear, jeans, a thick jumper and lined boots. Even with my coat on it felt cold outside, and I hurried down to the station.

The address was in a part of north London I had never visited before, a typical suburb of large Victorian and Edwardian houses on tree-lined roads. Anna Vale's looked little different to any other, save for the ancient car parked outside it. Natasha had been discreet, giving nothing away to them, not even my name, and I was wondering how to introduce myself as I approached the front door. As a grown-up baby girl I like to be called Miss Gabby, or just Gabby, and it seemed best, especially if they lived permanently in role.

I pressed the bell, a huge thing with a ceramic button set in brightly polished brass, and was rewarded with a deep chime from inside the house. There was a lump in my throat, which I swallowed, telling myself it was foolish to feel nervous. A shadow appeared beyond the coloured diamond panes of the door, a latch clicked open, and it swung wide to reveal an exceptionally pretty young woman. She was only a little older than me at perhaps thirty, small, with short, curly black hair, a snub nose and a full figure. She was also in a maid's uniform, a dark blue dress with a white pinny over it.

'Poppy?' I ventured. 'Hi, I'm Gabby.'

She smiled and ushered me in. I followed, my hopes rising rapidly. Other than being considerably shorter than me, she was close to my physical ideal as a nanny. I was already feeling submissive, and wiped my feet carefully before following Poppy into what was obviously the living room.

Inside, the house was anything but typical. For a start, just about everything was brown, either paint, or wood. There was a radio, a huge wooden thing with an elaborate veneered front, but no television. There were several aspidistra, glazed tiles, old fashioned furniture and fittings, right down to the light switches. It was also immaculate, polished brass, gleaming wood and spotless floors.

Poppy took my coat and left me. I spent a moment looking at the embroidery samplers and prints of hunting scenes they had chosen for decoration, before I heard footsteps and she came back with another woman, evidently her mistress.

Anna Vale was tall and slim, too slim for a nurse really, but I was more than willing to accept that. Otherwise she really looked the part: ramrod straight, with a lean, haughty face and long, shiny brown hair pinned up into an elaborate bun. Her clothing consisted of a tweed twin-set, the skirt reaching to just below her knees, a crisp white blouse, sensible shoes of brown leather, and fully fashioned stockings. She took charge immediately, greeting me with the briefest of nods.

'Do sit down,' she said, gesturing to one of the armchairs. 'You are a friend of a friend of Penny, I understand?'

'Natasha? Through Percy Ottershaw?'

'I have never met the young lady, but as I have Penny's recommendation that you are genuine in your needs I shall accept you on trust. You understand that I administer genuine corporal punishment in this household?'

'In a way, yes. Natasha explained. One moment, please. I thought you were a friend of Percy Ottershaw?'

'I do not have male friends. I was contacted by Penny, who assured me that you were . . . a playmate of a friend of hers.'

I nodded, wondering why Natasha hadn't explained, but too interested to really care.

71

'I am somewhat wary of journalists,' she went on, 'and those who would take a prurient interest in my affairs. Therefore, I insist that young ladies who come to me take a mild punishment to prove they are genuine, as I'm sure your friend explained.'

'No. She did not. What sort of punishment?'

'Nothing severe, my dear, there is no need to look so worried. Six of the best.'

'With a cane?'

'Naturally.'

I nodded. I could see the logic behind her argument, but I was wishing Natasha had told me, also wondering if the omission had not been intentional. I'd seen Natasha caned and it had left her in tears. I was not at all sure if I could take it.

'You accept?' she asked.

'I do, yes,' I said quickly. 'I accept your reasoning anyway. It is just that I have a very poor tolerance for pain. I am also quite bruised. Perhaps you could just spank me, if it is really necessary.'

'It is absolutely necessary,' she insisted. 'I must be sure of my girls. Yet you say you are bruised?'

I nodded. There was only one thing to do. I stood to take down my jeans, only to realise that with my body stocking on I was going to have to strip very nearly naked to show her. Soon I would be nude, so it seemed pointless to quibble.

They watched, Anna cool, Poppy smiling to herself as I stripped, peeling off my jumper so that I could shrug my body stocking down off my shoulders. I had no bra, and ended up topless as I opened the button of my jeans. Turning, I pushed it all down to show my bare bottom, complete with the smack marks applied by Monty with his spoon.

'I see,' Anna stated. 'You have been punished, haven't you? And how did that come about?'

Given her attitude to men, it seemed unwise to tell her the truth. It was also an opportunity to arouse her.

'I was spanked for impudence,' I said. 'By Natasha.'

'So you are punished regularly?'

'Fairly. She likes to punish me. She is too cruel to make a good nurse, which she understands.'

'Cruelty has no place in such a relationship.'

'Yet you use the cane?'

'I use the cane for discipline. There is, as I am sure you know, a natural hierarchy among women. It is naturally for those higher in the hierarchy to punish those below them. There is no cruelty in this.'

It was not the time to argue. Standing there, holding my jeans and body stocking down to show off my bare bottom, with both of them fully dressed, my sense of exhibitionism was rising steeply. If she insisted that I fit in with her complex mind games, I was prepared to do my best. For a moment she stayed silent, contemplating my rear view.

'Tell me more,' she demanded.

'She beat me across the kitchen table,' I explained, 'with a bread bin under my stomach to lift my bottom. It was done with a spoon, a big spoon.'

'How many smacks?'

'I do not know.'

'I would have made you count them out loud.'

'I couldn't have kept count. It hurt dreadfully.'

'Yet you took it.'

'I had no choice. She held me down by my hair.'

'Nonsense. You are how tall? Five foot ten?'

'Five foot nine.'

'And you are certainly muscular. She is big, this Natasha?'

'Not really, no.'

'If you lay over a bread bin, my dear, on top of a kitchen table, and she only had a grip in your hair while she beat you, one can be certain that you were willing. Or at the least you must have been aware that you deserved your punishment. Don't lie to me, my dear, I have a great deal of experience.'

'I am sorry. I took it, yes.'

She went silent again, and stood up. I shut my eyes as she came up behind me to run her fingernails over the skin of my bottom. They were long and sharp, making me shiver. Poppy giggled.

'It seems to me, my dear,' Anna stated, 'that if you can take a good spanking with a spoon, you would have no real difficulty accepting the cane.'

'I cried a lot,' I admitted. 'I have never been caned.'

'Never been caned?' she said. Poppy made a smacking noise with her lips in blatant anticipation.

'Well, I think we all know what ought to be done about that, don't we?' Anna said.

'Must you?' I asked and I heard the catch in my own voice.

'I must,' she said. 'You are genuine, I can see, but you have a lot to learn about discipline.'

'I hate pain,' I protested.

'Naturally,' she answered. 'If you didn't, there would be little point in punishing you, at least by this method. Poppy, run and fetch my cane, there's a good girl. Bend over a little more, Gabby, and pull in your back. A young lady never forgets elegance, even while she is being punished. Now, I am glad you seem to know how to behave. The first thing to understand while here is that you remain absolutely under my discipline and Poppy's. You may leave at any time obviously, but there are no stop words or any such nonsense.'

I nodded.

'The house rules,' she went on. 'You will call me Miss Vale at all times. Poppy you will address as Nurse. She will be responsible for you. I will remain aloof, except to administer any discipline which may be required. Poppy may spank you, if it proves necessary. Anything serious enough to require more will be brought to me.'

Poppy had scampered out. I could have left. I nearly did. Everything seemed to revolve around discipline. I'd been there a few minutes and I was about to be beaten, exactly what I didn't want. I was also naked from my neck to my thighs, and if I took what Anna wanted to give me I would shortly have two extremely attractive women to look after me. If I didn't, I would be out in the cold street, frustrated. I decided to take it, biting down my fear and trying to tell myself that it was only six strokes.

So I got into the position Anna wanted, with my back tucked in to stick out my bottom. She paid no attention and her face betrayed no emotion as she stepped back a pace. I pulled my back tighter in, opening my cheeks to show off both sex and anus. A barely perceptible nod acknowledged my change.

For maybe a minute I stood there, my fear and vulnerability rising, until my toes were twitching in my boots. There was a sick feeling in my stomach, and I would probably have run if it had gone on much longer, but Poppy came back. She was holding not one cane but several, in a bundle tied with a piece of red ribbon. They were horrible-looking things, thin and deep brown, marked with darker stains which it was impossible not to imagine as the sweat of the poor girls whose bottoms they had been applied to. I had put my hands on my thighs and found my fingernails digging into my flesh as Anna pulled a cane from the bundle.

'Relax, if you wish it to be less painful,' she instructed. 'It is unwise to tense your flesh.'

I obeyed, forcing myself to let my bottom and thighs go loose. She nodded and lifted the cane to tap it against my skin. My muscles jumped at the contact and I shut my eyes, trying to tell myself I could bear it, that it was worth it, that I could control my bladder during the beating.

The cane was lifted. I heard my own broken sob and it hit me, a sharp, sudden sting, so abrupt that I had jumped up, clutching my bottom, my mouth wide in a soundless scream, before I even really knew it. There was a line of fire across my bottom, the skin roughened as I held myself, hissing between clenched teeth and hopping up and down on my toes. For a moment the pain was unbearable, but it faded and I managed to get back into position, my bottom stuck out.

'I would not normally tolerate such a display,' Anna remarked. 'However, as it is your first time . . .'

She hit me again on the last word, once more sending me into a dance of pain, jumping up and down on my feet with my breasts jiggling about and my mouth wide open. Poppy giggled.

'There is nothing humorous in this situation, Poppy,' Anna warned. 'Do you find it funny when you yourself are beaten?'

'No, Miss Vale,' Poppy said hastily, backing a couple of steps towards the door.

She hung her head and I could see the trembling in her fingers, making me wonder what she could expect if Anna decided to punish her. After her open show of pleasure and amusement at my own distress, it was impossible not to hope that it would happen and that I would be able to watch.

'Position,' Anna ordered.

I stuck out my bottom, screwing my eyes up tight and telling myself I would stay still.

It was hopeless. The instant the cane bit into my flesh I was back on my toes, hopping up and down and clutching at my burning bottom. I had three lines now and I could feel all of them, making me wonder how I now looked from behind.

'Do try and maintain some dignity,' Anna said. 'Position.'

Once more I stuck out my bottom, and once more that awful cane was lashed down across my buttocks. I did try hard but still ended up doing my silly little dance as she waited patiently for me to get control of myself.

I'd had four, more than half, and as I stuck my bottom back out for the fifth I was telling myself it would soon be over. The cane came down, hit, harder still, and I screamed, jumping up once more before sinking to my knees in raw agony with my hands behind me clutched to my bottom, indifferent to the fact that I was effectively holding my cheeks apart.

'Silence!' Anna snapped. 'I thought at least you could control your noise.'

I shook my head miserably as I climbed to my feet. The tears were threatening to start in my eyes, but there was only one to go. I bravely stuck out my bottom, trying to think of soothing cream and the comfort of being held to another woman's breasts.

The stroke came down and for the sixth time I jumped to my feet, squealing and making a show of myself, but this time with a sense of triumph running through my head. It hurt a lot, but less than what Monty had done to me and more importantly I had passed the test. I was still filled with self-pity at the thought of what had been done to me, and the tears were trickling freely from my eyes, yet it was over, and that was what really mattered.

'Yes, well, I can see that you're a baby,' Anna said. 'A big baby, but undoubtedly a baby. Poppy, see to her.'

I was still sobbing and I let Poppy take me by the hand without resistance. I was led upstairs, clutching my lowered clothes and trailing my bag behind me, one flight, then a second, to a plain attic room, clean and neat but without ornament.

'This is where I'm sent when I'm bad,' Poppy explained. 'It'll be your nursery while you're here. Come this way.'

She gave me a gentle tug and I followed to where a full-length mirror stood in a wooden frame. It reflected my whole body, near naked. I looked rather forlorn with my jeans and body stocking pulled down, and the little pink crease of my bare sex showing between my legs.

'Turn around then, no time for vanity,' she said.

I obeyed, craning back as I turned to inspect my bottom. It was a mess of colour, yellow, black and dull blue from Monty's beating, along with six perfectly parallel red lines, each broken across the crease of my bottom, where I'd been caned.

'That,' Poppy said, 'is what a caned bottom looks like. Before we send you home, we'll take a picture so that you can stick it on your bedroom wall as a reminder of what happens to naughty girls.'

'I wasn't naughty!'

'So?'

I replied with a weak smile, knowing exactly what she meant. It didn't matter why I'd been caned; a picture like the one I could see in the mirror would have made any girl better behaved if she thought for a moment it might happen again.

'You are staying, aren't you?' Poppy demanded. 'Overnight, I mean.'

'I could . . . I don't know. I wasn't really expecting to be caned like that. I like gentle things.'

'I'll be gentle,' she promised, her hand coming out to stroke my hair. 'Even if you need your little bottom smacked I won't be too hard. Please stay over.'

I nodded, managing a weak smile and wishing fervently that things had been arranged so that it was Poppy looking after me, without Anna. The beating had got to me, though, and if I felt resentful I also felt submissive. Certainly it was going to be very, very easy to give in to Poppy.

'We'd better have your clothes off, then,' she said, suddenly all brisk efficiency. 'Can you do it yourself?'

I shook my head. She clicked her tongue and pulled me towards the bed, on to which I was pushed down.

She kneeled to take my boots one by one, pulling them off. My body stocking and jeans followed as one, pulled up and off my legs to leave me stark naked.

'We won't be needing these,' Poppy announced, bundling my jeans and boots together and throwing them towards the door. 'But this might work.'

She was holding up my body stocking and smiling faintly.

'Yes,' she stated. 'You can go in this and a nappy, naturally.'

'I've brought some,' I said. 'They're in my bag.'

'Good,' she said. 'Although we do have some. I get put in them sometimes. As a punishment.'

'A punishment? Don't you like it?'

It was a silly question, which she answered with a smile. Like Natasha, she evidently became aroused by humiliation. She had gone to my bag and lifted it on to a chest of drawers, where she began to examine the contents.

'Nappies, bottle, cream, powder, pins . . . you are well prepared. I suppose you expect me to soothe your bottom after your caning?'

'Yes, please . . . Nanny.'

'Nurse, please.'

'Please, Nurse Poppy. I am sore.'

She nodded, trying to hide a smile as she picked up the tube of cream.

'Over my lap, I think,' she said. 'Come along.'

She sat, patting her lap. I crawled over eagerly and she took me around the waist very gently. Immediately my tension started to drain away, to be replaced by the most delicious feeling of surrender. As I felt the cold cream squeezed out on to my bottom, I knew I had been right to stick with it, to take the cane, however much it had hurt. I winced as her fingers touched my bruised skin, but I was also sticking my bottom up to let my cheeks open to her and make my surrender absolute.

79

'You are eager, aren't you?' she responded.

I just purred. She had begun to rub the cream in and it felt so soothing, making me want to melt into her. It wasn't just the cream, either. I could feel her big breasts pressing to my side and feel her flesh through her dress, soft and resilient.

She knew what she was doing, too, smearing the cream evenly over the full area of my bottom and rubbing it in with slow, circular motions of her hand. Nor was she coy about it, allowing her fingers to move down into my bottom-crease, a little deeper each time towards my anus, until I was dying to be touched. I held my peace, sure she would give me what I needed, later if not immediately.

After a while she began to sing, so quietly I could barely hear the words, a lullaby I'd never heard before. I lay still, listening, my body absolutely relaxed across her lap as she continued to rub in the cream, round and round, ever closer to the centre, but never touching, teasing me, to bring me slowly on to full heat.

By the time she finally began to get properly rude, Monty, or any man, would have had his cock up me, come and probably gone to sleep. Not Poppy. She was enjoying herself immensely, but she was in no hurry. With my whole bottom creamy and warm, but no longer painful, she finally began to see to my sexual needs. She knew what to do as well, lifting a knee to bring my sex into prominence. Her fingers found my anus, tickling the little hole before smoothing cream over it and pushing just a little way up. I would have let her put her finger up, or more, as much as she wanted, until it began to hurt. She didn't try, but squeezed out a fresh squirt of cream into the palm of her hand and turned her attention to my pubic mound. I'd shaved in the bath that morning and was completely smooth, as a grown-up baby girl should be. Poppy appreciated it, enjoying the feel of my sex as I moved myself in her hand, wiggling my hips against the gentle pressure as she massaged me.

When her thumb finally found my clitoris I was ready to come anyway. It took moments, a casual, unconcerned act of masturbation, giving me exactly what I needed, exactly when I needed it. The orgasm was long and abandoned, with my pussy clenching and my bottom-hole opening and closing in little spasms, utterly uninhibited, the way it should be. When I'd finished she giggled and gave me the gentlest of pats on my bottom.

'That's better, isn't it?' she said. 'Now into your nappy, and you can have a little nap before lunch.'

'Yes, Nurse,' I answered, 'and thank you. That was wonderful.'

'Now, now, no need for that,' she replied. 'Miss Vale knows you need these little things, but she doesn't approve of talking about it. Come on, up you get.'

She slapped my bottom again a little more forcefully, and moved to roll me off her lap. I climbed down to sit on the floor as she went for my nappy. I was really still coming down from my orgasm, but watching her was still good. She was quick, matter of fact and smiling happily as she picked up what she needed and gestured to the bed.

'On you go,' she ordered. 'Lie down.'

I got on the bed, lying full length, acutely aware of my nudity and what she was about to do to me. I was used to being taken by the ankles and lifted bodily so that the nappy could be slid under my bottom. Poppy was less physical.

'Bottom up,' she said as she flipped the nappy over to make a neat triangle.

I lifted my bottom off the bed, allowing her to push the top of the nappy underneath. As she moved her hands I lay down, feeling the sensitive, smacked flesh of my bottom settle into the towelling.

'Legs wide,' she ordered, 'and up.'

I lifted my legs and opened them, showing her absolutely everything, completely vulnerable to her. She casually took the bottom corner of the nappy and pulled it up between my legs, pressing it to my tummy.

'Legs down a little, and together,' she said. 'Hold your nappy for me, there's a good girl.'

She reached out to take a nappy pin, placing it between her lips. I did as she told me, squeezing the nappy between my thighs as she tugged up the sides, wrapping them together over my tummy to swaddle my hips in the soft towelling. It was tight, more so than when I had been experimenting, and it felt better still. Poppy pinched the material to make it bulge and allow her to push the pin through all three layers, securing my nappy firmly in place.

I lay back, stretching, letting the feel of being naked but for a nappy flow through me. My breasts were bare and it didn't matter, not in the least. In fact, it would have been silly to cover me, except for warmth, and they had the heating full on. Naked was best, except for my nappy, and that only for the most simple and practical reasons, which had nothing whatever to do with modesty.

'There we are,' Poppy said happily, 'all snug and cosy. Now, you get into bed, and I'll wake you before lunchtime.'

I scrambled quickly into the bed, which was warm from our body heat, with fresh linen beneath the plain blankets and coverlet. Poppy kissed me and tousled my hair, then stood. She began to walk away but paused, turning back to me.

'You want to do this properly, don't you?'

'Yes, Nurse.'

She cast a quick, uneasy glance towards the door, then leaned closer.

'Out of role, yes?'

I nodded.

'You're not going to be awkward when I want a little something myself, are you?'

'No. I promise.'

'I'm sure you do but, whatever happens, you mustn't tell Anna. OK?'

'I promise. Just remember, I really cannot take much pain, and I am quite badly bruised already.'

'No more beatings, I promise.'

She kissed me full on my mouth, then again, the tiniest of pecks on one cheek. As she got up she was grinning and there was a bounce in her walk as she crossed to the door. I wondered what she wanted and why I couldn't tell Anna Vale. Whatever it was, she was welcome. After the way she had treated me I could do nothing less.

I snuggled down into the bed as the door closed behind her and stuck my thumb in my mouth, sucking happily as I wondered what was in store for me. Having passed Anna's test, it seemed fair to hope that there would be no more beatings from her, so long as I was good, and Poppy had promised. That meant I didn't have to worry about my poor, abused bottom any more and could get thoroughly into role, relying on Poppy to do what was needed. She seemed to have a considerable understanding of my fantasy, presumably because Anna treated her the same way during nappy punishment, even if it was to humiliate her.

It was warm and cosy, and I felt completely relaxed. I hadn't intended to sleep but I did, waking to the sound of the door being opened. It was Poppy.

'Lunchtime,' she announced. 'Miss Vale says you're to come down and eat with us. It's your favourite, bangers and mash.'

I managed a smile and stretched, still trying to get my head around the situation as I returned to consciousness. Poppy went to pick up my body stocking, shaking it out.

'In your suit,' she ordered. 'Sit on the bed and I'll help you.'

I swung my legs out, still sleepy as she began to invert the body stocking. As always, she was brisk and efficient, after inverting it, pushing on one foot, then the second, before rolling it up my legs. I stood to allow her to pull it up over my nappy, and helped with the last bit.

It wasn't something I'd tried before and it felt strange, but undeniably good. For one thing it made my nappy feel tighter and created an unmistakable bulge around my hips, leaving no doubt that although I was decent I was still in nappies. Fairly decent anyway, because it was tight across my chest and the outlines of my breasts showed, along with my nipples. It felt appropriate too, babyish, or rather grown-up babyish, as there was no doubt at all it looked sexual.

Poppy took me by the hand again to lead me downstairs. As with the rest of the house, there was nothing modern about the kitchen. Even the refrigerator was an old-fashioned model, and I began to wonder what it would cost to live the way they did, before pushing the thought out as inappropriate. Poppy had been cooking and it did smell good, although bangers and mash would not have been my normal choice for lunch. The amount she'd made was not normal either, a huge pile of mashed potato, stuck with sausages and topped with boiled cabbage and a large knob of butter. I thought it was for all three of us until she had sat me down and put the plate in front of me, along with a wooden spoon.

'Do you need to be fed?' she asked.

'I ... I am not sure I can even eat that much, Nurse,' I managed.

'Nonsense,' Anna Vale spoke from behind me.

It was a single word, but it carried a strong implication of caned bottoms. I was not going to argue.

'Yes, Miss Vale,' I answered her.

'There's a good girl,' she said, 'and my, don't you look pretty?'

'I'd better feed her,' Poppy said. 'Just to make sure.'

'Absolutely,' Anna agreed.

I waited as Poppy served out their own plates, both with about a third as much food as was on mine. Poppy took my spoon and scooped up some mashed potato and cabbage, so much I had to gape wide to take it in.

'Good girl,' she said as I struggled to swallow it. 'There we are, that wasn't so bad, was it?'

It was actually excellent, which was just as well. I was made to eat every single bit, until the plate was scraped clean, and wash it down with a pint of orange squash. By the time I'd finished my stomach was a hard, round ball beneath my body stocking, uncomfortably full. I actually felt slightly sick, and was praying they didn't intend to make me do anything energetic in the afternoon, or at least not for several hours.

Nor was it the end. There was jelly and custard for dessert, and again I was spoon-fed by Poppy and made to swallow down every single mouthful. Neither of them had any, and I was left feeling dizzy and bloated, holding my tummy through my body stocking. I was even wondering if making me sick was part of what they intended for me and whether I could cope.

It wasn't. After lunch I was sent to my room and simply left to my own devices. I lay on the bed, curled up, just sucking my thumb and thinking. It felt beautiful; detached, safe. Even the strain in my tummy subsided to a pleasant sensation of fullness after a while. Outside my window the sky was a clear eggshell blue, criss-crossed with vapour trails. I watched them dissipate, a new one form, and that in turn dissipate. Nothing else served to mark the passage of time, allowing me to slip into a pleasant, half-aware state, absolutely relaxed.

Nothing was going to disturb me – not Monty, with his hard cock and cruel fantasies; not a client, in distress because her boyfriend had wanted her to go halves in a restaurant, or refused to go halves; nothing. There was no tension, no pressure, no phone to ring, no emails coming in. If Poppy wanted something of me, that would be all right; she was my nurse. Even then it would be she who took charge, she who decided what to do. For me, there was simply no responsibility whatever.

Before long the orange juice I had been made to drink began to take effect. I simply let go, with my eyes closed in bliss as my pee gushed out into my nappy to leave the towelling soggy and warm around my bottom and sex. That felt better still, just lying in my wet nappy on my side, with a wet patch spreading slowly out across the rear of my body stocking. I put my hand back to touch, feeling the bulge of my nappy, the heavy, squashy feeling of the wet towelling and the damp wool where my piddle had leaked out.

I turned bottom up, and for a while I just stroked myself, letting the erotic side of my fantasy rise up once more to find a balance with the delicious sense of irresponsibility. I knew I was going to masturbate eventually, when I needed it, but there was no hurry, none at all. For one thing my body suit would have to come down, and I liked the feel of it, especially the way it made my nappy tighter and the wet patch that now covered my whole bottom.

Both hands went back to squeeze my cheeks through the nappy and pull it tighter up into the crease of my bottom and against my sex. It felt delicious and I cocked my legs apart, lifting my bottom further to get the material in between my sex-lips. I felt the pee squeeze out as I tugged, to trickle down and on to the bed. Briefly I wondered if I'd be punished, but the wet towelling was against my clitoris and it was too late. It was too late to stop either, and I realised that I was not going to have to take my bodysuit down at all.

I began to tug at the rear of my nappy, each jerk rubbing the wet material on my sex and squashing out more pee over my bottom. It was difficult, but I knew it would happen, and focussed as I began to tug faster, and harder. I thought of the condition I was in, in nothing but a body suit and a wet nappy, absolutely surrendered to the pleasure of my fantasy. I thought of Poppy and the way she had creamed my bottom so lovingly and masturbated me so well. Suddenly I was there, coming in a long, dizzying orgasm that left me limp on the bed, purring to myself, with my sodden nappy still clutched tight up between the cheeks of my bottom.

It was nearly dark before Poppy came up to find me still in my wet nappy. She tutted a little but set to work. She stripped both me and the bed, and I was sent to stand naked in the corner while she produced fresh sheets and blankets. With the bed done, she changed me, bustling around the room to fetch water and flannels, washing me, powdering my bottom and sex, and applying a touch of cream. I was spanked but ever so gently, just a half dozen pats delivered with my bottom stuck out, before being put in a new nappy.

'Better?' she asked as she fixed the pin into place.

I nodded, sticking my thumb into my mouth as I sat down on the bed.

'Anna's had to go out,' she went on, 'so I'm going to have a little fun with you, Gabby. Now remember what you promised – no sulking, and no sneaking.'

I nodded once more. She smiled.

'Does your bottom still ache?'

'Yes, Nurse,' I answered, as it was obviously expected of me. It was also true.

'Oh, dear,' she sighed, 'well, I don't suppose it's anything that a spoonful of cod liver oil won't cure.'

'Cod liver oil?'

'Now, now, Gabby, what did we just say about sulking?'

I nodded weakly, thinking of all the jokes about cod liver oil and wondering what it actually tasted like. One or two of my clients took it. I'd never tried it. Now I was going to.

Poppy had gone to a cupboard, the only thing in the room painted white. It was set high on the wall and marked with a large red cross, evidently a medicine cupboard. It wasn't just for show either. She opened it to display a range of old-fashioned bottles and tins, along with several carefully folded paper packages and one or two worrying-looking devices.

The largest bottle of all was the cod liver oil, and if the contents couldn't have dated from the fifties, the label certainly did, or earlier. She had also taken out a spoon, a full-sized tablespoon, into which she poured a full dose of the oil.

'Open wide,' she said happily.

I obeyed, and in went the spoon. As I closed my mouth it filled with the most revolting taste. I screwed my face up in response and swallowed, forcing it down and struggling to stop myself from gagging. Poppy watched, trying to hide the amusement in her face and not really succeeding.

'All gone?' she asked. 'Good. Now, you do look a little flushed, so I think I'd better take your temperature. Roll over on the bed, bottom up.'

I obeyed, watching as she returned to the cupboard, replacing the cod liver oil bottle and taking out a mercury thermometer, which she shook before holding it carefully up to the light. I knew exactly where the thermometer was going, up my bottom.

Sure enough, she came over and sat down beside me to tug the back of my nappy down. She spread my cheeks between finger and thumb and applied the thermometer to my anus. I was already creamy and it went in easily, to leave me lying flat with it sticking up from between my bottom-cheeks as she carefully timed five minutes, all the while holding my nappy down. Finally the thermometer was pulled out, and again she held it up to the light.

'A little high,' she stated. 'Not much, but I think we had better keep you in bed. I think an enema would do you good as well.'

'Yes, Nurse.'

She got up, trying to keep a serious expression on her face as she crossed to the medical cupboard, but not entirely succeeding. There was a large bulb among the various bits of apparatus, and as she took it I was already imagining it being pushed up my bottom-hole, only for a door to thump shut below us in the house.

'Shit!' Poppy swore. 'She was quick.'

'Does it matter?'

'Not for the enema. I want sex with you, Gabby, rude sex.'

'Can we?'

'Not unless you want another beating.'

'Oh.'

'It's complicated. If I want sex it comes at a cost. The same applies to you.'

'I see. What were you going to do?'

'Give you your enema, maybe play with your bottom a bit. Something nice and dirty. I love your bottom.'

'Thank you. I might be able to say the same if you showed me.'

'I daren't, not with Anna ... Miss Vale downstairs. Look, I'll come to you tonight. We should be safe.'

I nodded my agreement, not speaking because I could hear Anna's footsteps on the stairs. A moment later she called for Poppy, who hurried away. Once more I was left, now wondering where Poppy's little medical game would have led, and what she meant by 'nice and dirty'.

About an hour later I masturbated again, thinking of how it would have felt to be given my enema by Poppy. Supper came soon afterwards, a reasonable amount this time, but in the same basic English style; cottage pie with brussels sprouts, followed by more jelly and custard. Poppy read to me afterwards and left with a wink. Within an hour I was asleep.

It was pitch black when I woke up to the feel of a hand on my shoulder. I realised it was Poppy even as I pulled out of sleep, from the sensitivity of her touch and her scent.

'Shh! Not a sound,' she whispered. 'Can I come in?'

I nodded, which she may not have seen, but which she felt and took as an invitation. As she pulled my covers back I moved against the wall, making space for her in my bed. She crawled in, pausing only to tug up her nightie before taking me in her arms. I cuddled into her, kissing at her face as her warm, soft body pressed to mine. Her mouth found mine and we were kissing properly, our tongues moving together eagerly. She was stroking my hair and back one-handed, the other lower around my waist, then lower still to cup my bottom, holding the seat of my nappy.

We stayed like that for a long while, kissing and caressing each other, Poppy with her hand always on my bottom, stroking me through the seat of my nappy. Finally she pulled her mouth from mine to cuddle into my neck, her mouth to my ear.

'You like to be wet, don't you?' she whispered.

'Yes,' I answered her.

'And . . . and more?'

'Yes,' I said, shivering at the implication of what she was saying.

For a long moment she was silent, just stroking my bottom through the nappy and holding me into herself. When she spoke it was quieter still, and there was a catch in her voice.

'Sometimes,' she whispered, 'I'm made to do it, in my nappy, you know, everything, and made to stand in the corner, with it all in the back. I want to feel you, like that, Gabby, please.'

I nodded, my chest flushing hot at the thought of what she wanted me to do.

'Are you ready?' she whispered. 'I bet you are.'

'Yes.'

'Then do it. Let me feel it. Don't say a thing, just do it while I hold you.'

I nodded, cuddling tighter into her. I was shivering, absolutely abandoned, surrendered to her. She was right about me being ready too. I could feel the pressure in my insides, low down, in my rectum. All it took was a little concentration, a little conscious effort to overcome that last vestige of what we are taught to think of as decent behaviour, and my anus was opening to let out what was inside. I sighed as it began to happen, my bottom-hole pouting and spreading to the pressure from within to stretch wide. The head was out but I could have stopped, and I did hold, savouring the moment, an exquisite instant of delicious abandonment before I passed the point of no return and let go. Suddenly it was coming out into my nappy, thick and firm, to push out the pouch of towelling beneath my bottom.

'Oh, you're doing it,' Poppy sighed as my growing bulge began to fill the cup of her hand. 'Oh, you dirty little angel.'

She kissed me and squeezed me tighter still, holding me close as my nappy filled, my mess pushing into a hard lump under my bottom, which grew quickly as I let out more and more. All the while she stroked my bulge, shivering against me and kissing with ever greater passion. I began to pee too, just a little, wetting the front of my nappy and Poppy's skin where she was against me.

'You've wet, lovely,' she sighed. 'Now more at the back, really push. I want to feel it swell.'

My mouth came open under hers as she began to kiss me again. My nappy felt heavy, dangerously full, but I knew there was more, and pushed, my bottom-hole opening again. Out it came, my bulge growing fatter still in Poppy's hand. She squeezed it gently, pushing it against my bottom, making me aware of just how much I had done. There was still more though, and I kept pushing, my sense of utter abandonment growing as I soiled myself, my arousal too, until at last it was all out, the full, fat load of dirt which came of being forced to eat so much lunch hanging heavy in my nappy.

'Have you done it, everything?' Poppy asked as she finally broke away from my mouth.

'Yes,' I breathed.

She moaned, squeezing my bulge again more firmly and wobbled it against my bottom.

'Dirty girl!' She giggled. 'Now you can rub me while I hold it.'

I moved a hand down over the swell of her little tummy and lower. She held on tight, shivering in my arms, her face pressed against my neck. Her sex was plump and very wet, my fingers slipping deep into the groove between her lips. She moaned as I started to rub and cuddled tighter to me, squashing my load yet more firmly against my bottom.

'That's right,' she sighed, 'just like that. Make me come, Gabby, make me come while I feel what you've done in your nappy. Oh, that feels awful. There's so much. It's so heavy. Dirty slut.'

She finished with a little choking noise and I felt her hand squeeze hard on the mess in my nappy. I began to rub harder, full on her clitoris, drawing more excited sounds from her as her breathing began to speed up. I was scared she would make a mess but didn't have the heart to stop her, letting her knead the filth in my nappy as I masturbated her until at last she came, with a little pained cried as her thighs squeezed on to my hand. With her orgasm spent, she began to babble.

'Thank you, Gabby. Thank you. Oh, God ... you didn't mind, did you? Tell me you didn't?'

'No,' I answered, moving my hand up to stroke her hair. 'Whatever you need, Poppy. Don't be ashamed.'

Her answer was a little snivelling sound and I realised she was crying. I held on to her, letting her spill out her emotions in her own time and all the while stroking her hair to soothe her and telling her that what she'd done was all right. We needed to clean up, but I waited until her snuffles had subsided before kicking the bedclothes off and propping myself up on one elbow. Immediately I noticed that a light had come on, visible as a line of brilliant yellow beneath the door.

'Poppy?' I whispered. 'I think Anna's awake.'

'Shit!' she swore. 'Oh, God! We're done for! Quick, pretend I'd come up to change you, pretend . . .'

'Pretend what?' Anna Vale's voice sounded from the door as she pushed it open.

The room brightened, then flooded with light as Anna turned on the switch, leaving me momentarily blinded. I shaded my eyes as Poppy moved beside me.

'Get up, both of you,' Anna ordered.

I hesitated, not at all sure if we were still playing, or if her anger was genuine. Her next statement made it clear.

'It's the cane for both of you,' she said. 'Twelve.'

We were still playing, but it was hardly reassuring. I swung my legs down from the bed as Poppy moved and got up. My load moved as I stood and sagged down in my nappy. I knew it would look blatant from behind, a great fat bulge, making it quite obvious what I had done. I stayed facing firmly forwards.

'Turn around, Gabby,' Anna ordered.

I hesitated only a moment, then turned, shuffling around on my feet to show off the rear of my nappy.

'Disgusting,' she stated. 'Go and wash your hands, the pair of you, then over the bed.'

I was actually all right, but I was not going to argue. Poppy and I took turns at the sink, with Anna watching all the while. She was wearing a long, flannelette nightie and slippers, with her hair down, so long it hung almost to her knees. In her hand she carried that same vicious-looking cane I had been beaten with earlier. Considering the state of my bottom, I couldn't imagine she would insist on beating me, and I was certainly going to have to clean up properly. The sink was a huge porcelain affair, big enough for me to sit in, but when I began to climb in she spoke again.

'That will not be necessary, Gabby. Come and stand by the bed.'

'You're not really going to cane me, are you?' I queried. 'Not like this?'

'And why should I not?'

'I'm dirty, Anna . . . I mean, Miss Vale, and I'm so bruised.'

'With me, Gabby, you must learn to accept the consequences of your actions. Your bottom is not the only part of your anatomy suitable for the cane. I intend to apply it across the backs of your thighs. Now, do you wish to accept your punishment or leave?'

'It is the middle of the night!'

'Four fifteen a.m., to be precise. Well?'

'I will take it, if I really must, but not too hard, please?'

She didn't answer me but tapped the end of the horrible cane on the bed.

'Bend down. Hands on the bed, bottom well out, and keep your legs straight.'

I bent, feeling the mess squash out over my pussy and up between my cheeks as I stuck my bottom out. I normally clean myself up immediately after making a mess and it was getting uncomfortable. If she knew, she evidently didn't care.

The cane was lifted; I shut my eyes, heard it whistle down and screamed as it bit into my upper thighs right under the sagging bulge in my nappy. Instantly I went into my little pain dance. I couldn't help it, even though it made my load bounce up and down behind me.

Poppy laughed, but it only filled me with self-pity and humiliation.

I hung my head, struggling to cope with the burning pain of my thighs. It hurt so much, far worse than on my bottom, and I could already feel the tears of reaction and self-pity welling up in my eyes. I reached back, touching my welt, my face screwing up in pain as a nail brushed the raw flesh where the cane tip had caught me.

'Oh, you do look a sight, Gabby!' Poppy said, and laughed again.

It was more than I could bear. Not that I minded so much standing in front of two other women with a kilo or so of filth hanging in my nappy, but to be caned like that and laughed at by the girl who'd wanted me to do it ... I just burst into tears, great racking sobs that shook my whole body and made my bulge wobble, drawing fresh laughter from Poppy for an instant before she realised I was crying.

'Don't cry, Gabby!' she said. 'We're only playing.'

'I can't take it!' I sobbed. 'It hurts too much!'

'Quiet! Hold your position!' Anna snapped.

'I . . .' I started, and the cane lashed down across my thighs again.

I screamed, jumping up to clutch at myself and hopping frantically on my toes, struggling to get control and tell her to stop it, that she'd pushed me too far, that it wasn't fair!

I never got the chance. Before I could recover myself enough to speak the cane hit me again. I went down over the bed, screaming and kicking out, only for a fourth to hit me and a fifth, cutting into the rear of my thighs so hard that everything was knocked from my head but the agony of my thrashing. My screams were ringing in my ears and I was kicking in a futile effort to dull the pain, but I dared not roll over or try and get up, for fear of getting that horrible cane across my tummy or breasts.

Maybe she gave me twelve, maybe more. It certainly felt like more. It did finish though, in the end, to leave me a tear-stained mess on the bed, with my face wet with tears and a long piece of mucus hanging from my nose. I couldn't even speak, only gulp in air and shake my head in my desperate need to make the pain go away.

They waited for me to calm down, and when I finally managed to wipe the tears from my eyes I found both looking at me, Poppy full of concern, Anna as emotionless as ever. During the beating I'd been furious, but if there's one thing I am good at it is controlling my temper, and I had managed to bite it down before I spoke.

'Thank you, Miss Vale,' I managed. 'Thank you for beating me.'

'Punishing you, Gabby, dear,' she replied. 'A punishment I am sure you will agree you deserved?'

'Yes, Miss Vale.'

'Good. I knew you were a sensible girl at heart. Now go and clean that filthy mess up while I correct Poppy.'

I nodded agreement, although my real feelings were very different, resentment and anger, for her and for Natasha, who I was fairly sure had deliberately set me up. Only for Poppy did I feel no resentment, and that was why I had held back. She had been so loving, so gentle, and so in tune with my baby-girl fantasy. I couldn't possibly have done anything to risk alienating her, even if she did think it was funny to see me in tears of pain.

My thighs were absolutely burning and I was limping as I crossed to the sink. I turned the single tap on and climbed in, wincing as freezing water swirled around my cane-cuts. It began to soak into my nappy too, and I quickly undid the pin to clean myself as Poppy was put through the same agonising ritual I had just endured.

She bent, as I had, hands on the bed and bottom well lifted. Her nightie had fallen and she was made to lift it, exposing ripe, cheeky buttocks, well parted to show the pouted lips of her sex and the tight dimple of her anus. She had bruises too, not as bad as mine and more regular, showing she had been caned perhaps two weeks before.

I watched her thrashing as I cleaned myself up, amazed at the way she took it. Twelve hard strokes were delivered to her bottom and upper thighs, each planted with exact precision and laid on with the full strength of Anna's arm. She never even squeaked, even when a cut caught her in the succal groove, right under the fat of her buttocks, to leave twin red marks on her sex-lips. Even that was met with no more than a hiss of expelled air from between her lips. She counted too, each one, and afterwards went to her knees to kiss her mistress' cane.

By then I was feeling slightly ashamed of my own overheated reaction. True, she was used to it and obviously enjoyed it, yet she had been so calm, certainly calmer than Natasha, who was the only other girl I'd seen caned. I was pretty well clean by then too, and finished off by running a sinkful of water to let my dirty nappy soak. Poppy was smiling, obviously aroused, and kept glancing at me. Anna waited calmly until I had finished, then pointed at the floor in front of her.

'Kneel,' she ordered.

I went, keeping my emotions to myself as I realised I was to be made to lick her. Down on my knees, I looked up to meet her cold, clear eyes as she stepped forwards. She never spoke or betrayed any emotion. Her nightie came up, displaying large, lace-trimmed knickers. Her panty-crotch was pulled aside, revealing a bushy sex, with her crevice pink and moist. I was taken by the head and pulled in to lick until she came, with no more than a soft sigh.

Four

I was limping when I left Anna Vale's the next morning, with my upper thighs a mass of purple bruising. There was no question in my mind that the entire incident had been intentional, with the possible exception of Poppy's little bit of medical fantasy in the afternoon. The rest had been carefully planned to suit my fantasy and theirs. I had anticipated a measure of compromise, but not ending up too sore to sit down and with a set of bruises that was going to mean I had to keep myself covered up for weeks.

I was also pretty sure Natasha had known what she was letting me in for. No sooner had I got home than I was certain. She had left a message asking me how I'd got on in between giggles. I was not in the mood to respond and ran myself a bath, into which I poured a generous amount of essential oils.

With an eleven o'clock appointment I had a fair bit of time, so I let myself soak and thought about their set-up and how it applied to me. Anna was clearly a stickler for maintaining role, even to the point of deliberately indulging in a sexual hypocrisy that belonged not to the mid-twentieth century but to the late nineteenth. Poppy was less fanatical and obviously keen to indulge some of her fantasies without always being in the submissive role. She also seemed pretty keen on me.

That was one of the good things about the experience. The other was the level of relaxation I had achieved during the afternoon. None of the various meditation techniques I had tried produced anything like the level of serenity I had achieved, and it had gone well beyond the way I usually felt in nappies. The reason, I was sure, was twofold, combining the knowledge that Poppy was there to look after me and the fact that I had been completely out of communication. I had also to admit the possibility of a third factor – my caning.

Even if it did take a punishment to really get me there it was something I badly wanted to achieve again, but preferably not at the expense of so much bruising. I might need spanking, but I did not need to be beaten until I lost all control of my senses. Poppy, I was sure, would treat me fairly, and despite a degree of guilt I found myself considering ways of playing with her in Anna's absence.

By eleven I was more or less ready for my client, despite a strong desire not to sit down. Fortunately she took this for an intense interest in her case rather than a need to spare a smacked bottom, and she left contented. What I was not ready for was the phone call that followed shortly afterwards. It was from a police station in South London. Monty had been arrested trying to steal panties from a washing line and was in custody. He had given my name as his therapist.

It was an extremely awkward situation. I had no official status and he was not even technically a client. Ignoring the ignoble temptation to simply deny ever having heard of him, I agreed to go down later in the afternoon. There was another appointment at one, and I left immediately afterwards.

Monty was in a cell, looking forlorn. They had caught him red-handed, sneaking out of somebody's back gate with a pair of panties in his pocket – baby-blue cotton with a lace trim, as he pointed out to me. He had at least had the sense not to carry any ID and had refused to give his address. What he wanted me for had nothing whatever to do with therapy. Passing me a carefully secreted key, he asked if I could clear up his flat, which I was not happy about.

I did it anyway, after having to go through a lengthy discussion of Monty's mental state with a police psychologist, which ended with me agreeing to a series of specific appointments for him. The panties were easy enough, just about fitting into my bag. The magazines and videos were beyond hope, and I contented myself with taking the two spanking magazines and the bondage one, also the hardest and most perverse of the videos. Even that left me heavily laden, and the trip back to my flat was a serious effort and highly embarrassing, for fear the suitcase I'd taken would burst open.

By the time I got back I was promising myself that Monty was going to take me to a very, very expensive restaurant, several times. I was also tired, and would probably have gone to bed had there not been another message from Natasha. This time she sounded at least a little apologetic, even worried. She was also offering to cook dinner for me.

It was exactly what I wanted after my afternoon – good food prepared by someone else, along with waitress service. She was also the only person I could talk to about Monty. I sent her a text message, changed and went straight to the station, arriving at her Primrose Hill flat in under half an hour. She was her normal self, vivacious and enthusiastic, greeting me with a mischievous grin as she stuck her head out of the window. I went up to find her grin broader than ever.

'Grab a seat,' she offered.

'I'd rather not.'

'Too sore to sit down?'

'Yes.'

She laughed.

'So what happened?'

'What happened is that Anna Vale caned me brutally, first across my bottom, then on the back of my thighs.'

'Ouch! But it was good, yeah?'

'The grown-up baby-girl play was good, yes. Poppy is as close to my ideal nanny as I have found. As you know, the beating does nothing for me.'

'It makes your pussy wet.'

'A physiological reaction, no more. Unlike you, I do not need pain for sexual arousal.'

'Nor do I.'

'You crave it.'

'More humiliation.'

'There was no shortage of that either. You should visit them.'

'Maybe I will. So let's see the damage.'

I turned to lift my skirt for her and took down my tights and panties. Her mouth came open as she saw the mess Anna Vale had made of my thighs, and she put a hand up to suppress a giggle.

'Maybe not, on second thoughts,' she stated. 'I'll stick to Percy.'

She was grinning and trying to hold back her laughter. I covered myself.

'Otherwise it was successful,' I admitted. 'Although I am not sure you have been entirely honest with me. They had never heard of you, nor of Percy Ottershaw. Who is Penny?'

'Penny Birch. She recommended Anna Vale.'

'And exactly what did you ask her?'

'For a nanny for a grown-up baby girl.'

'And only that?'

'Well, no. I said to find somebody stern. Sorry, but I just love the way you react to punishment. It's such a turn-on and you're so funny, the state you get into!'

'Does my pain really amuse you, Natasha?'

'Oh, come on, Gabby, lighten up. You've got to admit that there's something funny about a girl getting a good bare-bottom spanking.'

101

'Not at all.'

'Well, it gets me off. Look, relax, even if it does mean you have to lie face down on the sofa. Have a glass of champagne and you have to tell me everything.'

'Thank you. There is another piece of news. Monty Hartle was arrested on Sunday afternoon for stealing panties from a washing line.'

'You're joking!'

'I am not.'

'Superb! Classic!'

'It is not funny, Natasha.'

'No, it's not funny. It's hilarious. Oh, come on, Gabrielle, think of the things he's done to you. What about that spooning he gave you?'

'Nevertheless . . .'

'Well, I see it as just desserts, whatever you think.'

'I understand your reasoning, Natasha, but consider. Had I been there, it wouldn't have happened.'

'You're taking the world on your shoulders again, Gabby.'

'I have a measure of responsibility.'

'No, you don't! Think about it. If we'd never met him he'd have probably been at it all this time, and he was bound to get pinched sooner or later. What are you going to do about it anyway?'

'I have agreed to provide therapy.'

'I hate to tell you this, but Monty probably sees panty stealing as therapy.'

'No doubt. Still, I must do my best to dissuade him.'

'I wouldn't bother. Let him stew.'

She had walked into her kitchen as she spoke, and came back holding a bottle of champagne beaded with condensation, and two glasses.

'I'm going to get you drunk,' she said casually as she began to work on the foil. 'Then you can let your emotions out and give me the spanking I need. I do deserve it, after all. I dropped you right in it with Anna

Vale. The thing is, what I actually told Penny was that you always got in a state, but really liked it hard, and that Anna should ignore you, however big a fuss you made.'

'That was hardly considerate, Natasha, and it doesn't make me want to punish you.'

'No? If you did that to me I'd be after you with a dog whip! Look, sorry. I misjudged your feelings, but I didn't mean it to be malicious. Forgive me?'

'Yes, but please don't do that again.'

'I promise.'

She had removed the foil, and as she gave the bottle a single precise twist the cork popped out into her hand without spilling a drop. She poured, passed a glass to me and took her own, coming to curl up at my feet, one arm resting in my lap. For a while we sipped champagne in silence before she spoke again.

'Wouldn't you like to punish me?'

'I confess that the thought had occurred to me. It was part of the reason for your trick, yes?'

'Yes. I was actually hoping you'd come round and just deal with me. Spanking is always best for real.'

'If you say so.'

'Oh, it is. You of all people should understand that feeling of helplessness, when something is going to happen and there's absolutely nothing you can do to stop it.'

'True.'

'Still. I'll happily come across your knee if it makes you feel better.'

'I'm not sure.'

'Come on, Gabby. Think of me wriggling and squirming across your lap, with my bum all hot and bare. You could make me lick your pussy afterwards, maybe sit on my face. I'm more than happy to lick your bumhole for you.'

'It would hardly be a punishment then.'

'No, but wouldn't it be nice?'

'Yes, and I'm not entirely at ease with the thought of punishing you anyway, despite your craving. Still, as you seem to find it so therapeutic, I think we had better have those trousers down. In fact, you can take all your lower garments off.'

'Yes, miss, but you have to take down my knickers, OK?'

'As you please.'

She stood up, smiling, to kick off her shoes, and quickly pushed the elasticated waist of her trousers down over her hips. Her tights came with them, down and off, to be kicked casually to one side. Turning her back to me, she put her hands behind her to lift the tail of her blouse and expose the perfect pear of her bottom, with the slightly fleshy cheeks bulging out of her minute silk panties below her tiny waist.

'Spankable?' she asked.

'Beautiful, certainly. Come across my lap, then.'

'Yes, miss.'

She came eagerly, with none of the reluctance I'd have shown in her place. I could feel her body trembling slightly as she lay down across my legs to lift her bottom with an inviting wiggle. Bent over, her hips and bottom seemed broader still in comparison to her waist, a wonderful view which I was going to enjoy regardless.

I let her wait for a moment, then took her gently around the waist to hold her in place across my knee. Her bottom was quivering slightly and her breathing was already becoming marked, before I had so much as begun. Remember how gently Poppy had spanked me after I'd wet myself, I began, using just the tips of my fingers, to plant little pats on her bottom. She responded with a sigh of pleasure, increasing my confidence, and I began to smack harder, still with my fingertips, and evenly, until as much of her bottom as showed around the edges of her panties had begun to flush red. She was beautiful in just panties, but I wanted to see more and it seemed a good time to take them down.

'Time to go bare, then,' I told her. 'Stick it up.'

She complied, raising her bottom even as I took hold of the rear pouch of her silk panties to peel them slowly off and invert them down around her thighs. Immediately I caught the scent of her sex, girl mixed with a trace of perfume.

Her whole bottom was flushed pale pink, no more than a shade darker than the unblemished skin of her thighs and back. She had no panty line; her skin was darker than mine and wonderfully smooth, like alabaster, the result of plenty of pampering. I began to slap her again, more firmly still. The sight of her bare and the feel of her skin was starting to get to me, also her scent, which was growing slowly stronger as the spanking aroused her.

I was watching the clock on her stereo as I spanked, and drew it out for a full ten minutes before stopping. By then her breathing was deep and even and her legs were wide, stretching her panties taut between her thighs. By moving a little I could see her sex, which was beginning to flower, the outer lips puffy and a little open, white fluid trickling down between the inner from her vagina, her clitoris on clear show.

'Warm?' I asked.

'Beautifully, thank you. You are good, Gabby. Men always have to rush it. Even Percy doesn't take that long to get me warmed up. I want more, though, and I want to come while you spank me and tell me what a bad girl I am. Use my hairbrush.'

It was on the table, which didn't surprise me, as she had been angling for her spanking from the moment I stepped through the door. I took it and gave her a gentle pat on the crest of one cheek. She sighed and wiggled, showing off her bottom-hole to me. I smacked her again, harder, and lifted my leg to bring her bottom up and make myself more comfortable. As I shifted position, the bruises on my thighs twinged and I laid in harder still.

She gave a little squeal but kept her bottom high, making no effort to escape as I began to spank her properly to set her cheeks bouncing and quivering, with the smooth skin beginning to roughen as goose-pimples appeared. She began to kick, her thighs moving to stretch her lowered panties as taut as they would go.

'Panties off, I think,' I told her.

'Yes, please, and let me come.'

'Not yet.'

I stuck my thumb into her lowered panties and tugged them down and off one ankle, leaving them hanging from the other. Immediately her thighs came wide to show off the full glory of her moist, ready sex. I touched, stroking the underside of her pubic mound, her swollen sex-lips, her vulva, at which she moaned.

'Please, now?' she said. 'While you spank me.'

'No, not until I'm done with you. Then you can do it on the floor in front of me.'

'Oh . . .'

Her complaint broke off as I smacked the hairbrush hard down on her bottom. She squeaked, but quickly pushed it up to give another of her inviting little wriggles. I began to spank her again, harder still, holding her tightly until her pleased little noises turned to gasps and hisses of pain. Her buttocks were reddening well and she was going to be bruised, if nothing like as badly as I was.

It was impossible not to enjoy it, with her beautiful bottom writhing in front of me and the smell of her sex strong in my nose. I was telling myself it was not the pain I was giving her that was exciting me, but it was hard to be sure, and there was more than a little guilt building up in me.

Not that it stopped me. I spanked until her whole bottom was a glowing red ball, with darker marks in places where the tip of the hairbrush had caught her. By then her cries were becoming truly pained and she had started to snivel, so I stopped before she could burst into tears and ruin my pleasure in her submission.

'You could do more,' she panted, 'if you let me frig.'

'Be quiet. I said to do it on the floor. Now hold still.'

I tightened my grip on her waist so that I could reach out for my bag. I was sure I had what I wanted in it, and sure enough, it was there, tiger balm.

'What are doing?' she asked.

'I'm going to soothe you,' I told her, 'by rubbing oil into your bottom, something to relieve the ache.

'Mm, yes, please.'

Her bottom rose, spreading her cheeks yet wider, her cleft making a deep, smooth valley, with the wet entrance to her sex plainly visible and her bottom-hole twitching slightly. I unscrewed the tiger balm, pushing back my instinctive pang of guilt, and carefully poured a little on to the crest of each hot, roughened buttock. She sighed at the feel of it and gave another little wriggle.

I began to massage the oil in her bottom, two-handed, using slow, circular motions to cover the smacked area of her cheeks, as Poppy had done for me. Her immediate reaction was a contented sigh, and I let my oily thumbs slide down into her crease, coating the sides where her flesh was still pale but missing her anus.

'That's warm,' she said.

'It should be, it's tiger balm. Just relax.'

Her cheeks twitched beneath my fingers as I rubbed a new circle on, this time allowing one oily thumb tip to brush her anus. She made an odd little noise, pained, and suddenly looked round.

'Ow! That's getting hot.'

'Good. Time for you to come, then. On the floor.'

She crawled off hastily to squat down on the floor, her bottom pushed out towards me with her sex and anus showing. Her hand went back to her sex so that I could see her busy fingers from behind, moving rhythmically in among the fleshy folds of her vulva. Her spare hand went behind, squeezing her bottom, then the other.

'Ow! My bottom's burning! Gabrielle!'

She was clutching at her cheeks, her face moving through a whole flurry of emotions.

'You had better masturbate, then.'

'Bitch! Oh, Jesus, OK.'

She began to rub again, her bottom now twitching, her anus too. Her hand had been on her bottom, and moments after she had begun to masturbate she was gasping, but still rubbing. It was beginning to get frantic, her bottom wobbling behind her, her rounded, glossy cheeks both quivering, her anus pulsing.

Suddenly she snatched at the hairbrush to take it behind her and eased the long handle into her vagina, as deep as it would go. Reaching back once more, her fingers pushed in between her bottom-cheeks, burrowing down to find her anus and push in. She squatted down low to keep the brush up her hole. I could see it, the handle ringed with wet pink flesh, and her anus, the tight little ring glistening pink as she eased her finger in and out. Her breathing was growing faster and her gasps more urgent and more pained.

She screamed in an uncontrolled blend of pain and ecstasy as she came, her muscles jumping and pulsing, the one finger jabbing in and out of her now mushy bottom-hole, the others clutching and slapping at her sex. It was intense but short. Even before her muscles had untensed she was climbing unsteadily to her feet to run for the bathroom. I heard the gush of the shower as I reached out for my champagne glass.

Natasha spent quite a while in the bathroom, and came back nude and already dry with a towel wrapped around her head. She was grinning, and took a swallow of her champagne before addressing me.

'That was beautiful. Thanks, Gabby, I knew you'd go for it. Am I forgiven?'

'If you mean does that compensate for the state of my thighs, the answer is no.'

'Whoops! More spankings for me then? Oh, dear.'

'No amount of spankings will compensate, Natasha. You enjoy it too much, and I could not justify beating you with the same severity Anna Valc used on me. Instead, you might try making an honest effort to find me a nanny.'

'I will. I promise. Now let me make you come, and don't tell me you didn't enjoy doing that.'

'Your bottom is truly glorious, Natasha, and yes, seeing you bare, and your reaction, has aroused me. The actual spanking, maybe . . .'

'Oh, what nonsense! Come on, dominate me. Sit on my face and make me lick your bumhole, that's rude.'

'I do not see why. But yes, it would be nice.'

'It's rude for me. On come on, I mean, what could possibly be more humiliating than being made to lick another girl's bottom-hole? Well, being made to lick a man's, I suppose, but still.'

'Anilingus is a beautiful, shared experience.'

'Having a big, fat bottom stuffed in your face and being made to lick the hole?'

'Yes, although I would not have phrased it like that.'

'OK, then, have your beautiful, shared experience, just get your bottom in my face.'

She had gone to her knees and lay back as she spoke, face up on the carpet. I stood to ease up my skirt and push my tights and panties down, then off. Naked from the waist down, I straddled her head and sank into a squat with my bottom to her face. She kissed me, one cheek then the other, before her tongue traced a slow line up the crease of my bottom. I sank lower, her tongue found my anus, and she was licking.

I shut my eyes, concentrating completely on the delicious feeling of having my bottom-hole licked. She was eager too, probing my ring and lapping at me with a wonderful urgency, as if she couldn't get enough of my taste and the feel of my anus against her tongue. However much it humiliated her, she was in no hurry, and nor was I. I began to stroke my breasts through my blouse, letting my pleasure rise slowly, and keeping firmly away from my sex until I could bear it no more.

Her tongue was well up my bottom, probing and twisting in my wet, open hole as I began to masturbate, rubbing myself gently, reaching down to slip two fingers into my vagina, rubbing again, faster and harder, feeling my orgasm rise, and burst. I held the picture of Natasha's face as I came, so delicate, so beautiful, and given over to my pleasure, her tongue well up my bottom in what to her was a gesture of utter surrender.

Monty Hartle was eventually released with a caution subject to attending four therapy sessions. I had agreed to submit a report on his progress to the police, which was going to require some highly creative writing. It also made me determined to do my best to wean him away from his habit. The first appointment was on the Thursday afternoon, for which he turned up early, beaming as he pushed into my clinic.

'Hi, Gabby, nice one, yeah?' he greeted me. 'Cool, yeah? I get to bonk you on police time!'

'No, you do not. For the next hour, this will be on a strictly professional basis. First, we need to discuss your obsession with female underwear. You may tell me the history behind it.'

'Oh . . . All right, as it's you.'

'Good. Sit down. Relax.'

He sat, and I lowered myself gingerly into the chair opposite. Monty's eyebrows raised a fraction.

'Not still bruised, are you?' he demanded. 'I know I whacked you, but . . .'

'Never mind the state of my bottom. Tell me about your obsession, from the beginning.'

'From the beginning? Where do I start? I mean, all blokes are into knickers, aren't they? They hide what you most want to get at, don't they? They look gorgeous too, wrapped around some little darling's nice tight arse, or even holding in a big, wobbly bottom. And the smell of fresh cunt . . . something else.'

'So you identify panties with female sexuality?'

'Yeah. Who doesn't? I mean, any bloke who's into cunt is going to be into panties. Stands to reason.'

'Perhaps, but very few steal them from washing lines. When did you start?'

'October the twenty-ninth, nineteen ninety-one.'

'That is very exact.'

'I'm an exact kind of bloke. You need to be to handle computers.'

'Tell me about it.'

'Sure. It was at school, right, this girl called Patsy. She was gorgeous, legs like yours, but a fatter arse, and tits like fucking footballs. She knew it too, flirting all the time, and wearing these skirts like you would not believe. She only had to bend forwards a few inches and you'd see her panties. Blokes used to throw pound coins on the ground so she'd bend down to pick them up. She'd do it too, the little tart, right down, with that gorgeous bum just straining those little panties out . . . It gives me a hard-on just thinking about it now. Can I wank?'

'No. Go on.'

'Spoilsport. Anyway, she was good, yeah, but she wouldn't put out for much, not full sex anyway. Some guys said they'd had her, but it was bullshit, although I think this bloke Gary did squeeze a blow-job out of her once.'

'And yourself?'

'What? Fat kid Monty, not a fucking chance!'

111

'So you resented her?'

'Yeah, sure I did, why not? She used to make this really big deal out of not wanting me around. Like when the boys were trying to make her show her tits one time, she agreed, but only on the condition I go away.'

'Hurtful, clearly, and this was why you stole her panties?'

'Partly. More it was for a laugh. It was before the tit-show anyway. A mate dared me to go into the girls' changing room and nick something. I did it, and her locker was open, with the panties she'd been wearing right on top. I took them. She had to go home in her gym kit.'

'It affected her, then? Her flirting did not extend to showing herself bare?'

'Yeah, it affected her. She was furious. She knew it was me, too, because my idiot mate told her. I denied it and I'd hidden the panties well, but she knew.'

'I see. Has it occurred to you that she excluded you from the display of her breasts precisely because you had stolen her panties?'

He shrugged. I went on.

'It seems to me that she may have resented you not so much for your weight, as because you had infringed the sexual boundaries she had drawn for herself. To show her breasts retained her own control, so did sucking a boy's penis, so long as it was on her terms. What you did, did not.'

'Maybe.'

'So your motive was resentment combined with a lack of respect for her personal boundaries?'

'Yeah, because she was a bitch to me.'

'Am I a bitch to you?'

'No.'

'Yet you clearly enjoy breaking my personal boundaries, also Natasha's.'

Again he shrugged.

'And there is no question that it arouses you. I suspect this is the root cause of your need to steal women's panties, so that they know something intimate has been taken. Otherwise, why not simply purchase what you want?'

'That would be no fun at all. There's a thrill in stealing them. You've got to know the girl's been in them, know her cunt's been up against the crotch.'

'Yet you steal clean pairs?'

'Dirty pairs are harder to come by.'

'I see. And what did you do with Patsy's panties?'

'The normal. Wanked in them a few times.'

'You always do this?'

'Yeah.'

'So there is a routine?'

'Yeah. I get a pair, find somewhere quiet and toss off with them. That's half the fun.'

'You then wash them, label them and add them to your collection?'

'Yeah.'

'And you feel the need for new pairs?'

'Yeah, of course. Half the fun's in getting them.'

'I see, and after the incident at school?'

'I didn't do it for ages after that, over a year. The next time was at a mate's. He had a really cute sister, and she'd sometimes walk around in just a top and knickers, like she didn't care. I thought she was coming on to me and I asked her out. She reacted like I'd suggested murdering her mother. So I pinched a pair of her panties.'

'Rejection again.'

'Revenge, I prefer. She was really snooty with me and she didn't have to be. I used to like thinking how cross she'd be if she knew I was using a pair of her knickers to wank in. After that I decided there were other girls who deserved the same. I stuck to my mates' sisters at first, because I could always get in the girls' bedrooms or nick something out of the laundry basket. I don't think any of them even noticed. Then there was this really stuck-up piece, at the place I worked immediately after school in my year off. She was the manageress, and she reckoned she was so fucking superior. Her boyfriend was a real jerk too, the worst. I hated them, but there was nothing I could do. Only I knew where they lived. So I sneaked into their garden one night, and pinched this pair of real fancy French knickers, real silk with a wide trim. Jerking off in them after she'd given me a hard time at work was just great.'

'These were all girls you knew?'

'Yeah. I only really got into it properly after uni, when I got my own flat. That's when I started collecting properly, but I'm not that bad, not really.'

'Something over one hundred pairs in over ten years. Less than one a month. You could be worse, I suppose. And over those ten years you've never been tempted to go further?'

'You know I'm not like that, Gabby.'

'I do. I will be stressing the fact that you have never escalated your behaviour in my report. I will also neglect to mention that you collect what you steal.'

'Thanks. Where are they, by the way?'

'In a drawer, on top of your other pornographic material. I have taken a considerable risk for you, Monty.'

'I know. Ta. You're great, Gabby. I owe you.'

'Consider it my social duty.'

'Well, you know ... any time you want your nappy on and that.'

'I will bear that in mind. So, I understand why you steal panties: a combination of fetishistic obsession, resentment of rejection by women and a desire to collect and order, together with a degree of anal fixation. Yes?'

'I suppose so.'

'You sound resentful. It is important to understand your urges.'

'I do. I just don't like the way you say it.'

'Then remember how often you have changed my nappy, also spanked me.'

That put the familiar grin back on his face.

'So what exactly did happen on Sunday night?' I asked.

'Serious bad luck,' he answered. 'When you said you weren't coming down it left me really randy, thinking about what we'd have been up to and that. Anything else seemed a real let down, except going out to do a bit of peeping. I tried these woods where there's often a lot of stuff going on in cars. Blokes'll sometimes show off their girls so other guys can watch from the bushes. There was nothing doing, maybe because it was so cold, and I gave up pretty soon. I went round some of my favourite flats after that, where there's a good chance of seeing in the windows. I got a bit, but nothing special, and just ended up hornier than ever. I was going to give up, but I got lucky, just as it was getting dark. I'd been on football pitches, to watch, and I was walking back to the car along this alley behind some houses. A light went on and naturally I looked, to see this woman come into a room in just bra and panties. She was good-looking as well, long black hair, nice tits, nice firm bum, a bit of a tummy, but I don't mind that. There was nobody about, so I ducked down and got out my binoculars to watch. It was good. She was doing ironing and kept moving around, making her tits jiggle and that. She had me so horny I'd have wanked off right there if I'd dared.'

'And the panties were hers?'

'No. I'd been hoping she'd strip, at least take her bra off, but she put a housecoat on after a bit. I moved on, hornier than ever, and I was going to go back to this bit of wasteland by the pitches and wank off when I saw the panties. There weren't many washing lines out, but it was dry, and this one house had one of those stand-up ones, with these little see-through blue knicks hanging there, just staring me in the face. All I needed to do was nip over the fence and snatch them. There weren't even any lights on in the house, and the back gate was half off its hinges. I went for it, snatched the knicks, stuffed them in my pocket, and came back out. There were two policemen walking up the alley. They came from nowhere!'

'Unlucky, I must admit. Leaving the moral issue aside for the moment, surely you see that the consequences of your actions outweigh the benefits?'

'Yeah, you're right – but, you know, it's fun.'

'It is also an invasion of women's personal space, which might lead to serious trauma . . .'

'What, losing a pair of knickers? Get real! I bet half the time they don't even notice.'

'Perhaps not, but when they do they will feel invaded.'

He shrugged, his face colouring as he looked away, not meeting my eyes.

'If I intended to judge you, Monty, I wouldn't have rescued your collection.'

'Yeah . . . sorry. You're right anyway, I suppose . . . it's not worth it. They've taken all my mags, you know, just stuff I bought in newsagents, nothing heavy, my vids too. What did you take?'

'About as much as I could safely carry. The two magazines devoted to spanking, and . . .'

'You got my *Blushes*, the one with the majorette?'

'Yes.'

'Ace! Thanks. That is my best. The look on her face when he's making her strip, fuck me! What else?'

'The bondage magazine, and many of the videos, the hardest, and the spanking one.'

'*Little Red Apples*?'

'Yes.'

'Good girl! I love that. The girl, the dark-haired one, she's just like you, little round arse and legs that go on for ever, and the way her arsehole winks while that dirty old bastard's spanking her! And the tennis scene, with those little skirts, and then she gets put over the net, with her little white panties showing, and spanked by the other girl . . .'

'Yes, Monty.'

He stopped, blew out his breath and adjusted his cock in his trousers.

'Do you play tennis?' he demanded.

'No.'

'Shame. I'd love to see you in one of those tennis skirts . . . I'd love to fuck you in one of those tennis skirts, bent over with your pants pulled down and your bare arse stuck up for me. Come on, Gabby, let's fuck.'

'No. I . . .'

'I'll put you in nappies, or you can go in that little pink baby-doll?'

'I'm afraid not. I am menstruating.'

'Oh . . . on the rag, eh? Shit. Still, you know what girls normally do for their boyfriends when they're on, don't you? They take it up the shitter.'

'That I doubt. And, as I have explained repeatedly, you are not sodomising me.'

'Blow-job?'

'Monty!'

He didn't answer immediately, but reached for his fly to pull out his cock. He was erect.

'Look what you've done to me,' he stated.

'That was not my intention. Put it away.'

'Come on, Gabby, get down on it. You know you want to.'

'I do not.'

'Yeah? You love it. You suck like a fucking angel, like you're going to eat me.'

'Perhaps. Not today.'

'I thought girls were supposed to get horny while they were on the rag?'

'Some may. I do not. More importantly, I am supposed to be finding out about your obsession with stealing women's panties, not indulging your sexual needs.'

'When I'm with you I don't need to steal panties.'

'I had worked that out.'

'Come on, Gabby, go for it.'

'No, but if you wish you may masturbate.'

'Well, at least pose for me, then.'

'As I said, I'm menstruating.'

'Get your tits out, then, or give me a panty show. I bet you've got nice ones on. What colour are they?'

'White.'

'Not the pink frillies, then?'

'Not today.'

'I wish you were. You do look cute like that, in a little pair of pink frillies and nothing else, or maybe a shirt, so your little bum-cheeks peep out underneath . . .'

He had begun to masturbate, tugging at his cock, with his belly held away as usual. It was impossible not to smile, at his sheer lack of acceptance of ordinary values. I could think of nobody else who could so casually expose their genitals and demand attention in such inappropriate circumstances. Abruptly he started to speak.

'I'm thinking of you in that tennis skirt,' he said, 'real short, so everyone can see up it. Only you're not wearing panties, you're wearing a nappy, a big, pink nappy, in the street, so everyone can see.'

I smiled again; it was impossible not to, thinking of the image. He grinned back, wanking faster.

'And I'd spank you,' he went on, 'in front of everyone, with your tennis skirt up and your nappy down at the back, with your bum spread wide and that lovely little arsehole on show . . .'

He stopped, puffing, to adjust his position on the settee and pull his balls out of his fly. For all his fat,

118

there was a powerful masculinity about him, with his big cock, which always seemed to be in a state of excitement, always ready for whatever soft, female receptacle he could find. He began to preen it, showing off for me, either oblivious or indifferent to the way he looked, perhaps even delighting in it. I watched, considering giving in to his demand and going down on the floor to suck him.

'Tits out,' he demanded suddenly.

I sighed, but reached for the buttons of my blouse, unfastening one, then a second. Monty began to wank faster again. I snipped open a third button, and a fourth, giving in to his need. My blouse came open, my bra up, exposing myself.

'Gorgeous, so perky,' he said, tugging harder still. 'Fuck, but I wanted to see those so badly last weekend. I'd love to spunk all over them. I'd been saving for you. I still am.'

'No, Monty . . .'

'This is for your tits. I've got to.'

'Really, no . . .'

'Your face, then. Come on, Gabby, I've got to, you're so fucking gorgeous.'

'I will suck, if I must, but you are not to do it in my face, or over my breasts.'

I was struggling to get my blouse off as he pushed himself up from the chair. It came, and my bra followed as he waddled forwards, to cock one fat leg up on the arm of my chair and push his genitals into my face.

'Monty . . .' I tried, only to have his cock stuffed rudely into my mouth.

He took my head, grunting as he pushed himself in, using my pursed lips as a slide. I tried to suck but he was too eager to let me take control, just ramming his cock in and out until I started to gag, pushing him away . . .

To receive the full load of his sperm in my face. The first massive spurt landed across my glasses and nose, the second lower, a third across my chin and chest, before he got hold of himself and milked what was left out over my lenses and the bridge of my nose. My mouth had come wide in shock and disgust at what he'd done and at the sheer volume of it. Immediately his cock was pushed back in.

He held me by the head, ignoring my muffled protests as the sperm began to run slowly down my face, and letting go only when fully satisfied. I gasped as he pulled back, swallowing what he'd done in my mouth before I could find my voice.

'I said not in my face, Monty!' I protested. 'Look at me!'

'Sorry, Gabby. I got a bit carried away there. Take it as a compliment. If you didn't have such a pretty face I wouldn't want to spunk all over it.'

'Fine, only now I have to completely redo my make-up, and I can barely see out of my glasses. Honestly, Monty, I don't mind sperm, but must you always save it up, and must you always do it in my face?'

'Like I say, pretty girls get their faces spunked over. It goes with the territory. Anyway, you pulled back. I thought you wanted it.'

'You were choking me!'

'Oh, sorry. Good, though, yeah?'

'For you, no doubt.'

I ran for the bathroom, holding a tissue under my chin to stop any sperm going on the floor. It was impossible not to look in the mirror. My entire face was plastered in sperm, my glasses heavy with it, a great thick slug lying across my nose and down to the edge of my mouth. There was more on my forehead and one cheek, bits in my hair and even in one ear. A single long streamer hung from my chin. It was on my breasts too, little blobs and streaks, one right on a nipple, hanging down from the erect teat.

It was hard to believe a single man could produce so much come, even after over a week of abstinence. Monty seemed to manage it on a regular basis, possibly because he ate so much, or because he devoted so much of his attention to sex, keeping his balls working overtime. I was not sure. The theory was beyond me. The fact was all over me.

I spent my weekend as quietly as possible, which I felt I deserved. My bottom and legs still ached, despite the amount of cream I had rubbed on and the various oils I had used in an attempt to soothe myself. I was still menstruating as well, and in no mood for sex, so declined Monty's invitation to visit him, along with a warning that if he managed to get caught stealing panties, peeping into women's bedroom windows or anything even vaguely similar, I would disown him entirely.

What I did get was a visit from Jo Warren, who had changed her mind about her novel yet again, having decided that the historical epic was due a comeback. She intended to transplant a female character, based on her ideal self as always, into a Second World War environment, complete with modern attitudes and a feisty, confident outlook on life. The plot followed the heroine's triumphs over assorted ministry men, partners and ultimately Nazis, all of whom were thoroughly misogynist in their attitudes. Finally she would sail for the US and meet a dock worker who would prove to be the man of her dreams; sensitive, caring and every inch a nineties-style 'new man'. It struck me as almost laughably bad, but I assured her of its likely success, certain that what she really wanted was praise. She also failed to mention Natasha for the first time since the enema incident, which was definitely progress.

Once she'd gone, I sat down at the computer to check my advert, although not actually expecting anything worthwhile. To my surprise there were three answers. One was from a transvestite who was sure he could accommodate my needs. I gave him a polite refusal. The second was from an obvious psychotic and completely irrelevant anyway, going on at length what should be done to gay men who had sex in toilets. I ignored it.

The third was actually interesting, if strange, offering me a chance to spend an evening as a grown-up baby girl in a house in Dulwich. It was from a woman calling herself Nurse Trainer, nothing more. There was an oddly impersonal tone to the message, which made me wonder if she was a professional. There was also a drawing of an enormous woman in an old-fashioned nurse's uniform, with a slipper held threateningly in one hand. Obviously she was yet another spanker, although if the picture was anything to go by suckling her would be heaven. Unfortunately I had my bottom to think about, and after a moment's consideration I decided against it, but forwarded the email on to Natasha, who was sure to be amused.

Five

I received Natasha's reply the next morning, responding in mock terror to the picture of Nurse Trainer, also asking if she could pass my mobile number on to Poppy. I agreed happily, looking forward to the prospect of seeing her again, although with a little guilt, as the request at least implied that any rendezvous would not include Anna Vale.

The week went smoothly enough, with nothing particularly challenging. Thursday was my second official appointment with Monty. I was already pretty clear on his motives, as I was on his attitude to women. After all, I had been on the receiving end often enough. So rather than delve further into his panty-pinching behaviour, we discussed peeping and voyeurism in general.

His attitude was that he had a moral right to look at anything which was on public display; women in revealing clothing, sunbathers and of course women undressing beside windows. The argument was simple – if they didn't want to be looked at, they shouldn't show off. My argument that women should be allowed to dress and behave as they pleased without interference met with laughter and an accusation of impracticality. I knew the argument and so did he, and as there is no solution we quickly abandoned it.

Again I found myself trying to persuade him that he should allow women their personal space. His resentment came out in response, arguing that if women failed to treat him with respect, there was no reason he should do so for them. It was difficult to counter, especially without suggesting that he identify himself as of lower significance, which was sure to be disastrous. So I switched to an individualist viewpoint, arguing that he had no cause for resentment against strangers on the grounds that he would not know what their response to him would be. He was going to say that the response was always the same, but he had Natasha and I as examples, and hesitated, shrugging, with the first hint of remorse for his behaviour I had seen. I stopped immediately. I had no intention of turning him into the sort of neurotic and brow-beaten specimen magazines so often portray fat people to be.

Returning to examples, I listened to his stories of spying on girls on beaches and through windows. To his credit, he always tried not to be seen or to scare the objects of his attentions. Contrary to some popular theories, his aim was neither to provoke fear, nor to gain some form of detached control, but simply to provide himself with a sufficiently sexual experience to reach orgasm, usually at a later time. One example illustrated his attitude perfectly.

He had been in Cornwall at some sort of convention, and staying at a hotel in which there was also a particularly attractive girl. She would spend a lot of time by the hotel pool in a bikini, and when Monty saw her walking down towards the dunes he guessed she intended to sunbathe topless or nude. He had followed and, hidden among the dunes, watched her change, oil herself and sunbathe. All he had seen were her breasts and a brief glimpse of her bare bottom, yet it had been enough to keep him in happy orgasms for the rest of the week. He had made no attempt to accost her, and swore that had she seen him it would have ruined it for him. What was interesting was that he evidently took as much pleasure, albeit not sexual pleasure, in the act of spying as in its results.

Inevitably he started to get aroused, and by the time he had finished describing an assortment of peeping incidents he had his cock out of his fly. Keen not to be given what he so eloquently described as a facial again, I turned in the chair and allowed him to masturbate over the sight of my bottom, with just my skirt pulled up. His response was to rise at the last moment, tweak out the back of my panties and come down them, full into my bottom-crease. As he had nearly overrun his time and I had another client immediately afterwards, I ended up spending an hour sitting in a pool of his sperm, which he thought hilarious. Clearly I had an uphill struggle ahead.

By the Saturday my bruises had faded to a few dull smudges and, while they were still noticeable on careful inspection, there was nothing to suggest I'd been caned. To celebrate, I decided to treat myself to an entire day at the Haven, naked, relaxed and free of all nuisances.

The morning was bliss, a little exercise, a swim, a massage, irrigation, before a lunch of lobster salad and a half-bottle of Chablis. I was on my last glass when a waiter put an ice bucket on my table with a second bottle in it. Before I could point out his mistake, Natasha followed, along with Poppy.

I was a little taken aback, and felt the most ridiculous flush of modesty at Poppy seeing me in nothing but a towel. Both kissed me, and I managed to respond without seeming too flustered, although from the look of mischief on Natasha's face I could guess it was no chance meeting.

'So you met?' I stated, hoping to get some background.

'We've been swapping emails all week,' Natasha answered. 'Since I sent your number and that Nurse Trainer thing.'

'As often as I can get down to the café, anyway,' Poppy put in. 'Anna won't let me have a computer, naturally. Sometimes she can be too obsessive.'

Natasha busied herself with the bottle, filling my glass, then the two she had brought for Poppy and herself. Poppy took a gulp as Natasha held her glass up to the light, swirled, sniffed and sipped, then nodded in appreciation.

'We thought Nurse Trainer sounded fun,' Poppy said.

'Perhaps yes, but . . .'

'So we're going,' Natasha cut in, 'and you're coming with us.'

'I am not sure . . .'

'No buts, Gabrielle.'

'She's too stern for me, Natasha.'

'Come on, Gabby, don't be such a baby!'

'That's the idea, to be a baby. Not to be spanked, at least not hurt.'

'Who says you're going to get spanked? She's into it, obviously, but all you need to do is say it's outside your boundaries.'

It took them nearly half an hour and the rest of the bottle of Chablis to persuade me to come, but they succeeded. After all, as they pointed out, I simply needed to be firm about my boundaries, and there would be three of us.

I did manage to ask about Anna, but Poppy's response was a shrug that conveyed both indifference and a touch of irritation that the question had been asked. Assumed that they had argued, I let the matter lie, although it was impossible not to ponder the possibilities of her being single as we walked to Natasha's car, or rather Percy's, her own being some completely impractical sports model.

It took us a while to find the house, in East Dulwich, halfway along a narrow straight road. As with Anna Vale's, there was nothing to distinguish it from its neighbours. Natasha parked as close as she could, double checked the address and marched boldly up to the front door, with Poppy and I behind her.

Natasha rang, and the door swung open to reveal a woman bigger even than the drawing had suggested, certainly fatter. She was also dressed the part, in a huge deep blue matron's uniform, complete with complicated little hat and upside-down watch. However, instead of welcome, her face expressed surprise and not a little embarrassment. It was left to us to speak.

'Hi,' Natasha ventured. 'Nurse Trainer? I'm Natasha, we swapped emails, yes?'

'Natasha?' she queried. 'Yes, but . . . Come in anyway.'

She made way and we trooped in. The house was typical enough, a little chintzy perhaps, but nothing out of the ordinary. We were shown into a comfortable front room with a sofa big enough for all three of us. We sat and Nurse Trainer followed us in to take a hard chair and perch herself nervously on the edge.

'You're not press, are you?' she asked.

'No,' Natasha assured her. 'We're genuine, one hundred per cent, aren't we, girls?'

'I don't want to be awkward,' she went on, 'but do you have any proof?'

I sighed inwardly. I knew what came next – the cane. Natasha saved me, grabbing my bag and starting to pull out bits of equipment, nappies, my bottle, powder, cream.

'There we are,' she said happily. 'Would a journalist carry all that stuff? She probably wouldn't know where to get some of it! Anyway, what's the problem? You seemed happy with us before. I answered your questions, didn't I, in the messages?'

'Yes, but . . .'

'So what is the problem?' Poppy demanded.

'Nothing,' she replied, 'only . . . I wasn't expecting . . . actual girls.'

'No? What were you expecting?' Natasha demanded.

'Transvestites?' Poppy suggested.

'Special girls is the term we use,' the woman said, 'but yes, transvestites, in a way. Up until now, all my clients have been men. More than half like to dress as girls and use girls' names. I respect that.'

'Clients?' Natasha queried. 'So you're professional.'

'Yes, of course. I offer a full service.

'Well, we're not going to pay!' Natasha exclaimed. 'No way!'

'Girls don't pay,' Poppy put in.

'I charge. It's my living,' Nurse Trainer answered.

'OK, sure, but you've got to be into it?' Natasha answered.

'Of course I am . . .'

'And you like real girls?'

'Yes, I do . . .'

'Then have some fun with us.'

The woman paused, evidently tempted as she glanced between us.

'Would you mind if I took some publicity photos?' she asked.

'No problem, sounds fun,' Poppy answered immediately.

'So long as my face is not visible,' I said.

'Likewise,' Natasha added.

Nurse Trainer smiled.

'Deal?' Natasha asked.

'I think so,' she said. 'Let me tell you what I offer. There's a playroom upstairs, almost brand new, as it goes, with full-sized equipment. Across the passage is my nurse's room, where I keep my own things, such as bottles, milk, spare nappies and, of course, paddles, if anybody's naughty. The only thing I won't do is change dirty nappies. Wet, yes, but not dirty.'

'I wanted to ask about discipline,' I said. 'Can we opt out? Are we able to set limits?'

'You can't opt out, no, or where would we be?' she answered me. 'It's something I'm used to using my judgement on.'

'Fair enough. I appreciate that you need to be fully in charge, of course, but please be aware that my pain threshold is very low.'

'All right. And you two?'

'Medium,' Natasha answered.

'Punish me as you think just,' Poppy added.

'Now that's the real answer,' Nurse Trainer said. 'So, we had better get you three little ladies dressed. I offer two choices, first stage, which means just your nappy, and training, which means panties and vest. Anything elaborate, you need to bring yourselves.'

'Training for me,' Poppy answered her.

'Me, too,' Natasha added. 'First stage for Gabby, I'm sure.'

I nodded, rising to follow the nurse as she made for the stairs. On the first floor landing we were shown into a room stretching the full depth of the house, with large frosted windows at either end. It was painted lemon yellow, both light and bright. The floor was wood block, and several pieces of obviously customised pine furniture stood about; a gigantic cot, a table with a top of padded plastic, a low chair, a great chest. A huge mirror covered nearly half of the long wall, with a robust wooden climbing frame in front of it.

'That's not just for play,' Nurse informed us, catching our interest in the frame. 'It's where very naughty girls go for punishment. Now, off with your clothes; I'll be back in a moment.'

She left us, and after a moment of hesitation we began to undress. It was my first chance to see Poppy fully naked, and I made no secret of watching as she peeled off. Her breasts were everything I'd imagined, full and heavy, slightly pendulous, with big nipples and in perfect proportion to her soft waist and slightly chubby bottom. Stood by the svelte Natasha, she looked small and ever so slightly plump, an enchanting comparison. Both were bustier than me, and fuller bottomed, adding to my desire to be firmly junior during what was to come.

Nurse Trainer returned while we were still undressing, and waited patiently for the removal of panties and bras before putting the bundle of pink material she was carrying down on the table. Our clothes were taken away and we were left nude, and in role.

All I had was a nappy, the same large pink sort I normally wore, nothing more, adding to the delicious sense of exposure already strong in my head. I was shaking as I pulled it into place and fastened the tabs, tight, to really bring home the feeling of being in it, and stood back to watch as the others investigated their panties and vests.

The panties were huge. They were also pale pink, see-through nylon, with an elasticated waist and legs, and layer upon layer of frills to create a frou-frou effect that pouted out from the girls' bottoms. Both of them had to tie them at the sides, leaving the material tight against bulging bottoms and stuck out in a big, frilly puff at either hip. The effect had Natasha giggling with erotic humiliation and sticking her bottom out in the mirror to get the best of the effect.

The vests were little better, also see-through pink nylon again, short and flared, to leave the girls' bottoms showing underneath the hems and doing very little to conceal their breasts. Again, both were really too large, but it only added to the vulnerability of their look.

Nurse had watched us dress without speaking, her face set in a placid smile. She was big, but with me in just my nappy she seemed huge, reassuring, yet threatening at the same time. There were already butterflies in my stomach, and I was wondering how it would feel to be fed at her huge breasts with the other two looking on.

'Photographs first,' she said, when Natasha had at last tired of posing in front of the mirror.

She already had the camera in the pocket of her uniform, a straightforward point-and-shoot. We were photographed in a number of babyish poses, crawling, sat splay-legged on the floor, curled up, always to make plenty of display of our bottoms. She was good about our faces and concentrated on Poppy, who inevitably was chosen for the punishment shots.

I was given the camera and watched as Poppy was draped across Nurse Trainer's knee with her bottom raised to show off the pink frou-frou at the rear of her panties. I took one like that, a second with the panties being levered down, and a third with them right down and the full bare globe of Poppy's bottom showing, along with a hint of her sex. It did look glorious and left me flushed and moist, very much ready to play.

A couple of firm swats put enough pink in Poppy's cheeks to let me take a proper spanking shot, and she was released to jump up, giggling as she pulled up her panties.

'Three shots left,' I informed the nurse.

'Best finish them,' she said. 'How about the three of you touching your toes?'

I nodded and got into position alongside the others as they bent obediently, well down, with our bottoms stuck out to the camera. I heard the click and imagined how it would look, with all three of us in spanking position, our bottoms lifted meekly to await punishment.

'Now bare,' the nurse said. 'Pop down your panties.'

Poppy and Natasha reached back to ease down their frillies and show their bottoms. It didn't seem fair for me to stay covered, so I did the same, opening my tabs and letting my nappy fall open at the back to add my own bare bottom to the line. Again the camera clicked and I knew we'd been recorded in our beautifully exposed condition.

'Legs wide for the last one, please,' the nurse said.

I could only obey, opening my legs to let the nappy drop to the floor. I was nude, showing my naked sex from the rear, my anus too, as I was photographed, everything exposed, between two girls scarcely less open. It left me shaking so hard I had trouble fastening my nappy tabs. I was thinking of all the men who would be seeing my naked body, especially my shaved sex-lips and the tight hole between my bottom-cheeks. They would undoubtedly masturbate over the sight, the same way Monty did when he made me pose.

'Thank you,' Nurse Trainer said as she extracted the film from the back of the camera. 'I think two hours is fair for that. Now, Gabby, naturally, must let nature take its course. You other two, if you need pee-pee, call for me and I'll bring a potty. Wet panties mean a spanking, and don't think I won't do it.'

'Yes, Nurse,' they answered in chorus.

The nurse left us, walking across to her own room, which meant she was still in earshot. I already wanted to come, although my fantasies were a little confused, as much exhibitionism as being in my nappy as owing a lot to the sight of Natasha and Poppy in their panties and vests. What I didn't want to do was get punished, but by the mischievous looks on their faces I could tell I was the only one.

'I'm quite ready,' Natasha announced. 'I want to do it in my panties.'

'Me too,' Poppy agreed.

Poppy had sat down cross-legged. Her face was flushed and her nipples hard, showing her arousal, and I could imagine that with her love of spanking the all-too-brief session across the nurse's knee would have been more frustrating than satisfying. Natasha was still standing and had her fingers in her mouth, excited but nervous at the prospect of what she wanted to do.

'I'm going to,' she said suddenly. 'I'm going to do it, watch.'

She turned and stuck out her bottom, stretching the pink panty material taut across her cheeks. Her legs were a little apart so I could see the harp-shaped rise that marked the outline of her vulva, with the pink nylon loose at the centre. I saw her muscles tense, and heard her little gasp, pleasure mixing with dismay as pee erupted through the crotch of her panties, spraying out backwards to patter on the floor.

Not all came through the material. More was gushing out at the sides of her panties, and I could see the bulge where the nylon was holding it in. What came out ran down her legs, both sides, to add to the pool rapidly forming on the floor. As it came, she reached down to slide a finger between her sex-lips, rubbing and sending her pee splashing in every direction. I watched, hoping she'd masturbate through her wet panties and let us watch her come, only for her to stop as the piddle died down. She turned, grinning, her eyes bright with pleasure.

'You are going to be in trouble,' I warned.

'I know,' she said proudly, and sat down right in the puddle. She put her bottom in the very middle and crossed her legs as the piddle began to soak into the seat of her panties. She was smiling and wiggling her bottom in the mess. The front of her panties were soaking, the material tight against her pussy-lips to show the shape of her sex to perfection.

'That's lovely,' she said. 'Now you, Poppy.'

Poppy just nodded and moved round a little so that both of us could see the front of her panties, with her pussy bulging out beneath the frills. Taking one heavy breast in each hand, she closed her eyes, stroking her nipples, her mouth slightly open. I watched, my eyes on her crotch, and suddenly the nylon was damp, a patch spreading down the groove of her sex before a little fountain of piddle burst from the centre.

She sighed, hanging her head as the pee began to gush, erupting from her panties in spurts and dribbles to pool between her thighs and soak in under her bottom. I could feel for her, imagining the sheer joy of wetting myself in panties, such an uncontrolled, irresponsible thing to do. She let it all out too, until, like Natasha, she was sitting in a big yellow puddle.

'Gabby?' Natasha demanded. 'Come on. I want to see that nappy bulge.'

'I haven't much . . .'

'Do it.'

'Or we rub your face in ours,' Poppy added.

'Yeah, and make her lick it up,' Natasha agreed.

'Don't be so cruel!' I retorted. 'I'll do it. Beasts!'

Like Poppy, I'd sat down, and for all my protestations I knew I had enough inside me. I would simply have preferred to wait until I really needed to go. They watched, grinning, as I opened my legs wide to leave the nappy pushing out over my sex in a fat pink bulge. I strained, willing myself to let go, and sure enough it came, running out into my nappy with a faint hiss. Poppy giggled, clutching on to Natasha's arm as they watched the puff of nappy material between my thighs slowly fatten and sag as the pee soaked in.

'Now you'll get it too!' Natasha laughed.

'No, I won't,' I protested. 'I'll just get changed. Should we call nurse, do you think?'

'No. She can hear anyway.'

It was true, but I hadn't expected her to appear so suddenly in the doorway, or so silently. One moment she wasn't there, the next she was looming over us, her hands on her hips as she surveyed the mess on the floor. For a moment there was silence, broken only by the sound of Poppy biting nervously on a fingernail. Finally the nurse spoke.

'Filthy little brats! How dare you, and all over the floor!'

'Sorry, nurse,' Poppy managed.

'You will be,' Nurse Trainer assured her. 'In a line, the three of you!'

'Me!' I protested. 'I haven't peed . . . Well, not on the floor!'

'And did you call for me when your friends wet?'

'No, but . . .'

'Precisely. Now into line, madam, or I shall have to fetch Mr Hairbrush, and you wouldn't like that, not one little bit.'

Poppy and Natasha were already standing, side by side, next to the big chair, where nurse had pointed. I joined the end of the line, shaking and wondering if I dared protest further. I didn't. I was going to get spanked again.

It was done like a production line, one by one, panties down, over the knee, spanked, and into the corner. Nurse came behind me first, ducking down. I shut my eyes as she eased my tabs, allowing her to tug my nappy down around my thighs. She refastened them to leave me bare-bottomed, with my legs held tight together and the pee-soaked nappy hanging heavy between my knees. Poppy followed, her panties jerked down around her thighs, where they hung below her bare, wet bottom, dripping pee on to the floor. I was watching from the side of my eye and expected Natasha to be given the same treatment. Instead, Nurse Trainer sat down on the chair and patted her lap.

Natasha hesitated, just a second, but a second too long. An instant later, she had been jerked down across the woman's knee, her soggy panty-seat kicked high and a hand brought down hard across her bottom. She squealed in shock and pain, drops of pee spattering in all directions as the spanking commenced, swat after powerful swat landing across her wet panties as she kicked her legs and clutched frantically at the floor.

Only after a good dozen swats did her panties come down, jerked off at the back with a complete lack of

135

ceremony to leave her bare bottomed and squirming in pain, for an instant before the spanking started again. Her buttocks were already red and really bouncing, her little fleshy cheeks squashing out with every slap to show off her anus and wring ever more desperate squeals from her throat. It was so hard and I watched in horror, thanking myself over and over for having the sense to ask for it gentle, as my friend howled and thrashed her way through the punishment.

By the time it finished, Natasha's bottom was cherry-coloured, really glowing and covered in finger-marks. She was gasping in reaction, unable to speak, and the tears were starting in her eyes as she stood, mouth open, to rub at her bottom.

'In the corner,' Nurse Trainer ordered, 'and you can leave your panties down.'

Natasha obeyed, shuffling miserably over to the corner of the room with one hand clutching at her lowered panties and the other rubbing at one tear-stained cheek.

'Poppy,' Nurse Trainer said firmly. 'Over you go.'

Poppy went without hesitation, allowing herself to be hauled across the nurse's lap and opening her legs in submission as a knee was raised to bring her bottom up. Nurse Trainer took a firm grip on her waist and began to spank, hard swats delivered to the big, fleshy cheeks to make them wobble and shiver and set Poppy gasping.

I'd seen her take the cane and I knew she was no baby, but Nurse Trainer still had her kicking from the pace of the spanking as much as the force. Slap after slap landing on the big, dancing bottom to a merciless rhythm which gave poor Poppy no chance at all to compose herself. She was brave, relatively, but she'd still made a fine show of pussy and anus before it was over. Like Natasha, she was sent cherry-bottomed and shaking into the corner to stand with her wet panties lowered, rubbing ruefully at her sore behind.

As Poppy took her place, I found myself swallowing in anticipation of my own punishment. I wanted to say something, but Nurse Trainer was already patting her lap and I found myself going down before I really knew what I was doing. Like the others, I was taken around the waist, firmly but gently, and her knee was cocked up under my tummy to lift my bare bottom.

There was a pause, a moment to contemplate my position and let my fear rise, before a heavy slap caught me right under my tuck, jamming my whole body forwards and wringing a squeal of shock from my lips. She never gave me a chance, not to speak, not to do anything but squeal and writhe and babble stupidly as I was beaten, spanked really hard. I didn't even manage to hold back as much as Natasha, but made a real show of myself, with tears and spittle and drops of pee. My trapped legs were kicking up and down together, my breasts jiggling crazily under my chest, my bottom opening and closing as I bucked frantically across her lap.

I got the same as they did, I think, but was left tearful and gasping on the floor, so that I had to crawl into the corner to stand beside them. I was dizzy with reaction and acutely conscious of my bare red bum. I wanted to protest but I found I couldn't, especially when Nurse Trainer spoke.

'There we are,' she said, 'three gentle little spankings for three sensitive little girls. Now, you, Natasha and Poppy may clear up the mess you made. Stay there until I return.'

We stayed, bare red bottoms presented to the room, hands crossed over our naked pussies, not even daring to glance back until we heard the sound of the nurse's footsteps on the stairs.

'That was hard!' Natasha protested. 'My poor bum!'

'No, it wasn't. Don't be a baby!' Poppy answered. 'And stop snivelling, Gabby, anyone would think you'd never been spanked before.'

'I hate spanking!' I wailed.

'No, you don't,' she answered, 'not really.'

I gasped as her hand found my belly, snaking down over my pubic mound to burrow between my sex-lips, lower still, and into my vagina. I was wet and her finger went in easily, pushed deep twice before being pulled out and lifted for inspection. It was covered in white juice, forcing a wry smile from my lips and a giggle from Natasha before Poppy popped it into her mouth to suck up my juices.

'I do hate spanking, I mean it,' I assured her. 'I know it makes me wet, but . . .'

I stopped at the sound of footsteps. Risking a glance back, I saw Nurse Trainer enter the room with a bucket in one hand and a packet of floor-cloths in the other.

'Over here, and do it properly,' she ordered, 'or it'll be a dose of the hairbrush, and then you'll have a reason to cry.'

They moved, getting down on hands and knees to clean up the piddle, bare red bottoms wobbling behind them as they worked. The sodden clothes were wrung out into the bucket, with nurse keeping a close eye on them, until the floor was properly clean. Her uniform was wet too, across the lap, and she made Poppy apply a cloth to it before either girl was allowed to clean herself up. Even then they were simply divested of their panties and given a wet cloth each, which I thought unfair until I realised why.

'Get that wet nappy off, Gabby,' the nurse ordered, 'and climb on the mat.' I obeyed, pulling my tabs free to let the nappy fall squashily to the floor, but picking it up hastily at a warning look from the nurse. She took it, left the room briefly as I climbed on to the mat to lie myself down on the cool plastic surface, awaiting one of my favourite parts of the fantasy.

Sure enough, Nurse Trainer came back with a fresh nappy and a large bag. I relaxed, limp on the changing table, as my legs were taken and lifted, to roll me up with my pussy and bottom on open display. She took a cloth, wiping my crease and sex, her fingers brushing on my pussy to make me moan and set me shivering. A towelling followed, applied with the same intimate thoroughness, which stopped just short of actually masturbating me. I thought she would do it, perhaps with the cream, in a wonderfully matter-of-fact way, just dabbing me off to orgasm, simply because it was what I needed. I was trembling hard as she used a big, pink powder-puff to pad my sex and anal area, and as cream was squeezed out on to my rolled-up buttocks I was shaking with anticipation.

She did my bottom, soothing my smacked cheeks before applying a touch to my anus and inserting the top joint of her finger into my hole. Feeling myself penetrated was more than I could bear, and I began to play with my breasts, eyes closed in anticipation of that final, special touch. What I got was a slapped hand, with both Natasha and Poppy giggling in the background. I swallowed my frustration, assuring myself that she was just staying in role and would oblige my very obvious need.

'Just you behave, there's no call to be dirty,' she said, taking me by one ankle and hauling my legs wide to spread my sex. 'Now, a dab of cream here.'

She took the tube, squeezing it gently to lay a long, cool worm on to my vulva, full between my lips. A strong shudder went through me at the touch, then another as her hand pressed to me, applying the cream to my pussy with short, deft touches. I felt my orgasm start immediately, my muscles tightening as it rose up, only for her to stop and pointedly close my legs.

'None of that, I said,' she chided.

'Please, nurse,' I managed. 'You can't do that to me and not make me come, you can't!'

'Oh, yes, I can,' she said.

139

'Please?' I begged.

'I don't . . .' she began and stopped.

'Oh, you must make us come, you must! You want to come yourself? Think what you could make us do.'

'Would you mind?'

'Of course not. Anything.'

'Then we shall see. For now, we'd better have you back in a nappy.'

As she spoke, she had lifted me by my legs. The new nappy was slipped in under my bottom and spread out before she lowered me into the soft embrace of the material. Once again my legs were hauled apart, and with a few deft motions my nappy was fixed into place, tight around my waist.

'Poppy next,' Nurse Trainer stated as she helped me down.

'I'm not going in a nappy, am I?' Poppy demanded sulkily.

'No,' the nurse replied, 'but you can go without panties to remind you of what you did in them, and if there are any more accidents it'll be the hairbrush, or worse. Now come up.'

She went, to be put through the same process as me, rolled up, cleaned, powdered and creamed, only unlike me she was left bare. Natasha was given the same treatment, and we were left as Nurse Trainer returned to her room briefly before going downstairs.

The girls looked very sweet indeed without panties, bare red bottom-cheeks sticking out from beneath the hems of their vests. Neither seemed to mind, both full of energy and excitement after their spankings, and keen for sex. So was I, and would happily have indulged myself with them had not Nurse Trainer warned us that any of what she called 'unnecessary hanky-panky' would result in a severe punishment. I had no intention of ending up tied to the climbing frame for a whipping, and held back, praying that she'd overcome her reservations about letting us come.

When she did come back, she had three bottles, each of which must have held a half-litre or more of milk. Poppy and Natasha took theirs, giggling and sucking happily on the teats. I hesitated, hoping for something better. She seemed diffident about actual bodily contact, but I had to try.

'Might I be suckled, nurse?' I asked.

She pursed her mouth, looking doubtful, then smiled as the girls burst into giggles.

'I think you had better come with me,' she said, holding out her hand.

I took it, allowing myself to be led out of the playroom and into her own. It was smaller and white, very clean and clinical, with a bench and cupboards around the walls, also a large, low chair like the one in the playroom, on which she sat down.

'I don't normally allow this,' she said as she began to unfasten her dress, 'but for a girl, I will.'

I nodded my understanding, fully aware of how strong her emotions would be. My own were certainly powerful and I was shaking as I watched her open her uniform and shrug it down over her shoulders to reveal a huge, solidly built bra. She was massive, her arms thick and brawny, what I could see of her waist ringed with bulges of firm, fat flesh, her breasts huge, each as large as my head.

She reached back, grimacing with the effort as she tugged open her bra-catch. It came, and the weight of her breasts sent them lolling forwards, one spilling almost free. I swallowed, my fingers shaking as she pulled the bra up and off, revealing her breasts, two fat globes of pale flesh, smooth and bulbous, each heavily veined and tipped with a broad, long nipple. She cupped one, holding it up in her huge hand, and patted her lap.

My shaking had grown uncontrollable as I went down to curl myself on to her lap. Her arm came around me, pulling me close, and the scent of her flesh

141

caught my nose. I opened my mouth, eager to take in the long, dark nipple in front of my face and opening my thighs to show my need.

'Is there something special you want?' she asked.

I nodded.

'Very well,' she responded, 'but if I'm to do that, you'll allow me some pleasure of my own.'

I nodded once more, accepting her right to have me serve her, however she pleased, just as long as she would masturbate me as I suckled. She moved her hand lower to cup my bottom, holding most of both cheeks in her splayed fingers, and I was pulled on. My head went in; the big nipple entered my mouth, my face squashed against fat breast-flesh, my lips closed. I was suckling, my eyes shut, in heaven as I mouthed on her huge, hard nipple, sucking and sucking with a desperate, fulfilling urgency.

Her only response was a gentle sigh, and a slight movement of her hand to press her breast more firmly into my face. For a long moment she simply let me suckle before the hand on my bottom began to move, stroking me. At that moment, I knew that the spanking had done me good. It helped me to surrender, to abandon myself that little bit more, precisely because the woman feeding me had taken control of me, spanking my bottom because she could.

I nuzzled closer, opening my mouth wide around her big nipple and pressing myself to her naked chest. Her hand was under me, cupping my bottom, her thumb in my crease, pressing down, opening me, to find my creamy bottom-hole. She touched, rubbing, and then she was in, the first joint of her thumb in my anus, delving deeper to take a firm grip on my rear. I felt juicy and open and spread my thighs for her, allowing her to watch as she fondled me and probed my anus.

I hadn't expected to be penetrated anally but I was hers; she could do as she liked and I accepted it, feeding happily at her breast while she explored my bottom. She was rough, too, pulling my ring open and squeezing my bottom with her fingers, until my flesh had begun to jump and shiver.

'There, there,' she soothed, as my body shook against hers. 'A little more, and I'll be nice to you.'

With her words her thumb pushed deeper, stretching my bottom-hole until I gasped. At that she stopped and slid it free to leave my anus wet and open. Her hand moved too, higher, her big fingers cupping my sex to spread my lips and ease my vagina open. She began to masturbate me, using her palm with her finger in my hole, then a second. It was rough, my body jerking to the motions, like the way Monty did it, frigging me as if I was a doll.

Not that it mattered. I was suckling her and I was in heaven. My thighs were wide, my whole lower body jerking to the movements of her hand, my anus still tingling from her rough treatment, my bottom-cheeks warm from spanking, my mouth engorged with nipple.

I came so easily, a long drawn-out orgasm with peak after peak of ecstasy as I gulped and bit at her nipple, with my bottom and sex in frantic contraction against her hand. She held me tight until at last it was over and I went slowly limp in her arms, still sucking and lost in pure, simple bliss.

'There we are, is that better?' she asked as her finger finally left my sex.

I nodded and nuzzled my face into her breast.

'Good,' she said, 'but let's not be too greedy, shall we? I think there's something else you need to do.'

'Yes, of course,' I admitted, pulling back reluctantly. 'Whatever you like.'

'Just do as I say,' she replied.

I slipped down from her lap as she moved forwards on the seat. As I had expected, she lifted herself to adjust her uniform skirt, pulling it high to reveal the tops of her stockings, suspender straps and the plump swell of her upper thighs, then her sex, encased in big, white panties. She lifted her bottom, put her thumbs in her waistband and pushed down the panties, exposing a plump, hairy sex, the centre red and moist. With the panties around her ankles, she opened her knees, leaving me no doubt whatever that I was to lick. I began to go down, but she shook her head, and slid a little way down the chair.

'Climb on,' she said, 'head to tail.'

I realised what she wanted, an awkward position for me – but then it wasn't me who counted, not now. Coming close to her, I bent across her body, allowing her to take my legs as my face went down between her thighs. She was strong and held me easily to pull me across her body and up, leaving my legs in the air and my face in her crotch. She took a firm grip on my waist, pulling my bottom and open sex inches from her face, and I set to work, kissing her, then licking, to taste the rich tang of her pussy. She moaned, spreading her thighs wider still as I burrowed my tongue down into the deep cleft of her sex.

Her grip changed, one brawny arm taking me around the waist. I felt her lips as she kissed my pussy, then her hand on my bottom, pulling open my cheeks. A finger-tip touched my anus, and I knew she was going to penetrate me again and explore my bottom-hole as I licked her. Sure enough, her finger went in, slipping easily past my still slimy ring and deep inside me. Her thumb found my vagina, pushing in and up to manipulate my flesh between finger and thumb, making me gasp into her sex.

'Lick me,' she demanded, 'hard, and don't stop.'

I struggled to obey, applying my tongue to her sex, far from comfortable and as eager to make her come as she was herself. She went on exploring, probing and squeezing at my twin holes, opening me. I could barely breathe, my face smothered in wet, hot pussy-flesh, my nose in the moist valley between her lips. Her clitoris was big, a hard lump of flesh under my tongue, moving as I licked, and she began to moan. I licked harder, clutching on to her big thighs as they squeezed around my head. A second finger found my anus unexpectedly and I gasped in shock as it was pushed roughly into my body to stretch my hole painfully wide.

'Lick!' she grated, and I forced myself to obey.

She was holding my bottom-hole open, really wide, and wiggling her fingers to make my cheeks shake. It hurt, but I could feel her sex starting to contract in my face, and ignored the pain, even when a third finger was forced into my reluctant anus, stretching me impossibly wide. She cried out in ecstasy, a wordless grunt of passion as her clitoris bumped beneath my tongue and her fingers jabbed deep into my rectum. Fluid squirted into my face as her sex contracted, and she was coming, and stretching my anus as she did.

I let her do it, holding me wide the orgasm went through her, my bottom-hole agape, so wide I was sure she would be able to see up into me. It hurt, a numb, heavy pain, like a bad bruise, and I was very grateful indeed when she finally eased her fingers out. By then she had relaxed and let me climb off to sit on the floor, breathless, my face plastered with her juices, my anus an open, sore cavity beneath me.

The bathroom was next door, and I went to wash my face, then my bottom and sex. Holding my cheeks wide in the mirror, I inspected my bottom-hole, half-expecting to be bleeding. I wasn't, but my anal ring was loose and puffy, the centre still a little open, showing wet pink flesh and reddened skin around it. It stung too, and I was limping slightly as I went back to find her washing at the sink in her room.

Throughout our sex, I'd been vaguely aware of noises from the playroom, giggles and the occasional wet sound. It was still going on, and as Nurse Trainer turned from the sink she put her finger to her lips. I nodded and waited until she had adjusted her uniform before following her into the corridor. She pushed the playroom door wide with one sudden motion.

Both girls were on the changing table, Poppy on her back with her thighs up and open, Natasha kneeling, face pressed between her friend's thighs. Poppy had her baby bottle between her legs, the teat in her pussy, milk bubbling and spurting from her vagina in time to her laughter. Natasha was trying to drink and lick at the same time, her face white with milk and pussy-juice, which had also formed a broad pool under Poppy's bottom. For a moment neither noticed, until Natasha stopped suddenly to lift her milk-smeared face from Poppy's sex.

'And exactly what do you two think you're doing?' Nurse Trainer demanded.

'Just playing, nurse,' Natasha said hastily.

'Just playing,' the nurse echoed.

Natasha nodded hopefully.

'Wasting good milk, more like,' Nurse Trainer went on, 'and indulging your nasty little habits. Punishment for both of you, I think. Get down.'

'Yes, nurse,' Natasha answered, swinging a leg off the table.

'Spanking clearly has little effect,' the nurse continued as they climbed down slowly, 'so we shall have to try something different, something appropriate. For you, Poppy, my girl, something to remind you that milk is for drinking. For Natasha, something to calm her down a little.'

Poppy had come down and was standing sheepishly in front of the nurse. Her vest was still up over her breasts to leave them peeping out beneath the folds of pink material. Nurse Trainer nodded thoughtfully.

'Yes, I think so,' she said. 'Come with me. Gabby, bring the bottles.'

The nurse took Poppy's hand, pulling at her. Poppy came, looking sulky, but meek enough. I gathered up the three bottles and followed, Natasha with me.

'What are you going to do?' Poppy demanded, suddenly worried as she was pulled into the bathroom.

'You'll see,' Nurse Trainer answered. 'Now bend down across the toilet.'

Nurse Trainer still had Poppy's wrist and pulled her down over the toilet bowl as she reached for something behind the door. Poppy had turned back to look, and I saw her expression change from apprehension to serious alarm.

'No, p-please, not that . . .' she stammered as Nurse Trainer drew down a bulbous red object like a hot water bottle, from which a long tube dangled to end in a nozzle.

'It's what you deserve, young lady,' Nurse Trainer said firmly. 'Gabby, if you would be so kind?'

'No, please,' Poppy answered, 'I hate enemas, I really do . . . please?'

She'd started to wriggle, but Nurse Trainer altered her grip, taking both Poppy's wrists firmly in one big hand and forcing her well down over the toilet. Her bottom spread to show off the lips of her sex and the soft dimple of her anus, the little hole already twitching in anticipation. I'd taken the rubber container and twisted open the top to hold it as a grinning Natasha poured in the milk, one bottle, the second, and the third, which Poppy watched in growing alarm.

'No, please, I can't take all that!' she babbled. 'A little yes, but . . .'

'Quiet,' Nurse Trainer ordered, 'what a fuss over a little enema, and you know it's good for you. Besides, there is no more than perhaps two pints of fluid . . .'

'Two pints! I only ever get one . . .'

'Then you should learn to take more, and also to consider the consequences of your actions, which you may now think on as you take your enema. The reservoir please, Gabby.'

I passed it to her and she calmly hooked it up on the shower rail. It was bulging, nearly full, with at least a litre of milk in it. Poppy looked back, almost panicking as she saw how much was going up her bottom, and she began to writhe and squirm in the nurse's grip. It did her no good. The nozzle was pushed in between her wriggling cheeks and up her bottom. She gave a little gasp of consternation and tried to rise, but she wasn't allowed to. Nurse Trainer held her down, bottom stuck out towards us, and reached up to switch on the valve to control the flow.

Poppy gave a last despairing moan as the milk began to flow up her bottom. Nurse Trainer planted a single, gentle slap on one big, quivering cheek, then took hold of the nozzle, holding it firmly in place in Poppy's anus as the enema was administered. In no time Poppy's breathing had begun to quicken, and I could see her belly twitching to the feel of the cool milk in her rectum. Before long she was panting, then gasping as her belly began to swell out beneath her to the pressure. Nurse Trainer paid no attention, holding the nozzle firmly in place, embedded in Poppy's pulsing anus, until at last the little ring began to dribble fluid down over the milk-smeared vulva. Suddenly, Poppy began to hop up and down on her toes, and to speak.

'That's all, stop,' she babbled. 'Stop, nurse, please . . . I can't take any more. I can't. It's going to happen, nurse, it is . . . it's going to happen!'

'Nonsense,' Nurse Trainer answered her.

'It is, I mean it!' Poppy squealed. 'Ow! Please!'

Poppy's anus had begun to bulge with the pressure in her rectum, and dirty milk was coming out in little spurts from the wet pink hole. She was clenching, struggling to hold it back, which I knew would only cause pain.

'Hold still!' Nurse Trainer snapped.

'I can't!' Poppy wailed. 'It's coming! I can't hold . . .'

She screamed, even as milk exploded out around the nozzle in her bottom-hole, splashing over the nurse's hand. Nurse Trainer let go of Poppy's wrists and pulled the nozzle free, but too late. Even as Poppy scrabbled desperately to get the toilet seat up, her enema erupted from her bottom, spurting out behind her to splash into the shower cubicle, on to the floor and down over her sex. Her scream of despair broke off to a sigh as she soiled herself and, with that, she just gave in. Slumping down over the toilet seat, legs wide, she let it all out, spurt after spurt of dirty milk, her anus pulsing and twitching between eruptions, one of the muscles in her leg jumping in reaction. Soon she was kneeling in a puddle of mess but, rather than finish or acknowledge the state she was in, she began to masturbate, rubbing at her wet, milky pussy. Fluid was still coming from her bottom-hole in spurts and trickles, but she took no notice, her eyes closed, her fingers busy between the plump folds of her pussy. The three of us watched, silent, as she brought herself to climax over what had been done to her, coming with a long moan and a cry of rapture.

'Filthy!' Nurse Trainer told her when it had finished. 'You're a disgrace. Now you can clean that up, and put your soiled clothes in the wash. You can go naked from now on.'

'Yes, nurse,' Poppy answered, and pulled herself slowly to her knees.

'Now for the other one,' Nurse Trainer declared, turning on Natasha. 'Back into the playroom, my girl.'

We followed, leaving Poppy to mop up her mess on her own. In the playroom, the top of the changing table was covered in milk, which Nurse Trainer dealt with in a typically thorough manner.

'Off with your vest,' she snapped at Natasha. 'Mop up this mess.'

Natasha made a face but pulled her vest up and off, to go naked. It was already wet with milk and failed to absorb much, leaving the top with an even smear of milk rather than pools. Nurse Trainer seemed indifferent.

'Now, Natasha, up on the changing station.'

'What are you going to do?' Natasha asked, starting to climb up.

'I'm going to give you an injection,' Nurse Trainer answered.

'An injection?'

'Yes. In your bottom. Don't worry, it's a new, sterile needle, and just distilled water. Quite harmless, but I find it a very effective punishment.'

'Yes, but . . .'

'Now, come on, no nonsense. Roll over, and let's have that little round bottom showing. It won't hurt a bit, and if you don't do as you're told it'll be spankies time. Then you'll be sorry, and you'll get your injection just the same, only with a hot red bottom to go with it.'

Natasha made a choking sound in her throat, but rolled over to show her bare bottom, flushed and beautiful, also quivering slightly in her fear. She was looking back as the nurse delved into her bag to pull out a packaged syringe, then a needle.

'Oh, Jesus,' Natasha managed and hid her face in her hands.

I watched, very, very glad it wasn't me as the nurse carefully pulled on rubber gloves and extracted first the syringe, then the needle. With the needle on, she took up a vial of distilled water, puncturing it to draw the contents down into the syringe. Natasha kept her face in her hands throughout, shivering, to keep her bottom quivering.

As Nurse Trainer expelled a tiny spurt of fluid from the upheld syringe, Poppy came in, naked, her face set in utter consternation, only to change to a smile as she

150

saw what was about to be done to Natasha. She joined me, linking arms, to press her flesh to mine. Natasha was shaking and suddenly put her hands back to cover her bottom. Nurse Trainer removed them gently, but they went back an instant later.

'Any more of that, Natasha, and I'm going to have to tie your hands and you'll be spanked. You won't be warned again.'

Very slowly, Natasha took her hands away from her bottom to leave the twin cheeks bare and vulnerable, trembling hard in her fear. Nurse Trainer came close to lay a hand gently on one bulging, girlish cheek. Natasha gave a sob, shaking her head, as Nurse Trainer took an ample pinch of soft flesh, making it push up between finger and thumb. The syringe was brought down; the needle touched Natasha's bottom-flesh, and pressed home. I actually saw Natasha's skin push in and break, the needle sliding into the soft flesh even as a choking sob broke from her lips.

Nurse Trainer altered her grip on the syringe to push home the plunger and draw a hiss from Natasha as the water was forced into her body. Done, the nurse eased the needle free to leave a single, tiny drop of blood welling from Natasha's punctured bottom. That was all, but it left Natasha shaking with emotion.

She got up slowly, lifting herself on her hands before swinging one leg down from the table, then the other. As she went to inspect her bottom in the mirror she was shaking. For a moment she stood, craning back to watch as the bead of blood ran slowly down over the smooth, flushed skin of her bottom. Then, without a word, she walked to the climbing frame, her legs planted apart, her bottom stuck out as she took a firm grip on the upper bars. She looked back, eyes wide among the tumble of damp curls framing her face.

I came close, sure what she wanted. Taking her in my arms, I slid my fingers down her belly to the wet folds of her sex, burrowing in. She sighed, pushing out her bottom. I slapped her gently, and again as I began to masturbate her.

'Harder, really smack me,' she demanded.

'I will,' Nurse Trainer announced. 'Keep her warm.'

I began to spank, smacking at Natasha's cheeks as I rubbed her. Poppy came close to take hold of Natasha's breasts, kissing and stroking them. I could feel the reaction, Natasha's muscles already twitching, her breathing deep and even.

Nurse Trainer had gone to the chest, delving inside to pull out a wooden paddle, a good foot long, wide and at least half an inch thick. It made me wince just to look at it but Natasha stuck out her bottom, all eagerness. I stopped spanking and pulled back my hand to give the nurse a clear shot as she stepped towards us. The paddle came up and down to land with a meaty smack on the offered bottom.

Natasha cried out but kept her grip on the frame. I tightened mine, as did Poppy, holding Natasha in place as the beating began, the paddle smacking down with firm, regular swats. I could feel the smacks going through Natasha's body and the way the muscles of her sex twitched to each. She was wriggling, shaking her head to the pain, but made no effort to stop it, keeping her bottom out as we masturbated her and she was beaten.

Her orgasm came suddenly, a cry of ecstasy and a violent contraction of her muscles, repeated as the paddle smacked down, harder still, and harder, to match the scream of her climax as it all came together. Instantly she jumped away, but the nurse had already stopped, and watched with a pleased smile as Natasha sagged slowly down into our arms.

I held her until she had stopped shaking and could pull herself up. She was still breathing heavily and her bottom was a mass of bruises, but she was giggling as she inspected the damage and flaunted it happily to the rest of us.

I would happily have continued to play, maybe just curled up in the cot in nothing but a nappy. The others seemed satisfied and happy to call it a day, including Nurse Trainer. I went with the majority decision, helping to tidy up before washing and dressing in normal clothes. The formality of our arrangement had been abandoned, and the four of us spent the next three hours in Nurse Trainer's living room, drinking tea and talking, as if nothing out of the ordinary had passed between us.

Her story was interesting, the mundane covering the strange in a way so typical of human psychology. Her real name was Rose and she had married young, to an older businessman who had expected to be treated as a baby after work. She had complied, reluctantly at first, but with greater enthusiasm as she discovered the benefits of her husband's sexual submission.

The marriage had turned sour, for other reasons, and they had eventually divorced, leaving her with the house but no realistic means of supporting herself. Without work experience or qualifications, she had been faced with the prospect of hard work for very little pay, or exploiting her skill as a nurse for grown-up babies. It had not been a difficult choice and she had managed to get a worthwhile clientele together within a year, largely thanks to the Internet. She had often considered the idea of sharing her fantasy with other women, but we were the first, and her sex with me an expression of a long-held fantasy.

We drove back in seriously high spirits, their sheer elation quickly overcoming my residual sulkiness over having my bottom smacked and my anus stretched. We ate at a French café off Sloane Square, salads of langoustine and goat's cheese washed down with a delicious pale wine selected by Natasha. By the end I was pleasantly drunk, and tired, but no more so than either of them. Abandoning the car, we made for my flat, walking arm in arm, with an unspoken agreement that they'd both be staying. It was close to midnight by the time we got in, and I was dropping. So were they and we ended up going to bed, all three together, cuddled up but too exhausted for sex.

Six

Sunday morning was very easy. Natasha had to deal with the car, but Poppy and I stayed at the flat, talking over toast and coffee in bed. She had seen my clinic and I explained my system of therapy to her. Slightly to my surprise, she had heard of Carl Rogers and was familiar with his ideas on the patient's wellbeing as central to therapy. That gave us plenty to discuss and created a new intimacy between us, so that before long she had begun to open up about her own relationship. It was apparently not going too well, after nearly eight years. Poppy had come to Anna Vale very young, a newly decided lesbian in need of order in her life. At first it had been wonderful, with the combination of authority and discipline exactly what she had felt was missing for her, and little or no male contact. Anna's obsession with the middle years of the twentieth century had been a piece of eccentric fun, and she had joined in with enthusiasm.

Unfortunately, Poppy had changed over the years and Anna had not. The regime remained rigid, where Poppy would have liked greater flexibility. Nor had Poppy been allowed to explore her increasing sexual dominance, except under Anna's supervision. There was also Anna's refusal to accept modern conveniences in the house and their increasing isolation from the outside world. My visit had caused a crisis, Poppy wanting a level of sexual intimacy Anna would not allow, which had sparked what sounded like a straightforward domestic row.

So Poppy had decided to see if I would play on her own terms, although she knew it would mean a heavy punishment when she got back. She still wanted to restore her relationship with Anna to normal, but felt the caning would be worth it. It was a piece of information which made me determined to give of my best before she left. She had contacted Penny Birch, and so Natasha, who had more or less taken things over in typical fashion. I knew the rest.

It was nearly noon by the time Natasha got back, and she had obviously been home because she had changed. She was as vivacious as ever and had barely stepped through the door before she took Poppy aside for a whispered conversation in my kitchen. Whatever they were talking about, it seemed likely to involve me and some sort of sexual indulgence – which was worrying, as I knew Natasha's tastes and they seemed to fit well with Poppy's.

I was half expecting to be jumped when they called me into the kitchen, but they were simply unloading the various bags Natasha had brought back with her, which contained nothing more suspicious than lunch. I began to help, feeling both relief and a touch of disappointment. Always fanatical about her food, Natasha had bought French bread, Channel Islands butter, a Munster and an Ami de Chambertin, York ham carved from the bone, salad ingredients, a dressing of Sauternes vinegar and fine olive oil with black pepper, and three bottles of Alsace, one already chilled. It was more or less what I'd have expected of Natasha, but Poppy was highly impressed and slightly doubtful, being used to Anna Vale's fanatically English approach to cooking.

We took two hours over lunch, and the food was spread out on a table so that we could choose what we liked. All three bottles were drunk, to leave me in a pleasant haze and wondering idly about an afternoon of gentle, lazy sex. Unfortunately neither of them seemed interested, drinking and laughing together as they finished the meal, then simply chatting as we allowed it to go down. Before long I was half asleep, and it came as a shock when Natasha suddenly stood up and came to stand over me.

'Right, Miss Goody-Two-Shoes,' she declared. 'You're in trouble.'

'Trouble, why?' I managed.

'Why?' She laughed. 'Why, Miss Gabrielle, is because while you got your pussy frigged yesterday, poor Poppy was given an enema, while I had a needle stuck in my bum and took a hard paddling! That's why.'

'That wasn't my fault. It was your own.'

'We don't care, do we, Poppy?'

'No, we don't. We're going to torture the little brat, aren't we, Tasha?'

'Yes.'

Poppy was beside me and they grabbed me, wrenching my jacket down over my shoulders to trap my arms. I struggled but I was laughing too much to make any real effort, which encouraged them all the more. They held me, wriggling, while Natasha dug my keys out of my bag and opened the door to my special bedroom. I was dragged in and thrown down on the bed, where Poppy sat on my legs and pinned me down. I could have pushed her off, but I was drunk and giggling, with part of my mind wondering what they were going to do to me and wanting it, despite the sure knowledge that it would be painful. So I stayed down while Natasha searched my room, taking the cord from my robe and pulling the pink ribbon from the neck of my largest teddy bear. I began to struggle again as I realised I was to be tied, but Poppy was heavy and surprisingly strong for her size.

'Sit on her tummy, Poppy, and hold her still,' Natasha ordered as she came back to us. 'No struggling, Gabby, you'll only make it worse for yourself.'

Poppy moved up the bed, settling her bottom on to my stomach. I tried to push her off, half-seriously, not really wanting to be stripped and tied up, but it did me no good. Poppy held on firmly as my shoes were pulled off. My skirt was unbuttoned and tugged out from under Poppy's bottom, my tights with it. I tried to kick, but they came down all together, my panties too, peeled off my legs to leave me bare. Briefly, Natasha pulled my ankles apart to show off my sex, before pushing my legs down and sitting on them, clutching hard at my ankles to keep me still. She got the cord around my leg, ignoring my frantic kicking as she tied it off before looping it around the other and forcing them together. I could do nothing, only squirm in futile, giggling remonstration as my ankles were lashed tight together.

'Hold her down while I undo her blouse,' Natasha said as she gave the knot a final tug.

She moved quickly and Poppy forced my arms wide, pressing me down on the bed. I fought back, thrashing my body from side to side and arching my back to stop it happening as Natasha fumbled for my buttons. She got them one by one, pulled wide to show off my chest and tummy, and with every bit of exposure I found myself giggling more and struggling less, too far gone to resist. Natasha twitched up with one contemptuous motion, baring my breasts to them.

I was rolled over, Natasha twisting my feet, forcing me on to my face. I squeaked at the pain, making her laugh, even as Poppy took hold of my blouse and pulled it off. My bra followed after a brief struggle and I was nude, with Natasha sitting on my legs as they grappled for my arms. I could have stopped them, I think, but I didn't, surrendering to having my arms tied tightly behind my back with the teddy bear ribbon, deliberately high to stop me protecting my bottom.

They climbed off, panting, and I was left helpless on the bed, stripped and tied, breathing heavily and shivering, half-scared, half-eager to let them take full advantage of my helplessness. Both of them were a little out of breath, but they were grinning and thoroughly pleased with themselves.

'And her glasses, I think,' Natasha said, reaching down.

'No,' I answered her, 'not my glasses. I hate not being able to see properly . . . No! Natasha!'

She had pulled my glasses off, leaving my vision a blur, with the two of them visible only as darker shapes against the general pink of my room.

'This is not fair!' I wailed.

'It doesn't have to be fair, Gabby, darling,' Natasha answered me. 'It just has to be fun. Anyway, it's for your own good. They might get broken.'

'Broken? What are you going to do to me?' I demanded.

'Just what was done to us,' Poppy answered. 'Well, a little more, maybe.'

'That is hardly fair!'

'Like we said, it doesn't have to be fair.'

'Exactly,' Natasha agreed. 'Right, sit on her, Poppy.'

Poppy climbed back on to me, straddling my back to press me down into the bed. Her hands found my bottom, gently kneading my cheeks and pulling them wide to show off the hole.

'What a pretty bottom, she has, so small and tight. A shame to spoil it, really.'

'We're not going to spoil it. Well, not for long, anyway.'

'What do you mean, spoil it?' I demanded. 'You're not going to spank me again, are you? You know how I hate it, and I really don't want any more bruises!'

'No spanking, I promise,' she answered. 'Bruises . . . maybe.'

'What are you going to do, then?'

'This.'

159

She had been burrowing in her bag as she spoke, and with the last word she pulled something out. I could barely see it, only two vague shapes, one pale brown, the other a brilliant viridian green, along with a glint.

'Injection first,' Natasha said. 'Now you can learn how it feels, seeing as how you thought it was so funny when it was done to me.'

'I did not!' I wailed. 'What do you mean "injection" anyway? What is that thing?'

'A hat pin,' she said casually. 'Here, look.'

She tugged at the thing in her hand and held it to close to my face. To my horror I saw that she was telling the truth. The green thing was a fat, ornamental pin head, holding a shaft of bright steel about ten centimetres long.

'No, you wouldn't!' I managed, with a knot of pure panic starting in my stomach. 'You wouldn't! Please, no!'

She just laughed and threw one leg across me to seat herself on the backs of my knees. I tried to struggle, writhing underneath them, with the bubble of pure panic growing in my throat until I thought I was going to scream.

'Now, now, no need to get in a state,' Natasha soothed, stroking my bottom one-handed. 'We're only teasing. We wouldn't really puncture your pretty bottom, would we, Poppy?'

A great wave of relief flooded through me at her words. My emotions came out in a long sigh, only for it to turn to a scream of pain as the pin was driven into my flesh without the slightest warning. Behind me, Natasha laughed, a truly evil cackle, Poppy giggling in time. They left it in, sticking up out of my bottom-cheek.

'Oh, you are funny, Gabby!' Natasha crowed when she'd got control of herself. 'And you do look good with the pin sticking up out of your cheek. Sorry, but I've got to do it again. Several times, actually.'

'No, please,' I managed. 'This is really unfair. Please stop it. It hurts!'

'Does she mean it?' Poppy asked suddenly.

'Not really,' Natasha answered, easing the pin from my bottom to draw a fresh gasp from me. I felt a fresh surge of panic hit me.

'She's just a bit of a cry-baby,' Natasha went on, 'and she's got a stop word, anyway.'

'Good,' Poppy said. 'Give her another, then.'

I tried to speak, but all that came out was a fresh scream as the needle was driven into my other bottom-cheek, deep, to leave me panting and twitching in reaction. I was trying to remember the stop word, but I was in such a state that I couldn't think of it, or anything but the awful prospect of having the pin driven into my bottom again. Finally I got myself under control.

'I mean it, really,' I babbled. 'Stop, please . . . please, Natasha, no more.'

'You'd almost think she meant it, wouldn't you?' Natasha said, drawing the pin slowly out of my flesh once more.

'I do!' I wailed. 'Stop, please, stop!'

I felt the wet on my skin as my blood beaded from the new hole. Both stung, an awful itching feeling, along with a dull ache at the crest of each buttock, around where the pin had been driven home.

'Once more?' Natasha said. 'Under her tuck, maybe, where it's nice and plump.'

'No, please!' I wailed. 'Mercy . . . No, I mean . . . What was it?'

'You know very well, little slut,' Poppy said. 'Yes, under her tuck, but don't hurry, and it's important that she should know how many times it's going to happen. Shall we say six more?'

'Six!' I wailed. 'No! Please!'

'Twelve, then, if six isn't enough for you.'

'No, please, girls, please . . . I can't . . . really . . .'

'Shut up!' Natasha ordered, 'or we'll tape your mouth shut and give you double. Here goes, then.'

I screamed again as the long pin sank into my bottom, deep under one cheek, to leave me gasping and writhing on the bed, panicking, my body beading with sweat and the tears welling in my eyes, as much from sheer, awful frustration as pain.

'I love the way her muscles jump when it goes in,' Natasha remarked. 'Do you want to do her other tuck?'

'Yes, please,' Poppy answered.

I was beyond speaking and could only lie there, shaking my head, my whole body trembling in reaction to what was being done to me. Poppy took the head of the pin, and I felt it drawn slowly from my body, only to touch again under my other cheek, making my muscles twitch. She giggled, bent down so that she could see properly, and pushed.

I actually felt my skin break and the steel shaft push into my flesh, even as I screamed. I was dizzy with pain, the muscles of my tummy and bottom twitching frantically, close to hysterics, blind with gathering tears, beyond which I could see nothing but a blur of pink and, where the Valentine teddy bear I'd propped by my pillow was clutching a satin heart, red.

'Red!' I screamed. 'Red, red, red . . . I mean it, I do! Red!'

'Ah,' Natasha answered me casually. 'Are you sure? I was enjoying that.'

'I'm sure, really,' I babbled. 'Just stop it, please, pretty please, anything, but not this, no more . . .'

'Oh, all right,' she said, 'but you're such a baby.'

I felt her take the pin and pull it slowly free. It stung and again I felt the wet of my own blood as the bead formed and broke to trickle down into the groove beneath my bottom. I was still panting, and the knot of fear and panic was still tight in my stomach, but easing slowly as I sank down, limp beneath them.

'I think she's quite brave to take four really,' Poppy said from above me. 'Aren't you, Gabby darling?'

I couldn't respond, my emotions too strong to find an answer. I didn't know if I hated them or was desperately and urgently in love with them. I was in pain, but was enervated too, trembling with need and filled with the delicious sense of being out of my own control. It still hurt too. My bottom felt swollen and hot, each prick an individual point of fire, stinging so fiercely my muscles were still jumping. I could feel the bruising too, dull and throbbing, adding to the sensation of my bottom being the absolutely centre of my body. I wanted to curse them, but if they'd decided to masturbate me I'd have done nothing to stop them, and I knew what would have been in my mind as I came.

'I suppose we'd better clean her up,' Natasha said. 'There'll be rubbing alcohol in her cupboard.'

She climbed off, and I pushed up my bottom, grateful for being able to move and keen to stretch my skin. Poppy gave me a playful slap and began to touch me, stroking my bottom between the four puncture marks and between my cheeks. I was wondering if she was going to bring me off, but she stopped as Natasha returned to bounce down on the bed. A moment later I caught the smell of the alcohol, then felt the soft wetness of the cotton wool as it was pressed to my injured bottom. It stung and I gasped at the sudden, sharp pain, but held still, letting her clean me properly. She did each cut carefully, ignoring my gasps and winces as Poppy applied sticking plaster to each in turn, not single pieces, but crosses, like something out of a cartoon, making Natasha giggle. With all four punctures done, they sat back.

'Cute.' Natasha laughed, and slapped my bottom. 'Oh, you should see yourself, Gabrielle, what a sorry sight!'

'You can . . . you can make me come if you want to,' I managed.

'Oh, no, not yet,' she answered. 'You're forgetting what happened to Poppy.'

'If you must, then.'

'Has she got enema equipment?' Poppy asked.

'Loads,' Natasha assured her. 'She uses colonic irrigation as a therapy, but I had something a bit different in mind. Come here.'

She got up, motioning to Poppy, who followed her from the room. I lay still, too overcome to even think of resisting, and bound too tightly anyway. All I could think of was that if they were going to give me an enema, they needed to get me into the bathroom. They were whispering and I heard Poppy giggle, but it was impossible to make out their words. Before long they came back.

'You'll love this!' Poppy assured me.

I managed a weak nod and a smile, hoping she was right.

'Now,' Natasha said, sitting down beside me, 'you're going to help us, aren't you, Gabby, or do we have to use the needle again?'

'I'll help,' I promised quickly.

'Good girl, very sensible,' she answered, with a pat on my bottom. 'Now, we need a nozzle of some sort, wide, to get her bumhole nice and open, and some good thick material. Come on, Gabby, any suggestions?'

'There are some cake decorators in the kitchen,' I said miserably. 'A linen bag too.'

'Good, I'm glad you're being so co-operative. Sit on her, Poppy, make sure she doesn't get away.'

She had risen as she spoke and left the room. A moment later her voice came from the kitchen, deliberately raised as she investigated the contents of my cupboards and fridge.

'Let's see, what's she got? Hmm, eggs, always fun, and tomatoes . . . That would make a nice mixture in her face and hair, wouldn't it, Poppy? We need butter,

164

of course, to grease her bumhole . . . Hang on, I've got it, perfect!'

'What?' I demanded.

'You'll see.'

There was a dull thump and the click of a drawer being opened, then another. She began to hum a pop tune happily, and came back into the bedroom a moment later holding my large mixing bowl. There were things in it, but all I could make out were shapes and colours. Poppy giggled and climbed off me as Natasha put the bowl on the floor.

'What are you making?' I demanded as Natasha poured out what looked like a whole packet of flour into the bowl.

'Cake mix, chocolate cake mix,' she said happily. 'You can do the eggs, Poppy; use them all.'

'No, please, not up my bum,' I begged, 'or, if you really have to, in the bathroom.'

'Do stop whining,' she said. 'One more word and we'll make you eat it afterwards, and I mean that.'

I went quiet, to lie shivering on the bed, trying to watch as they worked. Natasha stirred as Poppy broke the eggs in, all six, then added chocolate flakes, and butter, making a thick brown paste that filled half the huge bowl and must have weighed over a kilogram. All the time I was thinking how it was going to feel up my bottom and about the mess it would make, feeling bullied and sorry for myself despite an undeniable arousal.

It took Natasha ages to get the mixture even, by which time Poppy had assembled the cake icer with the thickest nozzle in place. When it was finally ready, she held the bag wide as Natasha scooped in the thick, brown mess, leaving the bag so full she had difficulty tying the ends off. They were giggling crazily as they stood up, Poppy holding the great sagging bag in both hands, and it still hung over at the sides, with the nozzle hanging down at the front like some huge, flaccid cock.

'Up on your knees,' Natasha ordered. 'Stick it out and remember, any nonsense, any nonsense at all, and you know what happens.'

I tried to rise, struggling to get my knees under me and lift my bottom as I'd been ordered. It wasn't easy and my efforts made them laugh, but I managed, kneeling with my knees as far apart as my tightly bound ankles would permit and my bottom cocked up towards them, open and vulnerable.

'Grease her up, then,' Poppy said.

'Sure,' Natasha answered. 'Oh, shit, we shouldn't have used all the butter. No, there's enough on the paper, I think.'

I couldn't see, but a moment later I felt the cold, greasy surface of the butter wrapper pressed between my bottom-cheeks, wiping, as if she was cleaning me. Butter smeared out over my anus and around it too, cool, then moist as it began to melt to my body heat.

'That should do,' Natasha announced as she peeled the wrapper away. 'Right, Gabby, let's get you open.'

My only answer was a tiny sob as her finger found my anus. I felt the butter smeared over my ring, and a little hard piece pushed up the hole, then her finger easing into me and up to wiggle in my rectum as Poppy giggled to see me penetrated.

'She has a neat little bumhole, doesn't she?' Poppy remarked.

'She powders it every night,' Natasha replied, 'and creams the hole. It seems to keep her nice and tight. Let's see if I can get a second finger in.'

'Ow!' I protested as she suited action to word, forcing another finger into my reluctant anus.

'Ever so tight,' she said. 'Springy, like a little fat rubber band.'

Poppy giggled as Natasha splayed her fingers, stretching my anus wide to make me gasp. For a moment she held me, gaping, before closing her fingers and sliding deep in.

'Plenty of room inside,' she said. 'Come on, up it goes, then.'

Her fingers came out, leaving my bottom-hole to close slowly and push out a trickle of warm butter, which I could feel as it ran down into my vagina. Poppy's fist touched between my bottom-cheeks, then the cold metal, right on my hole, slimy with butter, pushing in, opening me, until I began to spread around it. It was thick and I tried to relax, taking as much as I could, but she kept pushing until my anal ring began to strain.

'Stop!' I begged. 'That's all I can take.'

'There's only a little bit in!' Natasha laughed. 'Nothing like a cock, certainly not Monty's cock.'

'Yes, but I haven't . . .'

'You haven't been buggered by Monty? Seriously?'

'I haven't. Not by anyone.'

'You're virgin, up your bum, really virgin?'

'Yes.'

'Oh, my, have you got a surprise coming.'

'No, I have not.'

'As you like, but it makes it a lot easier when this sort of thing happens to you if you've had a cock or two up the bum. Come on, Poppy, let's do her. Push it in a bit more and never mind her squeals, she's just being pathetic.'

'Please,' I begged, 'just fill me like this, if you have to . . .'

'Shh, nursie knows best,' Poppy said. 'Now stop wriggling like that. Just stay still.'

I hadn't realised I had been wriggling, but tried to do as I was told and push out my bottom-hole as the icer was forced deeper up, stretching me until I was gasping.

'What a baby!' Natasha said. 'OK, that's enough. Hold it in, I'll squeeze.'

Poppy changed her grip, holding the nozzle tightly in place in my bottom-hole. The bag of mix had been hanging down between my thighs, and I felt Natasha pick it up. She made a disgusted noise at the feel of the thing and I heard a squashy, wet sound as she started to squeeze. I felt it immediately as the thick paste was forced into my rectum, not like an enema, but with the sense of weight and strain coming immediately, if slowly.

'It's going up,' Natasha said. 'Can you feel it, Gabby?'

'Yes,' I managed.

I could, my rectum already bulging as it struggled to accommodate what was being forced in. My bottom-hole was pouted out and there was an awful sense of urgency building in me, my body telling me that something entirely different was happening and that I should be on the loo, not kneeling on my bed in bondage. I'd started to shake quite hard too, enough to show and make the girls giggle.

It began to hurt and I gasped, but Natasha just squeezed harder, delighting in what she was doing to me and in my reaction. I pulled my cheeks in, trying to take the load deeper, and the pain died, only to rise again as she squeezed once more.

'Not so fast!' I begged. 'Let me try and take it.'

'Stop whining, I said!' she snapped back. 'Just pretend you've been caught short in the street and you're going to fill your knickers unless you hold tight.'

Poppy laughed and I tensed again to feel my lower belly swell as the mixture went deeper up me. An awful bloated feeling started, in my head as well as my gut, making me feel fat and vulnerable, horribly insecure. I began to pant and wriggle my toes, overwhelmed by my feelings as yet more mixture was forced into my straining rectum. They'd made so much, and I was sure most of it was already inside me, and that I could not possibly take any more. I could feel it around my bottom-hole too, squeezing out around the nozzle, despite already being so badly distended.

168

'You're not trying,' Natasha complained. 'Come on, Gabby, you can do better.'

'I can't,' I panted. 'Please . . .'

She squeezed. I gasped as my rectum strained, mixture squashing out around the nozzle to soil my bottom-crease and roll down, thick and sticky, over my pussy.

'Come on,' Natasha urged. 'Take it, Gabby.'

I tried, tightening my bottom and actually feeling my load shift in my guts, up towards my tummy to tighten my skin and put a sick feeling into my throat.

'No, more, I beg. Red,' I gasped.

'Oh, all right,' she answered me, 'but it's nearly all up anyway. One more squeeze.'

She did it even as she spoke, making me gasp as the last of it was forced up my bottom. Some went in; more squashed out around the nozzle, most squeezing down between my sex-lips to hang from my pussy for a moment before falling to the bed with a plop.

'I think she is actually full,' Poppy remarked.

'Nonsense,' Natasha answered, 'she could fit loads more. It's just a question of getting it up. Hmm, maybe we should have put some milk in the mixture?'

'Maybe,' Poppy admitted and tugged the icer out of my bottom-hole.

She hadn't warned me, and I nearly did it on the bed, but managed to tighten up just in time, so that only a little came out. I could do nothing without their permission and help, and I was too cautious of Natasha's cruelty to dare to ask. So I stayed in position, my breathing slow and heavy, trying to keep myself under control and fight down the awful, bloated feeling inside me, and the desperate need to go to the loo. I could feel my swollen belly hanging beneath me, heavy and fat. There was a strange, crawling feeling in my tummy, and my bottom-cheeks had started to twitch again.

'Very cute,' Natasha said, 'and now, for the climax.'

'Yes, do it,' I managed.

'Not your climax, slut,' she answered me, 'although I suppose we might let you come eventually. I mean the climax of your torture. Now, let me see . . .'

She stepped away, and I looked back, to see her drop the icing bag into the mixing bowl. Going to my drawers, she pulled the top one open, rummaging inside. I could see no more than a blur, but I knew what she was doing, and sure enough, when she came close again she was holding a pair of my panties in her hand, dangled between forefinger and thumb, a white silk pair trimmed with lace.

'You're going to do it in your knickers,' she told me, 'in front of us.'

'No, please,' I managed. 'Not those, anyway. They're silk. Use a nappy. Please, Natasha?'

'No. I want to see them bulge as it all comes out. I want you to ruin your fancy knickers, too; it'll add to your feelings.'

'She's being very lippy, isn't she?' Poppy put in. 'Not at all the right attitude for a girl with her hands and feet tied and two pounds of cake-mix up her bum. If I was her, I'd be polite and respectful.'

'So would I,' Natasha admitted. 'We'll just have to punish her, I suppose, to teach her a lesson. For her own good, of course.'

'Not a spanking, please!' I babbled. 'Not like this.'

She just laughed and dropped the panties on my back. Her hands went to the knot securing my ankles, tugging at the cord until it came loose. I opened them immediately and nearly let go of the load in my bottom, clamping shut just in time once more. Natasha pulled the panties on around my ankles.

I let her tug the panties up my legs as I slid to the floor. Poppy took my shoulders, helping me to rise as Natasha tugged the panties higher still and around my

170

bottom. I stood, slightly dizzy, my bottom-hole held tight.

'I suppose we're going to have to untie her hands if we want any work out of her,' Natasha said. 'Shame.'

'What work?' I asked as she began to fiddle with the ribbon securing my wrists.

'Cleaning up, for starters,' she answered, 'and I could do with a glass of wine. It's hard work torturing you, you know.'

'Could I come first, perhaps?'

'No. We want to watch your panties fill. Then you can come.'

'But . . .'

'Gabrielle.'

'OK. I'm sorry.'

'Good. Fetch us our wine, then, and you then can clean up this mess.'

She gestured idly to the floor and reached out for Poppy's hand. Together they walked from the room to settle themselves on my couch. I quickly retrieved my glasses and followed, hobbling, with the strain in my bottom close to unbearable. I could already feel the sticky mixture against my sex where Natasha had pulled my panties up tight, and between my bum-cheeks, but I knew that it was only a small part of what I was holding in, and could imagine how it was going to feel in my panties.

In the kitchen I found a fresh bottle of wine and opened it, pouring their glasses and bringing them out. It nearly happened as I bent to serve them, and I had to jump up quickly. The result was a stab of pain in my belly, making them laugh as I clutched at myself.

'Just do it, if you want to,' Poppy advised.

'Yes, do it,' Natasha added. 'I want to watch you work with your load in your panties. Come on.'

'Don't rush her,' Poppy said, 'let her wait if she wants to, until she really can't hold it any more.'

'I can't, not much longer,' I said. 'My tummy! Please can I get in a nappy?'

'No. Your knickers are soiled anyway,' Natasha answered me. 'Now, come on, chop chop, there's tidying to be done and washing up.'

'Yes,' I managed and hobbled quickly into the bedroom.

My legs were shaking as I picked the things up and scraped the chocolate mix off the bedcover. Twice I nearly did it before I managed to get everything in the sink and the cover in the wash. Bending was worse, my body responding to the position, desperate to let it all out. I held it, though, with my pain and confusion growing, until I was panting and wriggling my toes.

They came to watch as I began to wash up. I knew I couldn't hold. The urge to just let it all out into my panties was becoming overwhelming, along with the urge to masturbate once I'd done it, with them watching as I utterly disgraced myself. They were sipping wine, their arms around each other, eyes twinkling with arousal and pleasure, faces full of mischief.

It was that which broke me, their sheer delight in the state they'd put me in. I was near nude, my only garment my panties, and those just so I could ruin them, my bottom covered in sticking plasters and smarting, my tummy swollen and aching, my pussy urgent . . .

I just let go, the way they wanted me to. My eyes shut; my mouth went wide and I dropped the things I'd been holding into the sink. I stuck my bottom out, straining the panties against my flesh, making myself round, showing off deliberately. Poppy giggled as I let out a tiny, broken sob and let my bottom-hole open. I gasped as it came out, my anus gaping to the point of pain as I let it all go out into my panties, pushing the seat out and squashing up between my bottom-cheeks as the material began to bulge. As my panties filled, so the air filled with the smell of chocolate.

172

Even as I let go of my bottom, my bladder went, pee spurting out through the front of my panties to spatter on the floor and dribble down my legs. They were laughing, both of them, as they watched me fill my panties and wet myself, the bulge growing, pushing back and down to sag below my bottom as the weight grew, heavier and heavier, also my puddle spreading to a wide yellow pool between my feet. I hung my head, letting it come, my anus opening and closing to a slow, lewd rhythm, each pulse admitting more mess into my panties. I was shaking with reaction too, relief and sheer arousal, as the awful heavy feeling grew, until my bulge had began to drag my panties down at the back, exposing the top of my bottom-crease. Unable to stop myself, I reached down under my belly to find my wet, ready sex.

'Oh, no, you don't,' Natasha warned. 'That can wait.'

'Please,' I begged. 'Now, while it's in my panties.'

'Wait, I said,' she ordered. 'Get your dirty little fingers out of your knickers, now!'

I obeyed, sobbing as I withdrew my hand.

'Now finish,' she ordered.

I nodded my head, my lip trembling as I pushed again and felt my bottom-hole open to squeeze yet more mess out into my panties. One calf had started to shake, and it was incredibly hard to fight down the urge to masturbate as I felt my mess squeeze out and the weight in my panties increase that little bit more. My anus closed but I pushed again, forcing out yet more, desperate to have the full weight under me, everything I could do. The strain had gone and my relief was simply overwhelming as I sank down, my breasts hanging in the dirty washing-up water, to strain once more, pushing out the last of the contents of my rectum into my panties. I stood, water dripping from my erect nipples, to look at Natasha and Poppy. They were hugged together, giggling, more delighted than ever.

'Enough?' I asked. 'Can I do it, please?'

'Not yet,' Natasha answered.

'It is all out. I promise. Look.'

I turned a little to make a full show of the huge swelling in my panties. My bulge wobbled as I moved, and the smell of chocolate in the air grew thicker still. My panties were so full I was sure they were going to fall down, which I didn't want, so I reached back to hitch them up a little to cover my crease, squashing mess up between my cheeks and into my pussy. It made no difference, the weight dragging them straight back down to uncover a good half of my bottom-crease. At any moment they were going to drop and spoil the moment.

'Please, now?' I begged.

'Feel it,' Poppy ordered.

I reached back to cup the obscenely huge bulge in my panties. The wet was coming through on to my hand, which came away sticky. Poppy giggled. I touched again, feeling the weight in my panties and squashing it up a little over my pussy. Glancing back at them, I let my other hand snake down over my belly.

'None of that!' Natasha snapped.

'Please!' I begged.

'Slut,' Poppy said. 'Punish her, Tasha. Slap her thighs.'

'No, please, just let me come!' I wailed.

'We'll see,' Natasha answered me. 'For the moment, what did I say about whining?'

'You said not to, but . . .'

'But nothing. You've whined constantly. You've never stopped whining.'

She had stepped forwards as she spoke, coming up beside me. I stayed still, trembling hard, looking at her as she let her eyes travel down my naked body to my bottom. She reached out, taking the waistband of my panties between forefinger and thumb fastidiously and pulling the back open. I felt the mess peel away from my skin and cool air on my damp buttocks.

'This,' Natasha said, 'is to teach you to do as you are told, and not to whine!'

She pulled out my panties further still, at the same time reaching for a spoon from the drying racks.

'No, please!' I managed, panic welling up inside me as I realised what she was going to do.

She took no notice whatsoever, pushing the spoon down the back of my panties to scoop out some mess, which she held up to my mouth.

'Open wide,' she said.

I closed my eyes, unable to watch, my lips shaking as my mouth came open. I felt the spoon go in, the mess touch my lip, then fill my mouth as I shut it, grimacing as she pulled it free. She laughed, Poppy too, watching me as I swallowed my mouthful.

'Oh, you are a dirty little bitch, aren't you?' she said happily. 'OK, that's enough, I think. You can come.'

'Thank you,' I sobbed.

'Not like that,' she said as my hand burrowed for the front of my panties. 'My way.'

I opened my eyes, to find her seated on a stool, patting her lap.

'Oh, no . . .'

'Over my knee, Gabrielle, and you can frig your pussy, while I give you the spanking you so richly deserve.'

'Like this?'

'Yes, like that. Over!'

I was whimpering as I went down, but I kept my hand down the front of my panties. My pussy was warm and wet, the hole clogged with chocolate mixture, my lips and clitoris unbearably sensitive. Natasha took me by my waist as I went down, easing me gently but firmly across her lap until she had me in place, with my bulging panty seat stuck up and out right towards Poppy.

'Here goes!' she said. 'Spankies time!'

Her hand came down, hard, full across my seat. Instantly the mess squashed out across my bottom and burst from the sides of my panties, over my thighs and over Natasha too. She gave a squeal of both delight and disgust and laid in all the harder, spanking away at my filthy panty seat, with cake-mix splashing in every direction, out of panty legs and the top too, and over my pussy to where my fingers were busy with my clitoris.

Poppy was laughing crazily and had stepped close to smack at my legs then dip down, taking my head and cradling me to her chest. I was coming, even as I felt the soft, warm pillows of her breasts in my face. My clitoris was burning under my finger, my vagina contracting, Natasha spanking harder than ever. I felt the warm sludge squeeze out over my sex; I snatched at it, to rub it in over my pubic mound and between my lips, smearing it everywhere but, most of all, full on to my clitoris.

'Filthy, dirty, little brat!' Natasha spat, spanking harder still, to send a great gout of mess spurting from the top of my panties and up over my back, even into my hair.

I screamed, my orgasm exploding in my head, a rush of overwhelming ecstasy at everything that had been done to me, everything that I'd been made to do to myself, stripped, tied, tortured, utterly soiled, spanked, and at last, cuddled into Poppy's wonderful, big, soft chest . . .

My whole body was bucking as I came, my muscles in frantic contraction, my senses completely overwhelmed. The pain had gone, leaving only warmth and an incredibly intense awareness of my sex, bottom, and face, every signal amplified and wonderfully erotic, from the tight feeling of my laden panties, to the softness of Poppy's chest, to the glorious sensations of my vulva.

I came close to passing out and ended up limp and panting across Natasha's lap, utterly exhausted, my hand still down the front of my panties, with chocolate cake-mix trickling slowly down my thighs and falling bit by bit from my disarranged panties to land with sticky plops on the floor.

Finally Natasha got up, pushing me off her lap to slap at the mess coating the front of her jeans. I felt weak at the knees and went down, kneeling, while my body slowly came back under my control. The mess was appalling, my whole lower body filthy, the floor a sea of pee and bits of mess, even some of the cupboard doors spattered with it.

I went to wash, hoping they'd clean up. My panties came off in the shower and I did my best to clean them in the vain hope that they'd be wearable after a good soak and a wash or two. I cleaned thoroughly, douched and gave myself an enema, which stung, making me realise how sore my bottom-hole was. By the time I'd finished, they'd got the kitchen clean. They'd also finished the wine and Natasha was in one of my skirts. I made no comment but went to fetch another bottle.

'Good, yeah?' Poppy asked as I came back into the clinic, where they'd settled down.

'Beautiful,' I admitted, 'but cruel.'

'Cruel to be kind,' she answered. 'It wouldn't have been the same otherwise.'

'Not like that, no, but really I prefer to be nursed. It takes longer to get there, maybe, but it can be just as strong. What is it that you like?'

'Being irresponsible and under another woman's control, yes. Nothing brings out my feelings like a punishment, though.'

'Suckling?'

'I've never really tried it. I think Anna finds it too . . .'

'Intimate?'

'No, not intimate. Revealing, really. She hates to show off and, to be entirely honest, she's a bit short up top. Maybe I should have asked Rose.'

'You should have. It was beautiful. It would be beautiful with you, too.'

She smiled, blushing ever so slightly, before suddenly giggling and cupping her breasts in her hands to show off their size.

'Sluts, the pair of you,' Natasha said, putting down the paper she'd been reading. 'More sex later, perhaps, but for now we need to think about food.'

'Food? We only just had lunch.'

'We had lunch hours ago, Gabrielle. It's nearly six o'clock. Judging from what's in your fridge, we're going to be on lettuce sandwiches . . .'

'No butter,' Poppy pointed out.

'That does it,' Natasha said. 'I'm going to walk down to the garage. I must be able to get something. Pasta, maybe, and some sort of spicy sausage to make a sauce. You've got onions and garlic.'

She had risen as she spoke, and was pulling her coat on. More than happy to let her make the decisions, I just relaxed into my chair, sipping wine. I was slightly surprised she hadn't made me bring her to orgasm, and Poppy, but again I was happy to wait. There was also an unworthy but I supposed inevitable need inside me to get my revenge. I filled Poppy's glass as the flat door banged behind Natasha, only then realising that I should have given her my keys.

'She is cruel, isn't she?' Poppy said. 'I suppose when you're that beautiful, you can get away with it.'

'She is no more attractive than you are,' I answered, 'just closer to the fashionable ideal. And yes, she is cruel, too cruel for me, really. It is not just sadism, she does it to goad people into taking their revenge on her as much as anything.'

'She said she prefers to be submissive.'

'Her ideal is to be spanked against her will or, rather, without her having any say in the matter, but under very specific conditions. I like to surrender my control; she likes it taken away from her.'

'But by the right person, yes?'

'Naturally, that is always the way, and something many people fail to understand.'

'So are you going to get her back, and me?'

'Not when she is expecting it. As for you . . . to be entirely open, I would rather make love to you.'

She didn't answer immediately, taking a sip of wine to give herself a moment to think.

'So would I,' she said, 'but I do need to be punished. You'd spank me, wouldn't you?'

'Yes, if you feel you need it.'

'I do, but would you enjoy it?'

It was my turn to pause. I didn't want to lie, but as I examined my feelings I found I didn't have to. Watching her punished had excited me, her reaction so openly pleasurable that there was no guilt or bad feeling at all.

'Yes,' I said.

She smiled, rising to cross to my chair and seat herself on the arm. I opened my arms for her, taking her in to hold her, our mouths meeting in a long, open kiss. We held on for a long time, cuddled close, eyes closed, delighting in the feel of each other's bodies and the intimacy of our embrace. Finally she pulled back to jump up from the chair, smiling, and more full of life than ever.

'I'm going to go to bed with you,' she said happily, 'only not tonight. I have to get back, or I'll be in even more trouble with Anna than I already am. But, before I go, if you're going to be nice, and you promise not to let Natasha be too horrid, you can both play with me.'

'Please, yes. Would you like anything special?'

'Well, yes, as you've got all the grown-up baby-girl gear, I'd like to be put in nappies, and spoon-fed my dinner, and spanked, and made to come in some lovely, naughty way. Yes, that would be perfect. In fact, I think I'll give Natasha a surprise when she comes back.'

Her whole face was lit up with pure mischief as she ran into my special bedroom. Not to put her in the nappy was more than I could resist and I followed her, finding her already down to her bra and panties. I took a nappy as she finished stripping and nodded to the bed. She went down, rolling her legs up to show off her sex and let me slide the nappy in under her bottom, and parted them as I tugged it up. It was a little tight on her hips, as I discovered as I fixed the tabs, but looked adorable, with the back puffed out over her chubby bottom and her sex covered with a fat, pink puff of material.

'Beautiful,' I told her. 'Do you want a baby-doll or anything?'

'No, I like to be bare except for the nappy. Why cover my chest? It's not as if I've got anything to be shy about.'

She smiled at me, cupping her breasts again, and leaning forwards to hold them out, plump and pink in her hands, the nipples pointing forwards, just dying to be suckled.

'Later,' she said, catching my thoughts, 'although I think what all three of us really need is a good stern nurse to keep us under control. Rose was good, wasn't she?'

'A little too stern for me. That paddle was terrifying.'

'You'll be going again? We'll be going again, yes?'

'If we are invited. For now, you will have to put up with me. Come on.'

I held out my hand, and she took it, allowing me to lead her back to the clinic. There, she bounced down on the couch, legs wide to show off the front of her nappy, her pretty face set in a happy grin.

'It's lovely, it just makes me want to wriggle my bum,' she said cheerfully. 'I'm going to wet my nappy in a minute, nurse, and sit in it while we eat, then the two of you can give me a really good spanking, a hard one, with the back of my nappy pulled down to get me bare . . .'

My buzzer went. Assuming it to be Natasha, I pressed it without really thinking.

A few moments later, Jo Warren's head appeared around the side of the door.

We were caught. Poppy was sprawled out on the couch, blatantly naked, except for something worse still, her nappy. Jo gave her a strange look, then turned to me. There was only one thing I could possibly do.

'I'm ... I'm sorry, Gabrielle,' Jo said. 'Is this an awkward moment?'

'Not at all,' I answered, struggling to keep my voice absolutely level and free of emotion. 'This is Poppy. Poppy, this is Jocasta. Poppy is helping me with an experiment into practical regression.'

'Practical regression?'

'Yes, You've heard of Regression Therapy, no doubt?'

'When you get taken back to relive childhood experiences? Yes. Isn't that really out of favour?'

'Yes, it has been largely discredited due to a tendency towards the creation of false memories of traumatic events derived from subconscious wish fulfilment on the parts of both patient and therapist, however ...'

I paused, realising that I was babbling. It wasn't a good explanation, especially when it was Sunday evening, but it was better that admitting we'd been playing grown-up baby girls. I took a swallow of wine as I ordered my thoughts, and continued.

'Practical Regression Therapy, by contrast, seeks only to relax the patient by restoring the lack of responsibility associated with infancy. The effect is essentially similar to meditation, allowing the subject to relax absolutely.'

'Wow. Does it work?'

'Yes,' Poppy chimed in. 'It's wonderful. I feel completely restored, so much so I haven't wanted to take my nappy off.'

'Wow. I have to try it! Why didn't you tell me about this, Gabrielle?'

'I'm only experimenting with the idea,' I said quickly, 'and I'm not certain it would be appropriate to your case.'

'Oh, but it would,' she answered. 'Even with your new mix of oils and shiatsu, I can never really get rid of my tension. It's in my head, more than in my body. What do you do, Poppy, is it stressful?'

'I don't actually work . . .' Poppy began.

'Oh, you lost your job, you poor thing,' Jo broke in. 'I know exactly how you feel. Never mind, though. Be positive, and you'll be back in no time. What is it you do?'

'I'm actually just a housewife, sort of,' Poppy answered.

'Never say "just",' Jo answered, 'not when you're running a household on your own. They estimate the work a woman does for her husband is worth five hundred a week, but I reckon . . .'

'I don't actually have a husband,' Poppy answered. 'I'm a lesbian.'

There was a moment's pause.

'Oh, how wonderfully bold!' Jo exclaimed. 'I admire you so much, Poppy, to have the courage to be so out, so proud . . .'

She trailed off, and began to fiddle with her fingers.

'So how's the book going?' I said quickly.

'Oh, right,' Jo replied. 'That was what I was meaning to talk to you about. I realised that I was getting too far away from what was motivating me, and I've decided to go back to my original idea.'

'Ah . . . but what about the difficulties with Natasha? Who, I should warn you, is due for dinner at any minute.'

'She is? Good. I want to speak to her. I've been too timid, Gabrielle. Like you say, I should put myself first.

I can't let this thing with Natasha continue to cloud my mind.'

'What's the matter with Tasha?' Poppy asked.

'It's complicated,' I answered. 'Jo and Natasha were good friends, but had something of a quarrel . . .'

'A quarrel!' Jo broke in. 'She's nuts, that's what the problem is. She wanted me to smack her bottom, Poppy, can you believe it? And, worse, she asked my boyfriend to! Then, when I wouldn't, she . . . No, I don't even want to go there. Without Gabrielle's help I think I'd have gone mad these last few months. As it is, I just can't get the whole thing out of my head. That's why I have to speak to her.'

'I think it might be wiser to think on the matter a little more before making any hasty decisions,' I said. 'Perhaps an appointment during the week? Or if you prefer to keep it informal, we could meet at the Haven for lunch?'

'No,' she answered. 'I have to speak to Natasha, and I have to speak to her now. Sorry, Poppy, but this is something I just have to do.'

'Speak to me about what?' Natasha asked, appearing in the doorway with my house keys dangling from her hand.

Seven

What should have been a truly wonderful evening ended up in disaster. It could, however, have been worse. For all their attitude, Natasha and Jo were in fact scared of each other, physically in Natasha's case, mentally in Jo's. So what might have been an extremely unpleasant situation was simply cold. Both of them took an entirely self-centred position. Jo demanded the photographs and an apology from Natasha, on the simple grounds that she was morally in the right. Natasha pointed out that this would leave her open to Jo spreading gossip about her sexual habits, and that all Jo had to do was keep quiet. This failed to satisfy Jo, and the argument swung back and forth or, rather, circled, getting nowhere.

Poppy very quickly gave up on the idea of playing and left. I walked her down to the station, apologising for the others, although she was more concerned about Anna's reaction when she got home. We parted with an intimate kiss anyway, drawing a few surprised looks from passers-by, and I walked back, feeling strangely alone and more than a little frustrated.

Natasha and Jo were still arguing, and both attempted to enlist my help as soon as I walked through the door. I refused, demanding peace, and suggesting that we eat together in an effort to be less combative. They agreed reluctantly although, with Natasha flatly refusing to make a vegetarian pasta sauce for Jo, I ended up cooking. For all the girls' efforts at cleaning up, the kitchen still smelled faintly of chocolate, and I found it hard to hide a grin as I worked, despite trying to puzzle out a solution to their disagreement. Finally, just about at the point when I'd got my sauce right, it struck me.

'Listen to me,' I stated firmly as I put their plates in front of them. 'This is what you will do. Natasha, you will give me the photographs and the negatives, which I will hold in safe-keeping. Jo, you will not mention Natasha's sexual tastes to anybody. Nor will you include any reference to spanking in your book. Is that fair?'

Both opened their mouths and closed them again. Finally Natasha nodded, then Jo.

'Good,' I stated. 'Now, let's eat.'

My firm attitude seemed to work and they were actually moderately being civil to one another when they left, which gave me a degree of satisfaction. I was also exhausted and annoyed that I had been unable to take Poppy up on her offer. Too tired and irritable to do anything else, I changed into pyjamas and collapsed into my ordinary bed.

Monday was busy, with three appointments and a lot of reading to do between them. The next two days were little easier, although Natasha finally delivered the photographs on the Wednesday evening, including the negatives, which had some extremely rude shots of her and Percy, which were unfortunately too small to make out much detail.

Thursday was Monty's day. I'd done some background reading, case histories of peeping Toms, and come across an interesting common thread. Again and again, the voyeurs asserted that at least a proportion of their victims had been passively or even actively willing. The attitude of the analysts was that this represented self-delusion to a greater or lesser extent. Given my own pleasure in exhibitionism, I was not so ready to reach what seemed to be a simplistic conclusion, but it was certainly interesting. Monty, by and large, was more self-aware and in any case preferred the women he peeped at to be unaware of his presence. However, he had claimed to have watched couples in cars with their knowledge, including penetrative sex. It seemed an avenue worth exploring, in an effort to find out just how honest he was with himself.

He arrived at his normal time, as casual and crude as ever, treating himself to a leisurely feel of my bum as I made coffee. I was already confident in my ability to send in a sensible and positive report, and fairly happy with my efforts to wean him from the more intrusive forms of sexual deviance, so let him grope for a while until his hand started to push in under the curve of my bottom.

'No, you don't, Monty,' I chided him, 'not until we have done our piece. Come and sit down.'

He did as he was told, not even sulking, and with us seated in comfort and cups of steaming coffee in our hands, I began.

'I want to talk about voyeurism again,' I told him, 'but specifically about incidents where you feel the people you are watching are aware of your presence and actively seek your attention.'

'You've been talking to Natasha, haven't you?'

It wasn't the answer I'd been expecting.

'No,' I said, 'or at least, not to discuss your voyeuristic behaviour. Why do you mention Natasha?'

'There was this time . . .' he began, and trailed off.

'Tell me,' I insisted.

'I took her to this place,' he said, 'for some fun, and made her suck a couple of guys off.'

'I see, but is that relevant? You weren't the voyeur.'

'Yeah, well, it wasn't the first time I'd been there. Some of the lads have got this thing going at work, right? We try and get girls down to this lay-by, and do it in our cars, or in the bushes sometimes, so the others can watch. I had a great time with Tasha, buggered her and made her piss in her panties . . .'

'Yes, she told me something of this, although not in detail. At other times you have been there as a voyeur?'

'Yeah, loads of times.'

'And the women know you watch?'

'Not usually, no. They're usually girlfriends, some wives. One or two know. They must, the way they show off. There's one woman who likes to suck cock. She does this little show, right, pretending to be a hitch-hiker and leaning in the window of her husband's car, so he can demand a blow-job for a lift. She does it squatting down, with the door open, so everyone can see.'

'Could that not that simply be for her own pleasure and her husband's?'

'He knows. He thinks it's a great laugh. He say she knows too, but he won't let anyone else have a go, bastard.'

'I suspect she doesn't know.'

'No way.'

'Perhaps. What I am trying to get at here, Monty, is the extent to which you are aware of the reactions of women you watch to your voyeurism, or the likely reaction were they to realise. The literature suggests that there is a tendency among voyeurs to delude themselves into thinking that the women enjoy their attentions.'

'Some do,' he answered, with a shrug. 'I mean, you like to show off, don't you? Tasha likes it too, even if she does get in a right state over it. Then there are loads of female flashing sites on the net, tits out at Mardi Gras, bum-flashing on the roadside, starkers in the middle of the road sometimes.'

'It does not occur to you that some of these women might be paid or coerced?'

'Bollocks. You can see they're having fun. What is this? You know as well as I do girls like to flash a bit of tit and arse. I reckon a good half the girls who do it in the backs of cars get off on being watched.'

'Half? That seems exaggerated. I also suspect it depends who is watching. Another couple is more likely to be welcome than a single man, let alone one who might be considered threatening.'

'OK, for couples, sixty, maybe seventy per cent are up for it. I should know, Gabby, I've been out enough.'

'I admit that there will be instances of deliberate exhibitionism, but I do think you are deluding yourself to an extent. I would be surprised if more than a small percentage of women in such circumstances enjoy being watched.'

'Half, easy. More. Come with me. I'll show you. Seriously, you should. What you shrinks don't realise, Gabby, is that once you've got some poor sod on the couch and you're giving them the third degree, they're going to say what you want to hear. I mean, only a nutter is going to admit he gets off on the girls he watches being scared, isn't he?'

'I do realise that situation can exist, Monty, and remember, that with you as the sole exception, my clients come to me of their own accord. I don't normally take cases where a report has to be made to an outside authority.'

'Yeah, I suppose so. It's true, though, in general, and you read too much too, and soak up all the theory. Now, if I was to take you out, I could show you that if we're together at least half the other couples we see'll want to swap a peep.'

'In this weather? We will be lucky to find another couple.'

'You'd be surprised. Sure, it won't be like in summer, but I know places.'

It was tempting, appealing to my sense of display and the gradual sense of frustration that had been building up during the week since playing with Natasha and

Poppy. At the least I would be able to go bare in his car, with the cold and darkness stretching away outside, while I was warm and naked . . .

'I will come,' I said. 'This weekend?'

'Saturday,' he answered me, 'always the best night, after the pubs turn out, and girls are pissed and feeling dirty. So what else do you want to talk about?'

'That was my main point, and we seem to have reached an impasse. I'm perfectly satisfied that you are not dangerous, merely irresponsible.'

'I can be responsible.'

'That is what I am hoping.'

'Cock time, then?' he asked happily. 'What do I get? A bit of T and A? A starfish show? Cunt?'

With a sigh I put my hands to the button of my trousers.

Monty collected me on the Saturday afternoon in his strange, box-shaped car. I had talked to Natasha and she had explained to me about the lay-by and wood near Reigate, which I immediately outlawed on the grounds that he could very well have set something up. He pouted a little but accepted my decision and drove out to the west instead of south. I had the maps, determined to deprive him of any chance to take us somewhere prepared in advance, and directed him out along the main corridor of roads leading towards Reading.

It took a bit of time to identify any suitable parking places and, as I'd suspected, it was really too cold. The first two proved completely empty and the third had only one car, which drove off the moment we appeared. We did glimpse the occupants, a fragile-looking blonde girl and her shaven-headed boyfriend, so I noted them down as a clear case of a couple not wanting to be watched. Monty argued that we had no proof they'd actually been having sex, or so much as a cuddle, so we ended up counting them as a half.

The third car park was more urban and busier, with five cars parked. Two appeared to be occupied, each parked well away from the others. Unfortunately, the windows were so heavily steamed up that it was impossible to see in, and must have been equally impossible to see out. Monty wanted to stick around and watch, suggesting that I'd be surprised by what went on. I declined. By then it was nine o'clock, and ice was starting to form on the puddles, making it seem very unlikely indeed that any men would be watching from the bushes, sane ones anyway. One thing was for certain, even the most determined voyeur was going to have serious trouble getting an erection, and flashers were going to be showing very little indeed.

We retired to a pub to eat and discuss what to do. Monty was insisting we were simply too early, and that it was worth going back to the best of the car parks after eleven o'clock. I was doubtful, but despite our lack of success there had been a certain thrill in the game and I agreed to his suggestion.

We'd had beer with our meal, and he bought me a Cognac afterwards while he prudently sipped tomato juice. A second followed, leaving me slightly tipsy and slightly aroused by the time we left at a quarter to eleven. We returned to the car park to find it as quiet as before, with the puddles now solid ice.

Monty backed the car into an area in deep shadow and turned the lights off. Opposite us was a low bank, illuminated dull orange by a single street light which penetrated the bare twigs of bushes growing on it and the trunks of a line of young cherry trees at the top. I could see that in summer it would have been ideal for men to hide as they watched the car park, but now anybody would there would be clearly visible.

I began to tease Monty, suggesting that all he really wanted was to have his cock sucked in the car and that I'd have happily done it in London. He threatened to put me across the bonnet and spank me, cold or no cold. I was going to answer him back, only to stop as he lifted a hand.

'There's one,' he said, nodding towards the bank.

Sure enough, a man was walking slowly along the top of the bank. He was short, hunched over in a black great-coat, sandy-haired, balding, maybe fifty, and certainly shifty-looking. He also had a dog.

'He is just walking his dog,' I answered.

'In those bushes? He's not. He's out for girls. The dog's a cover. Loads of men have dogs.'

'That doesn't make them voyeurs.'

'A voyeur's a guy who likes seeing girls in the raw, or being dirty. Find me one who doesn't.'

'Fair enough, but still . . .'

I stopped, because the man had ducked down as a new car swung into the car park. It stopped at the far end, well away from us. Nobody got out.

'If they want to be watched, they'll turn the interior light on,' Monty said. 'Look, watch him.'

The man had disappeared, over the crest of the bank but moving towards the car. For a moment nothing happened, before I glimpsed a new movement and caught the pale oval of his face among the bushes, just for a moment. It felt strange, sinister almost, but compelling to think of what was presumably a normal couple having sex and the man watching. Monty took my hand to comfort me, or so I thought until he pulled it closer and guided it on to his bare cock.

'Wank me,' he said.

I began to stroke at his already growing shaft. He twisted the control of his seat, letting it down so that I could get at his cock properly.

'Nice, like that,' he said, 'Maybe I should spank you over the bonnet, then fuck you from the rear. He'd love that.'

'Don't, no.'

'Only joking. Yeah, that's nice, just gently.'

I continued to pull at him, feeling his cock swell and stiffen in my hand. Across the car park, the man seemed to have lost interest and the car remained dark inside. I was beginning to lose interest and thinking of sucking Monty's cock when a second car pulled in, again selecting an empty area of the car park. This time, the interior light came on almost immediately.

'Here we go,' Monty said. 'Watch.'

He pulled himself up, squeezing my hand and his erection in under his gut. I kept tugging and focussed on the car. They were sideways on to us and I could see the occupants, a girl in the near window, brown-haired, freckled, probably still a teenager. He was beyond, and harder to see, but I could make out a loose grey top and his face. He was black, his hair cropped short, grinning as he said something to her. Her response was to pull up her top over naked, pert breasts, one with a tiny tattoo.

'Wow, nice,' Monty said. 'Go on, mate, make her strip.'

His cock was now rock solid in my hand, his eyes fixed on the girl's breasts. The boy was talking to her, apparently telling her what to do. She responded with a shy smile and began to stroke her nipples, bringing them to erection. It was very clear that he was deliberately making her show off and that she was enjoying it.

Still tugging at Monty's cock, I leaned forwards to peer at the bushes. Sure enough, the man was visible at the edge of the pool of light, cautious but moving closer. I wasn't sure if the couple had seen, but with the light on inside their car it was obvious they didn't mind.

The girl had cupped her breasts and was running her thumbs over her nipples, really showing off. The boy was staring at them, then glanced suddenly away out of the window. He turned back, grinning, and said something. The girl giggled, put on a pout and held her breasts out, showing them off even more blatantly, with her face set in an expression of exaggerated ecstasy.

'Teasers,' Monty whispered.

'What?'

'They're teasing him. Watch, and keeping wanking.'

I nodded, tugging at his erection. The girl was putting on quite a show, but it looked staged rather than for her pleasure, with a lot of writhing and lip-licking. In the bushes, the man was moving closer, presumably gaining confidence as the couple were obviously showing off. He moved fully into the light and I saw that he had his hand in his coat, with his arm moving to a familiar rhythm.

I saw the boy speak. Suddenly the girl pulled down her top, her expression changing to a sulky pout as fake as her ecstasy. The boy pushed open the door to stand, one fist raised.

'You looking at my girlfriend's tits?' he demanded.

'Yeah, you were, you filthy pervert!' she shouted from the car.

The voyeur fled, stumbling off through the bushes. The boy ducked down, laughing, to kiss his girlfriend as he pulled his door to. An instant later the engine caught, the interior light went out and they left with a screech of tyres.

'Teasers, like I said,' Monty remarked.

'Do people often do that?' I asked.

'Quite often. There are always some who like to wind the men up; get them randy, then have a go at them.'

'Well, that certainly alters the picture of the voyeur as aggressor.'

'Yeah.'

'Do you think he will be back?'

'I don't know. Let's find out if he's got guts.'

'What are you doing? Monty!'

He had turned our interior light on. Suddenly it was far harder to see what was going on outside. I felt a shiver of apprehension, thinking of the man out in the darkness.

'Get down on my cock,' Monty ordered. 'The sort of bloke who teases almost never gets it out.'

'Hold on, Monty . . .'

'Come on, give him a show, yeah? He deserves it, after that.'

'Perhaps, yet . . . Hey!'

He had taken me by the hair and was pulling me down on to his crotch, gently but firmly. I went, not at all sure if I wanted to be watched sucking his penis, even as it was pushed into my mouth. He held me down, easing his cock in and out of my mouth, and I waited, my stomach crawling a little, wondering if the man would come.

Monty's hand had gone to my bottom, squeezing me through the thick woollen skirt I'd chosen, then starting to inch it up. I managed a muffled protest around my mouthful of erection, but he carried on.

'We've got to give him something to see, yeah?' he said. 'He'd like to watch you suck, sure, but he doesn't want to see my cock, does he?'

I didn't try to answer, thinking of how I'd feel bare. He was right. If it was going to happen at all, I needed to be showing, intimately. Monty chuckled as I shifted my hips to let him take my skirt up more easily. It came up, over my thighs, over my bottom, until the rear of my tights was showing, stretched taut over my cheeks. Monty began to feel me, stroking my bottom through the tights.

'These are coming down – you know that, don't you?' he said.

I nodded, and shifted position, pulling one knee up on to the seat. It was awkward but my bottom was stuck right up, obviously deliberately on show. Monty chuckled again and moved round to take me by the hips. His fingers dug into the top of my tights and they were coming down, eased slowly off my bottom, my panties with them, to leave me showing, bare and open. My bottom was sticking out right at the window, and I could imagine the view from outside, a bare, pale moon framed in dark cloth, with the lips of my sex showing between. Anybody close would even be able to see my bottom-hole.

'He's there,' Monty said.

A shudder went right through me, really strong, at the thought of the man, watching me, bare, knowing I was sucking on Monty's penis.

'He's not sure,' Monty said. 'He's staying back. Wiggle your bum.'

I obeyed, thinking of the lewd, crude way Monty liked girls to be, dirty, sluttish, displaying bottoms and breasts for men's amusement. He'd got me just like them, panties down, showing off to him and to a dirty old man. His hand found my bottom, pulling at my cheeks to stretch my anus wide, then lower to hold open my pussy, deliberately exposing the pink, fleshy interior.

'He liked that,' Monty said. 'He can see me. I think he realises we're not teasing. Yeah, he's coming over.'

Another shock went through me, anticipation, and a little fear. Our doors were locked, but the man was going to be just inches away from me, from my bare sex, watching me in my arousal. I sucked harder, wanting the man to see me take Monty's sperm in my mouth, to watch as I surrendered myself.

'He's here,' Monty said.

The tap on the window still made me jump. I looked up as I heard the purr of the window motor, and there he was, his red, eager face peering in at the window. Not knowing what to do, much less say, I went back to sucking Monty's cock.

'Hi,' Monty said. 'Want to watch her suck, close up?'

'Yeah,' the man answered, his voice thick with lust. 'Pretty little bitch, ain't she? How far does she go?'

I'd thought Monty objectified me. This man was worse, far worse.

'All the way,' Monty said, 'but for now, you watch her wiggle her arse while she sucks me off.'

'It's cold!' I complained, pulling up.

It was, freezing air wafting in despite the heater.

'Watch from the back, yeah?' Monty offered, and before I could protest he had pushed the button to open the rear door locks.

'Ta, mate,' the man said.

I went back to sucking as the man climbed in. I was shaking hard and feeling very vulnerable indeed with my bare bottom raised for their attention. I wasn't sure if I wanted him to touch me or not, but I wasn't going to ask. His zip rasped down, and he made an odd little grunting noise as he started to pull at his cock, not even bothering to ask.

'She's got a nice tight arse, ain't she?' he grunted.

'The best,' Monty answered.

They went silent, both with their eyes fixed on my bare rear view. The man was right behind me, peering around the seat so that he could look between my buttocks, his eyes feasting on my bare sex and the tight dimple of my bottom-hole. Monty took hold of my head, feeding his cock to me with increasing urgency.

'Shaved,' the man grunted suddenly. 'I like 'em shaved. She's creamed her ring too, ain't she? I bet you love to fuck her arse.'

His words filled me with a new vulnerability and the worry of a finger in my bottom-hole. I pulled up, with some difficulty.

'No touching. Just look,' I said.

'Yeah, right,' he answered as my face was pushed back on to Monty's erection. 'I can talk though, eh? I bet she loves dirty talk, eh?'

Monty simply grunted. He was close to orgasm, jamming his cock in and out of my mouth, his great belly quivering with the effort, his breathing deep and fast. There was silence again, except for the wet sounds of my mouth being fucked and the slapping noise of the man's masturbation, until he spoke again, as suddenly as before.

'I would just love to see you fuck her up that tight little arsehole, mate,' he drawled, 'right up her dirt-hole, and give her a cream pie, all over her cunt and up her tube. Fuck me, I'd like to do her myself, right up her tube . . . spunk up her arse . . . I've got to, mate. Hold her, while I fuck her arsehole.'

I shook my head frantically at his words, trying to pull off. Monty just tightened his grip, jamming his cock deep into my throat to make me gag even as I writhed my bottom away, expecting the man to take hold of me, to jam a finger into my bottom-hole, or worse.

'Stop wriggling, I'm coming!' Monty gasped.

'Yeah, that's right, mate, spunk in her mouth!' the man called. 'Right down her fucking throat. Make her swallow it, the dirty bitch, make her swallow the fucking lot. Then you can hold her down while I fuck her arsehole for her, oh, yeah . . .'

He gasped, and at that instant his hand found my bottom, clutching one cheek, his fingers slipping down into my crease. I jerked frantically away, wrenching my head off Monty's cock.

'No!' I shouted. 'I said not to touch!'

The man didn't answer. He had gone back, his body arched against the seat, his eyes mouth wide, a stiff little cock gripped in his hand, and white come spurting and bubbling out of the tip. I waited, watching, until he had finished.

'Now just get out,' I ordered.

'Bitch,' he answered, but he went, still trying to stuff his cock back into his trousers as he climbed out of the door.

I blew my breath out. I was shaking all over and there was a sick feeling in my stomach. I was confused, too, uncertain of my own feelings and struggling to come to terms with what we'd done.

'What's the matter?' Monty asked.

'What's the matter?' I echoed. 'What do you think the matter is? He wanted me held down while he raped me anally!'

'Yeah, but he didn't do anything, did he?'

'No, but he wanted to . . . he would have done.'

'It's what I'd like to do, not against your will, but . . .'

'What, hold me down while some complete stranger has anal sex with me?'

'No.' He laughed. 'I'd rather he held you down while I had anal sex with you.'

'This is not funny, Monty.'

'Come on, Gabby, you've got to allow a guy his fantasies. It doesn't mean he'd actually do it. I mean, I fantasise over giving you one up the arse all the time, but I haven't forced you, have I?'

'No.'

'Then calm down and get your head back on my cock. I was nearly coming there.'

'Were you thinking about what he was saying?'

'Yeah, I was, as it goes. You should lighten up. It would have been good.'

'You would have done it? Held me while he sodomised me?'

'Not if you didn't want it. But yeah, I'd like to hold you and watch you get your arsehole fucked . . . Yeah, I would. Come on, get sucking.'

'No. Not with him out there.'

'All right. We'll go somewhere else, yeah? But I've got to have it, Gabby, I was that close.'

'If you really have to, but go.'

'Yeah, sure. Still, you've got to admit, Gabby, if you go around with your arsehole creamy all the time, you can only expect blokes to want to bugger you. I mean, talk about a fucking invitation!'

'It is not an invitation! You know why I cream my bottom-hole.'

He gave a snort of laugher. I'd already pulled up my panties and tights as we spoke and was smoothing down my skirt. I was still shaking a little but it was dying down, leaving me with my arousal and confusion. My pussy was soaking, but I was absolutely certain I had not wanted the man's penis up my bottom. That didn't stop me thinking about it, and how it would have felt to have my anus stretched around his intruding shaft, to hear him grunt and pant as he sodomised me, to feel his sperm splash over me as he came between my buttocks and over my sex, what he'd called a cream pie.

I sat silent, looking out of the window as Monty pulled out of the car park and turned on to a main road. What had happened had certainly opened my eyes, and made me realise that voyeuristic sex was not simple and certainly not just a case of dirty old men peeping at unwilling women. Monty was right, too; nobody without direct experience had the right to theorise. I now had that right, some right anyway, but for me the experience had been entirely too personal. Showing off was one thing, having a strange man with an erect cock say he wanted me held down so he could rape me anally was another. He'd treated me like a piece of meat as well, barely speaking to me, except to call me a bitch. Even his agonisingly intrusive comments on my body had been addressed to Monty.

What I needed was a drink and a cuddle, something to reassure me that people, and men in particular, could actually be caring. What I didn't want was to spend the night on my own. So I suggested to Monty that we return to my flat, with the unspoken admission that once there I would provide for him sexually.

It began to snow as we pulled on to the M4, big, heavy flakes falling from the windless air and swirling around the car. Monty slowed, concentrating on the road and the traffic, leaving me to huddle into myself, thinking about nakedness and the fine balance between erotic display and sexual vulnerability.

Conditions grew steadily worse, and I was relieved when we finally stopped, parking in an alley no more than a couple of hundred yards from my flat. It was gone midnight and the snow was thick on the pavement, the other cars and the high, blank wall beside us.

'How about here?' Monty asked as he turned the ignition off.

'Sex? Here?'

'Yeah. You've got me into doing it in the car now.'

'I think not . . .'

'Come on, Gabby, there's no one about, and I really fancy it. I just keep thinking of how you looked sucking on my cock with your tights and panties pulled down.'

He had leaned towards me as we spoke, and suddenly twisted the chair control, spilling me backwards. I squeaked in surprise, and the next moment he was leaning over me, kissing at my face, his fat hand groping for the hem of my skirt.

'In the flat, please,' I managed, pushing back at him.

'Come on,' he urged, his fingers fumbling between my legs to rub my sex through my tights.

'No,' I answered him. 'Please, Monty. It will be better indoors. I will put on a pinny if you wish, and serve you.'

'Sure,' he said, 'but at least I'm going to have your knickers down again, right now. You can walk home like that, bare under your skirt, bare and hot, 'cause I'm going to give you that spanking.'

'What spanking?' I squeaked.

'The one I was going to give you over the bonnet,' he said. 'Come on, Gabby, it's been weeks since that cute little arse got a good whacking.'

'No, please!' I gasped, but he was already grappling, me, pulling me by the arm to force me to roll face down. 'Monty, no, not a spanking.'

'Yes, a spanking,' he said firmly. 'You need it.'

'No, I do not!'

'Oh, yes, you do! Come on, over!'

'Ow!'

I was being turned and there was nothing I could do against his strength and weight. I tried anyway, kicking and squirming as I was forced slowly over on to my belly. My struggles only encouraged him, but when I finally managed to inject some anger into my voice he stopped. He held on though, with me pushed down and his hand gripping my skirt.

'Ah, come on, Gabby, don't be a spoilsport,' he whined.

'I am not!' I answered. 'It is just that I don't want to be spanked. Why do you always have to spank me?'

'You know why. Your bum's so cute and you wriggle so nicely. Look, I'll tell you what. Let me spank you and you can do your business in your nappy before bed and I'll change you. How's that?'

'I'm not really in the mood for that,' I told him. 'I feel a bit insecure, after that man.'

'Don't worry about it. Come on, cheer up.'

'It is not . . . Ow!'

He'd smacked me full across my bottom. The next instant his weight was on my back, crushing me into the seat and knocking the breath from my body. I gasped, struggling beneath him as he wrenched at my skirt, tugging it high to plant another slap on the seat of my tights.

'No!' I squealed. 'Monty!'

He just laughed, snatched at the rear of my tights and jerked them down, panties and all, halfway down my bottom. I felt the cold air on my skin and struggled harder still, writhing in his grip as he took a firm hold on my panties and pushed them low, taking my tights with them to lay bare my bottom.

'Got you!' He laughed happily.

'Please, no, not again ...' I managed, but he only laughed and set to work.

I gave in totally, too fragile, too submissive to really fight him. He really spanked me too, smacking away at my cheeks open-handed and laughing as he did it. All the while I was kicking my legs in frantic reaction and wriggling my bottom in a desperate, futile effort to escape the pain. It only made him worse, his laughter growing as he beat me, aiming the smacks to make my cheeks part and show off my bottom-hole, or up under them to bring the blood to my pussy. It got me too, my sex growing urgent even as the tears welled up in my eyes, until they finally broke, and I burst out sobbing, even as he stopped to slide one fat finger into my sex from the rear.

'You're sopping, you little liar!' he said. 'You love it, don't you?'

I shook my head in hopeless denial, knowing full well that he would never understand how much I could hate it despite the reaction it caused in me. He gave me another pat, then another, harder.

'No, please, enough,' I gasped.

'Can I fuck you, then?'

'Yes ... you know you can. In my flat.'

'No, here, like this, from behind, with your hot little arse in my lap.'

'No, in bed ...'

'No? More spankies, then.'

He began to spank again, laying in gently at first, then harder, until I'd started to squeal and kick, begging him to stop. He did.

'Well?' he demanded.

'OK,' I sighed. 'If you have to. I surrender.'

'Sensible girl. You do look good like that, Gabby. Nothing like a bare red bum for a girl, is there? Are you hot?'

I nodded miserably. It was true. My whole bottom was burning, and felt unnaturally big and swollen.

'Maybe I should cool you off,' he said and I heard the purr of the window going down.

'Hey, I'm bare!' I protested, only for my words to turn to a squeak of shock as a handful of snow was slapped on to my bottom.

'Here we are,' he said, 'just the thing for a spanked girl, eh?'

I answered with a sigh. The snow was freezing cold but immensely soothing, easing the hot pain of my spanking. He began to rub, letting it melt on my cheeks and run down between them, making me gasp again as a runnel of ice-water touched my bottom-hole. He took a second handful, then rolled the window up before slapping it on to my bottom. His fingers delved down between my cheeks, spreading them, and more snow fell down between, on to my bottom-hole and also my pussy.

'You rub it,' he said, 'and pay plenty of attention to the starfish, while I wank up.'

I nodded in meek acceptance, reaching back to stroke my bottom, rubbing the cold snow over my cheeks. It was melting fast and dribbling down into my tights and panties, under my tummy too. I didn't care, content to soothe myself and wait for Monty to take me.

He had his cock out, wanking as he watched me play with my bottom. I put my second hand back to spread my cheeks, making a show of my bottom-hole, the way he liked me to. He grunted in satisfaction and the slapping sound of him pulling at his cock grew faster. I lifted my bottom and turned a little, allowing one finger to touch my anus, tickling, until my ring began to twitch.

'Oh, you do not know what you do to me, you dirty little bitch,' he moaned. 'Such a cute arsehole, and you will not let me fuck it! Right, here I come.'

He moved to climb on top of me, his fat legs spreading over my thighs to push me down into the seat, my bottom bare to him, to his cock. I felt his knuckles as he adjusted himself, then the hot, fleshy shaft as he pressed it between my buttocks.

'Ah, nice ... your bum's all cold on my cock,' he sighed. 'Come on, stick it up, I'm going to fuck you.'

He took my hips, pulling at me to force my bottom up. As my cheeks spread I felt his cock go down between them, the head in my crease, sliding down, over my anus to my vagina, and in. He grunted as his cock filled me and began to push, humping himself on to my bottom, each time jamming me down into the seat. I could only take it, panting and breathless under his weight, with his balls slapping on my thighs.

'Nice,' he groaned. 'You are so juicy, so sloppy ... I'm going to rub in your slit for a bit.'

He pulled out, laying his slimy cock back between my buttocks to rub himself on my flesh. I kept my bottom stuck up, enjoying the feel of his erection.

'Come on, frig off,' he urged. 'I love it when you come with my cock in your cunt.'

He lifted and I slid my hand down under my tummy, resigning myself to masturbating as he used me. I knew he wouldn't stop until he came anyway, and I was wet and urgent, while the windows were caked with snow, making it impossible to see into our dark, cosy nest.

'Yeah, that's my girl, dirty slut,' he drawled as I began to rub at myself.

I was so turned on that there was wet on the seat under my pussy, and not just water from the snow, but moist and sticky juice against my fingers as I began to masturbate. Taking hold of my bottom, Monty spread my cheeks and went back to rubbing in my crease, only to suddenly dip down and slide himself up into my vagina.

'I need more cunt-cream,' he said. 'I want to slime it right up your crease.'

He was holding his cock, dipping it into my open hole to pull out juice and smear it on to my anus. His cock-head was rubbing against the most sensitive areas of my skin, firm and slimy with my own juice, making me want to rub harder, to come with his cock pressing to my flesh, or rubbing between my buttocks, or up my pussy, any way he wanted it.

I could feel it starting, a bubble of pleasure growing slowly in my head as I began to wriggle my bottom, to get more contact with his lovely cock. He went up me again, deep, only to pull out, to rub his load of juice up between my bottom-cheeks, on to my anus, and push . . .

'Monty!' I gasped.

It was too late. My bottom-hole had already begun to pulse with the onset of orgasm, and maybe I was just too loose, from the way the girls had treated me. Before I really knew it, the head of his cock was in my anus, stretching out my ring, piercing me, until with a sudden stab of pain it was in, the whole, fat penis-head inside my rectum, with my sphincter clamped tight on the neck.

'Sorry, Gabrielle,' he said, and pushed.

I gasped as his cock was forced up my bottom, a wordless cry of indignation and helplessness. I was slimy, too loose to stop him physically, and too high on my surrender to really fight. So up it went, jammed inch by inch into my straining rectum to the sound of my panting, gasps and grunts. I could only lie there, gaping, my fingers still deep between my sex-lips, my clitoris still twitching in anticipation of the orgasm he had broken by invading my anus.

He put it right up, until I could feel the coarse brush of his pubic hair between my spread buttocks and the weight of his balls lying between my thighs. His belly was pushed hard against me too, spread out over my bottom and lower back to envelop me in fat, soft flesh, all of it centred on the cock in my rectum.

I felt bloated, breathless, out of control, utterly overwhelmed. He felt huge inside me, filling not just my poor bottom but my whole body, right up to my head, as if I were no more than a doll, stuffed full of thick male penis. My mouth had come wide, and as he began to move inside me, it came wider still, agape in mindless reaction to my sodomy.

'That is good,' he sighed, 'so good. You do not know, Gabrielle, how many times I've imagined putting my cock up your arse, and now it is. I'm going to bugger you until I spunk right up your dirty little hole!'

His pushes had grown faster as he spoke, until I was gasping and panting beneath him, my head a whorl of emotions, all centred on my straining bottom-hole. It did hurt a bit, but I was greasy, open. Maybe the girls had stretched me, because there wasn't the agony I'd expected, only a dull throb and the extraordinary bloated feeling of having a penis in my bottom.

It was just as emotional too, my first time, and my tears were coming even as I started to push my bottom up to meet his thrusts. I was being sodomised, buggered, my anal virginity gone, and there was nothing I could do but take it and react. Without really knowing it my fingers had begun to work on my pussy again, in absolute, final surrender to what was being done to me. Monty felt the change and chuckled.

'That's it, frig, you dirty bitch,' he gasped, 'frig while I'm up your arsehole. Come while I'm in you, and I'll spunk in your dirt-box while you're still coming. Do it, you little bitch, now!'

I didn't need telling. I'd been close before, and I was coming almost immediately, his filthy words ringing in my head as I masturbated, harder, faster, while I panted out my emotions to the cock being jammed into me, ever deeper, ever more firmly, bloated out my rectum like a full load, filling me with desperation, helplessness, surrender . . .

'I'm coming!' I gasped as I felt my contractions kick in.

My anus locked on his cock as it hit me. My mouth came open in a scream of uncontrollable ecstasy and I was coming, bucking and writhing beneath his weight, pushing my bottom up and squirming it into his crotch, indifferent to the sudden growing pain as he hammered himself into me, deep and hard, grunted and came himself, filling my rectum with sperm even as I cried out in the rapture of my second peak.

He kept on pumping, emptying himself up my bottom, even as I went slowly limp beneath him. Exhaustion swept over me, mental and physical. I felt him pull out, his cock leaving my bottom-hole to close slowly, sore and dribbling sperm, a cream pie, just as the voyeur had threatened to give me.

Monty rolled off me and began to clean up, using tissues from my bag. I lay still, feeling very, very emotional. I had every right to. I'd been sodomised, sat on and buggered, a big, fat cock forced up my bottom. The evidence was still oozing out of my poor, aching hole and down over my sex. I could find nothing to say and no energy to rise, my head spinning in confusion, tears rolling slowly down my cheeks.

'How d'you feel?' Monty finally asked.

My answer was a sob.

'Lighten up,' he said. 'You got your kicks, yeah? No bollocks, Gabby, I felt your arsehole clench.'

'I'm sore,' I answered him.

He laughed. I heard the purr of the window motor and turned, wondering what the hell he thought he was doing, with me still lying there with my bottom bare. What I saw was him scooping up a big handful of fresh snow, which an instant later had been slapped on to my bare behind and rubbed well in between my cheeks. I managed a gasp of protest as the shock of the cold hit me but, as always, he took no notice.

'Must you?' I managed as he began to rub it directly against my aching bottom-hole.

'Relax, it'll cool you down,' he said. 'Hey, no need to look so sulky, yeah? Every girl gets one up the arse in the end. It's nothing to get in a state over. It's just a laugh. Hey, you'll love this.'

Another handful of snow was slapped on to my bottom, a big one. A third followed, piled up on the rest.

'Stay still,' he ordered as I turned to remonstrate.

He'd grabbed my panties, and pulled them up, over the snow. He laughed at my indignant gasp, and squashed out the bulge against my flesh. Taking my tights, he pulled them up too, and gave me another slap before tugging my skirt down.

'Do you look like you've filled your panties or what?' He laughed. 'Come on, you can walk back like that. What an evening, eh? What a laugh!'

Eight

Monty had to go. He had sodomised me, more or less forcibly, and come up my bottom. That was bad enough, but totally unacceptable was the way he had thought it was so, so funny. It was simply too much. The sex I could take; the lack of comfort and the cruelty, I couldn't. I needed somebody caring who would look after me, and if they really felt I needed punishment, or to be sodomised for that matter, at least to cuddle me afterwards. He needed somebody tougher than me, somebody for whom becoming sexually aroused was not so closely linked to a need to surrender herself to her partner. He had also broken our original agreement – or, more exactly, it had broken down. True, it was my own decision not to continue to demand that he be my nurse, but he had carried on indulging his own fantasies, using me as a sex object.

Unfortunately I felt a moral obligation towards him, and was fairly certain that rejection by me would make him return to peeping and panty stealing, which I did not want. So I ended up shelving the problem and allowing him to stay on the Saturday night. He was oblivious to the emotional effect he had had on me by sodomising me, or by making me walk through the streets with my panties bulging with snow. Nobody saw us, but that was not the point. I had been made to walk through the streets looking as if I had soiled my panties.

He should have taken over, perhaps fed me from a bottle, put me to bed in my nappy, stroked my hair until I fell asleep, something kind and gentle. What he did was make himself the most enormous pile of sandwiches while I got the snow out of my clothes and cleaned up. He then sat there, eating them, watching cartoons on TV and making the occasional obscure and supposedly witty remark about the characters. In the end I went to bed to lie in the darkness, sucking my thumb and feeling used, until I went to sleep, still with the TV on in the background.

It was the same in the morning, with him bumbling around the flat looking for food, then coming into the bathroom to watch me shower while he ate cereal from a mixing bowl. Before long he'd got his cock out and I was made to suck him off, down on my knees in the shower with the water cascading over my back and bottom. He kept on eating as I sucked, only putting the bowl down when he was close to orgasm so that he could take his cock and spunk in my face and hair. Having come, he simply wandered away.

I knew full well that if he stayed I would be spending my Sunday as his sex slave, or more accurately as his slave full stop. What I needed to do was think and relax, so I bundled him out late in the morning, letting him take a final leisurely grope of my bottom and breasts by the door before he went. I was still in my robe and feeling sensitive and rather fragile. An afternoon in nappies seemed a good idea, as I badly needed the relaxation it would bring and knew that I was going to have to masturbate before long.

A second cup of coffee was a still more urgent priority, and I went to make it, all the while thinking about Monty and the fact that I was no longer anally virgin. Rationally, I knew the concept was meaningless, that the fact that I had had a cock put up my bottom made no difference to who I was, or anything else.

Emotionally, it was impossible to be detached, with the memory of how it felt to have a man's penis working in and out of my anal passage burning in my head. It was also impossible to deny that it had felt good, and that the real problem was not that I'd been sodomised, but that I hadn't been cuddled afterwards.

By the time I'd got to the couch with my coffee, it was getting very hard to hold myself back. I wanted to touch my bottom-hole, to feel where Monty had put his cock, and to soothe my poor aching ring. Giving in to my feelings, I fetched cream and arranged myself on the couch once more, my panties off, my legs wide and my robe open. Squeezing some cream on to one hand, I went back to drinking coffee as I began to explore.

My bottom-hole felt sore and a little loose, slightly open and exceptionally sensitive. I stroked myself for a moment before dabbing the cream on and starting to rub, in little circular motions, soothing myself, my eyes closed. Before long my finger was in the hole, just the top joint, probing gently, to open myself as I concentrated on how it felt to offer my bottom for penetration. Monty had pushed his cock up without giving me much choice, but so many times he had made me bend to show off my bottom-hole, always imagining how his cock would feel where my finger now was, in the hot, tight hole of my anus. Finally it had become too much for him, and he'd sodomised me.

I put the cup down and pulled up my legs, spreading myself wide to the cool air. My finger probed deeper, well into the cavity of my rectum, to feel the hot, slimy interior where Monty's cock had been, which he'd filled with sperm. I pushed in a second finger, holding myself open, now in full, blatant anal masturbation, fingering myself with my creamy little hole held wide to the air. I thought of how Nurse Trainer had opened my bottom-hole, three big fingers holding me wide as I licked her sex. I thought of Poppy and Natasha, and how they'd forced the icing nozzle into me and filled my rectum with cake-mix, then made me push it out into my panties.

Poppy had been right when she'd said they'd been cruel to be kind. It was what I needed, sometimes, to let me surrender completely, to be taken charge of, to be punished even. Only that way could I reach the deepest pleasures, the most beautiful experiences, total abandonment.

My fingers were deep in, as far up my bottom as I could push them, until I felt something hard, deep inside me. Easing back a little, I began to push my fingers in and out. My anus was straining and sore, but I was too far gone to care. I felt so wonderfully open, with my newly buggered bottom-hole spread to the air, and my sex too, wide, without the slightest concealment, totally exposed. My thumb went to my clitoris, rubbing; I clutched tight, holding myself by my pussy and bottom-hole, delighting in the sexual response of my body, my nudity, my penetration, the knowledge that I could fuck, that I could be buggered . . .

I came, gasping out my orgasm, my thighs high and wide, my fingers deep, deep up my bottom, wriggling in the hot slimy interior of my rectum, my thumb flicking over and over on to my clitoris, riding my climax, on and on. At the very peak I imagined being caught in the position I was holding by a man, taken by my ankles, buggered and spunked up as I masturbated, to let me come on his cock, or with sperm spurting and dribbling from my anus.

It took a long time for my orgasm to subside, and it left me feeling a great deal happier. I always do my best to persuade my clients of the benefits of masturbation, and it is something I firmly believe in, wonderfully self-indulgent, pleasurable, soothing and completely harmless; an ideal therapy.

I showered and dressed, then began to tidy up the mess Monty had made of my flat. Tidiness comes naturally to me, and I hate things out of place, while Monty seemed to regard the world as his personal dustbin. Certainly he'd treated my flat as one, which was particularly galling when I considered the fanatical precision with which he had categorised and labelled his collection of stolen panties, as well as such things as his CD collection.

Thinking of his panty collection reminded me that I still had them, and that they could probably now be safely returned, along with his magazines and videos. That meant a trip to his house, with the inevitable consequences, something which raised seriously mixed emotions.

I had just about restored the flat to order when the buzzer went. Expecting somebody in an emotional crisis, as likely as not Jo Warren, I went to answer it with considerable irritation. Sure enough, as soon as I heard the misery in the voice at the other end I knew my guess was right, only it wasn't Jo, or any of my clients. It was Poppy.

She came up at a run, but stopped on the landing to look at me, her face tear-streaked and miserable, her lower lip trembling uncontrollably. In either hand she held a large, old-fashioned suitcase. I put my arms out for her and she came into them, instantly bursting into tears on my shoulder. All I could do was hold her and stroke her hair and back, until finally she brought her sobbing under control and stepped back to dab at her eyes.

'What's the matter?' I asked, although with the two suitcases I had already guessed.

'I've left Anna.' She sniffed. 'Can I . . . can I come in?'

'Yes, of course. Let me help you.'

I ushered her in, following with the suitcases. Obviously she was hoping to stay with me, and there was a little voice in the back of my head shouting with elation, despite my outward feelings of sympathy and surprise. She let me take her coat, and followed me into the clinic. She didn't sit, but she stood by my couch, looking utterly forlorn.

'Do you want to talk?' I asked.

She nodded.

'Coffee?' I offered. 'Tea?'

'Anna beat me,' she said, 'for last weekend. Really hard.'

'But, you knew she would, yes?' I answered cautiously.

'Not like this,' she said, and turned her back.

She was in a dress, cotton with a print of big, red flowers, knee-length and belted at the waist, fifties style. Underneath her legs were bare and so was her bottom, a sight which would normally have had me thinking sex as she rucked up the dress to the level of her waist; not now.

When she had said she'd been beaten hard she had not been exaggerating. The entire surface of her bottom and the backs of her legs were a mass of bruises, dark, angry cane-welts, purple and black between raised lines of rough, red skin. Just looking at it made me wince, and it was only too easy to imagine her pain and distress, and sympathise.

'I don't know how many strokes,' she said, her voice catching. 'More than a hundred though, with a heavy cane. She made me wait all week, and she was really cold. Then, this morning, she told me it was time, and that I'd have to be tied to take my punishment properly. I let her. I was looking forward to it. She made me kneel on a chair, and she tied my ankles to the legs and my hands to the back, low down, so I was bent right over, and couldn't protect myself at all. She pulled up my dress and took down my pants, and left me there, for ages, until I was shaking and really uncomfortable. When she came in with the heavy cane I was scared, but

I still wanted it. I thought I'd get twelve, maybe twenty-four. She told me I was getting thirty, and that I'd be made to count. I can, normally, but she did it really hard, and fast too, so that I lost control, and lost count too. She started again, as hard as before, and not on my bum, on my legs. After twenty I lost count again, and she just started again, and she wouldn't stop, not even when I started crying, which I never, ever do, and . . .'

She burst into tears again, and I came forwards to cuddle her. For a while she clung on to me, sobbing, then began to speak again.

'She only stopped when I started to scream and, afterwards, she wouldn't comfort me, but told me to stand in the corner. I needed a hug so badly, but she wouldn't, she just wouldn't!'

'I understand,' I said.

'I just wanted a hug! The bitch!'

'You can cuddle me, Poppy, for as long as you like.'

'I left,' she said, and once more started to cry.

I held on to her, stroking her head and whispering to her, letting her cry until she stopped of her own accord. I could feel for her, absolutely, having been through the same experience, if not so extreme. I was also angry because Anna had abused her trust and hurt her, but it was impossible not to feel pleased as well. She had come to me. She could have chosen Natasha, or who knew how many other friends, but she had come to me.

It took two days for Poppy to start to recover emotionally, which I actually thought showed a lot of strength after the collapse of an eight-year relationship, never mind the caning. I let her stay in my special bedroom, and spent a lot of time cuddling her and generally looking after her. She wanted me to cream her bruises, which I did, and managed to keep my hands away from her pussy, although it drove me to distraction. I forced myself, though, even when she began to show signs of pleasure, determined not to take advantage of her while she was feeling fragile and to allow her to make the first move.

I knew it would come and it did, sooner than I expected. On the Tuesday night I put her to bed, with her bottom and legs creamed and wearing nothing but a short nightie. My hands were shaking as I went back to my ordinary bedroom, and I knew that I'd be masturbating myself to sleep over her for the third night running. I did, only to be wakened in the early hours of the morning by a gentle kiss.

Nothing was said. She simply slipped in under my covers and we began to kiss, just holding each other at first, then with greater passion as our hands began to stroke at necks and hair, backs, breasts and bottoms and, finally, each other's sex. We came together, kissing as our fingers worked in our pussies, an experience as loving and intimate as any I had ever had. We slept in each other's arms.

In the morning, she was back to her old self, more or less, full of life with only the occasional moment of moody introspection. She'd been nude when she came into my bed, and she stayed nude, completely at ease with me, only dressing when it was time for the first of my clients to arrive. She stayed quietly in the bedroom while I worked, as before, and afterwards made lunch for me and insisted on doing my shopping in the afternoon.

By then there was no question that she was going to be staying with me. What little she had brought with her was unpacked, and I was adjusting my lifestyle to her presence without the slightest regret or ill feeling. That evening we went to bed together in my special bedroom, by mutual agreement, and both naked. As before, sex was loving and intimate, if a touch less spontaneous, as we came head to tail, licking each other's pussy. We snuggled down together afterwards, with me in her lap. I was on the edge of sleep when she whispered into my ear.

'I'm going to pee, Gabrielle.'

Even as she spoke I felt it, the warm gush of fluid, spurting out between the cheeks of my bottom and running down my skin into the bed. She sighed as she did it, nuzzling and kissing at my neck as her pee came out, over me and into our bed. Soon I was in a warm pool, my bottom wet and my hip pressed into soggy, sticky sheets.

'Now you,' she said as her gush died to a trickle. 'Do it all over me.'

I rolled over to take her into my arms, even as my legs came up, opening my sex to her. It took a moment of concentration, but it came, my pee squirting out to patter against her skin and the sheets, spraying out over us. I could feel her trembling as I urinated on her, and her kisses were growing rapidly more passionate. When I'd finished we came together, thighs locked, to rub our pussies, squirming and wriggling, delighted in the puddle we'd made, until we came, Poppy first, then me, rubbing on each other's legs with our bottoms and bellies and legs wet with our pee.

Inevitably we had to change the bed and clean ourselves up, which was done with a lot of giggling and bottom-slapping. I threatened to put her in a nappy, and would have done, had I not been so tired by then. As it was, I decided to be sensible and we ended up going to sleep, still naked, in the other bed.

Thursday was Monty's day, his fourth and final session. There was really very little to say, even when it came to his attitude to my feelings. After all, I could hardly deny enjoying anal sex, when I'd come with him inside me, and as I was with Poppy, I was no longer particularly concerned with his lack of post-coital emotion. He had, in any case, promised to give up the panty stealing, although more due to what he now saw as an unacceptable risk of being caught than for any moral reason.

As usual I ended up on my knees, sucking his cock with my skirt pulled up at the back and my panties well down to show off my bottom. I half expected him to tip me over my couch and bugger me, but he contented himself with coming in my face and leaving my glasses coated with sperm, a sight which left him grinning with delight, as always. Fortunately Poppy was out shopping at the time, but she came back while Monty was still there, and exchanged a few polite words before he left.

'So that was the infamous Monty?' she said as the outside door banged below us.

'Yes,' I sighed.

'Did he . . .' she asked, glancing at my face.

'Yes,' I admitted, not wanting to lie to her.

'I thought so,' she said. 'You've still got come in your hair.'

I went for the tissues, thoroughly embarrassed. She merely giggled.

'Natasha said he likes to do it in girls' faces,' she said as I frantically cleaned up the little bits of sperm which had escaped my initial attention.

'Lots of men do,' I said.

'It's a power thing, I suppose,' she said. 'Like marking women as their own by putting their sperm over our faces, showing off their virility.'

'Possibly,' I answered, 'with Monty I think it is more that he likes to deny a woman's right to sexual concealment. He loves to make women display themselves in blatantly sexual situations.'

'I suppose he'd like to have us all walking around topless.'

'Probably, but I think he prefers it if the woman's embarrassed as well. He finds women being exposed funny as well as arousing. That is one of the things I find hard to take about him.'

'Tasha said much the same. Still, I think it was unfair of her to palm him off on you like that.'

'Palm him off? She introduced me to him in the hope that he would make a suitable nurse for me. He did not.'

'No, she didn't. That's not what she told me anyway. She said she couldn't handle him, and so she set you up with him instead.'

'She did?'

'That's what she told me. Her boyfriend was about to come back from France apparently, and it was going to be awkward if he was around. So she introduced you. I thought you knew?'

'No. I did not. I had guessed, yes. I asked her. She lied . . .'

I trailed off. Poppy was telling the truth; there was no possible doubt. I had wondered about Natasha's motives, and whether her denial had been truthful, but now I was certain, and equally certain that she would find the situation hilarious, especially when she discovered that I had surrendered my anal virginity to Monty. I am not normally vindictive, but the situation cried out for revenge.

'So are you going to drop him now?' she asked. 'Now that we're together, I mean.'

It was her first real acknowledgement that we were lovers, and it pushed everything else out of my head. I smiled and nodded, then went to kiss her. She responded, and in minutes we were in a tangle of discarded clothing on the floor, kissing and licking at each other's body, until we had both reached orgasm. Afterwards we lay together for a long time, until the approach of another appointment for me forced us to break apart.

I spent an hour listening to my client's difficulties with her boyfriend, who was apparently obsessed with the small size of his penis and constantly required reassurance, often during the middle of sex, also having his cock measured. Ignoring the temptation to suggest gagging him during sex, I dug out some statistics to show that he was actually more or less average in size, and suggested she praise his cock during foreplay in an effort to forestall interruptions later. She left happy, or at least interested, studying the sheet I'd given her on cock size with fascination.

That was it for the day, so I came in to Poppy in the special bedroom. She was lying face down on the bed, naked, with her bruised bottom and legs glossy with cream. The colours had started to change, dull yellows and blues replacing the black and angry red she'd first shown me, but she was still a mess from immediately below the base of her spine to the backs of her knees, and when I came to touch her, it was very gentle. What she said surprised me.

'I do need to be beaten, Gabrielle. You will beat me, won't you?'

'Not like this,' I answered.

'But you'll spank me?'

'Yes, and you are to spank me too, when I need it, but never hard.'

She answered with a sigh, and nodded. I began to stroke her bottom, smoothing in the cream.

'Would you like some more?' I asked.

For a moment she said nothing, just purring gently as I stroked her bottom.

'Four days you've been looking after me,' she said, moving suddenly on to her side. 'It's about my turn. Come on, Miss Gabby, off with your clothes.'

I nodded, my excitement starting to rise immediately. She got up, and walked to the drawers in which she'd put her things. I began to undress, as I'd been told to, and I watched her as I stripped. I knew she had a nurse's uniform, a genuine one from the fifties, very neat and prim. I'd never seen her in it, but as she pulled out a carefully folded bundle of white cloth I knew I was going to. Stockings followed, and a girdle, a solidly built bra and a pair of large white panties.

She began to dress, the girdle first, fastening it behind her back to give her waist a smooth, elegant curve, enhancing her bust and the flair of her hips. Her stockings followed, each carefully pulled on, to fit her tiny feet snugly and keep the seam precisely at the back. Each reached only a little more than halfway up a thigh, and once they'd been clipped off her suspender straps were left straining, with her stocking tops running in long arches between the buttons. Only then did she put her panties on, easing them up over her suspender straps and tucking them into place beneath her girdle.

By then I was nude. I took my clothes to the wash basket, and came back to find her buttoning up her dress, with her feet already in her sensible, square-toed shoes. She looked perfect, and I could feel myself melting as I sat down on the bed to suck my thumb and wait until she had finished. Her final touch was to pull up her hair, into a tight bun, adding just a little severity.

'Done,' she said, 'and I'm glad to see you're ready. Now, until I say otherwise, Miss Gabby, you are under nurse's orders.'

'Yes, nurse.'

'Good. Now, first of all, we had better get you in a nappy.'

I nodded, and swung my legs on to the bed as she approached. She took a nappy from the drawer as I moved on to my back, opening it and smoothing out the tabs. My legs came up, and I found that I was already trembling as I got into that beautiful, exposed position, my legs rolled high, to let everything show, not for sexual display, but simply because it doesn't matter what I show when I'm a grown-up baby girl.

Poppy took hold of my legs, gripping me around my knees, and lifted so that she could slide the nappy in under my bottom. As she released me and my cheeks settled into the soft material, my sense of reliance really took over. I relaxed absolutely as she parted my thighs to pull the nappy up between them and encase my sex in the material. It was smoothed out on my tummy, the tabs fastened to either side, and I was ready, as I should be, stark naked but for my nappy and completely under her control.

'There we are,' she said. 'Now, time for your milk. A bottle, or are you still on the breast?'

'Breast, please, nurse,' I answered.

She gave a little sigh, but sat down. Her fingers went to the top of her uniform, unbuttoning one, then two and three buttons, leaving it open to her belt. Pulling it wide, she exposed half of her bra, which she pulled up, spilling out one plump breast, the nipple already stiff. I swallowed as she patted her lap, my eyes fixed on her long, swollen nipple and the wide, puffy areola. My mouth was already open as I crawled quickly across her knees, and into her arms. She held me, as Nurse Trainer had done, around my back as she lifted her breast to offer the nipple to my mouth. I took it, my lips wide, to suck it all in, to taste her skin and feel the firm, engorged flesh. She pulled me to her and, as my eyes closed in pure bliss, I began to suckle. Poppy gave a contented purr and ever so gently began to stroke my back.

For what seemed an age I just suckled, feeding at her teat, my eyes closed, everything focused on the nipple in my mouth and her gentle, soothing caresses. I'd been worried she might not be big enough to feed me, but she was, her breasts plump and heavy, the way a woman's should be, her nipple enough to let me really feel that I was suckling.

I was completely surrendered to her, and did nothing when she moved her hand from her breast to my legs, save to cling on to her more tightly. She began to caress my thighs, between them, right under the bulge of my nappy, gently stroking, until the instinctive need to spread my legs began to grow. I gave in, with no reason at all to resist, opening myself to her, my legs wide in my need. Her response was a little tutting sound, as if accepting an inevitable but slightly tiresome truth. Immediately her fingers went higher to push in under the edge of my nappy and find the smooth, bare expanse of my skin.

As she began to masturbate me I cuddled tighter still, holding her, my mouth wide on her nipple, suckling on her with my legs spread wide, completely abandoned to my needs. She slipped a finger into my vagina to open me and spill my juice out and down over my anus. A second followed as her thumb found my clitoris, moving on the tight bud to send a strong shiver of pleasure up my spine.

She was still stroking my back, soothing me as she masturbated me, with my pleasure growing as I slipped deeper into surrender, utterly and completely hers, to do with as she pleased, in the full knowledge that she would look after me, feed me, hold me, change my nappy, smack my bottom and, best of all, take control of my sexual needs.

I came so easily, just slipping over the edge into orgasm, my pussy tightening on her fingers as she masturbated me with such casual skill. She held me as the contractions went through me, still stroking me, and whispering to me until at last I went limp in her arms, my thighs closing slowly around her hand.

'There we are,' she said, 'that's better, isn't it?'

I snuggled into her chest, still sucking, yet more relaxed as my orgasm faded. She let me feed, not hurrying me at all, but holding me to her until at last I disengaged to leave her nipple wet and glistening, the teat sucked out, really straining. For a moment she held me to her chest before gently easing me up and off her lap. She put her breast back in her bra and covered up casually, although I caught the trembling of her hand as she fastened her buttons.

'Bed now, Miss Gabby,' she said, 'while I go and have my supper. And not a squeak out of you, or it'll be spankies time.'

She wanted to do it, I knew she did. I also knew she'd be gentle, that she'd punish me, but not hurt me. Not that I could have denied it to her anyway, not after the beautiful orgasm she had given me, but for the first time, as she tucked me into bed, I found myself actually looking forward to a spanking.

Not that there was any reason to hurry. It would happen when it did, when it was necessary. Until that time came, there was nothing in the world I needed to worry about. I brought my legs up to my chest and stuck my thumb in my mouth, allowing myself to drift into the sleepy, half-aware state that I can only achieve when I'm in my nappy.

It was early, with the last of the grey, winter light still fading from the sky beyond my curtains. Outside it was cold, the streets full of slush and people hurrying away from work, full of cares. I had none. I was warm, comfortable, absolutely at ease, with Poppy between me and everything outside – perfection.

I didn't mean to sleep, but I did, waking to darkness. There was a feeling of pressure in my bladder, and I simply let go. My pee burst free to soak into my nappy, swelling it out over my pussy and bottom. I was on my side, one leg raised, so that I could feel the weight grow as I peed, sighing in relief as I did it, until my bladder was empty and my nappy was full, bulging out around my bottom.

With my nappy nice and wet I lay still, sucking my thumb as a delicious sense of arousal began to build in me. I had no idea what time it was, but there was light coming under the door and I could hear Poppy outside, walking across the floor of my clinic, then the chink of china as she put down a cup. Soon enough, I knew, she would come in to find that I'd wet my nappy. She would change me, powder me and cream my pussy and bottom-hole. Possibly I'd be spanked; it was her choice completely. Yet it seemed unlikely, simply for doing what came naturally.

I could do more too, or I would be able to do soon, and knew she wouldn't mind. She'd asked me the first time we'd met, and held me while I did it, and while I made her come. It had been important to her, something she'd needed to balance her own feelings about being made to do it herself, and the way she was punished when she had, made to stand in the corner, with her nappy seat heavy behind her, bulging out to show what she'd done . . .

Just the thought put a shiver right through me. I was already wet, and soon I'd be dirty. She'd come in and she'd deal with me, in whatever way she felt appropriate, changing me, or making me do it myself while she watched in disapproval. Maybe she'd want me to make her come while I was still in a mess. She had the right to. I was hers.

I lay there, imagining it and letting the pressure in my rectum slowly build. It was important not to hurry, to let it come naturally, not to force it, but to do it because I had to. It was going to happen too, before long, pushing out, filling the pouch of my nappy, until I was thoroughly soiled.

The temptation to slip a finger up my bottom-hole was close to overwhelming. It would have felt so good, to push it deep in until I was open and slimy, and masturbate as I filled my nappy. Without Poppy I would have done it, but I held off, feeling the strain build, until my anus had begun to pout. At the feeling my mouth came open in a little sob. I closed my eyes, wondering if I could hold any longer, and decided I couldn't, just as the door catch clicked. I opened my eyes to find Poppy standing in the doorway, silhouetted against the light. Her hands went to her hips.

'Not asleep yet, Miss Gabby?' she demanded.

'No,' I answered. 'I'm wet.'

She answered with a sigh and came into the room, turning the light on. A single tug pulled down my covers, exposing me. She shook her head.

'Wetting your nappy I can forgive,' she said, 'because I know you can't help it, but you should have called me. You made a wet patch on your sheets, and now I'll have to change the bed!'

'Sorry, nurse,' I managed.

'You may well be, young lady,' she snapped. 'Off the bed and on to your mat.'

I climbed off, glancing at the tiny wet patch I'd made on the sheet, an arc no more than a few inches long where my nappy had leaked slightly. She spread out one of my plastic sheets on the floor and I sat down to suck my thumb as she changed the sheets, tutting all the while. Only when the bed was made did she turn her attention to me.

'Right, miss, on your back,' she ordered.

I got down immediately, opening my legs to make it easy for her. She took the powder and cream down from the shelf, along with a new nappy, and came to kneel beside me.

'You should have called out for me,' she repeated, pulling a nappy tab open.

I didn't answer, lying inert as she opened my wet nappy and pulled it out from under my bottom. I felt air, cold on my wet skin, and suddenly the urge to pee welled up inside me again. An instant later, a little yellow fountain burst from my pussy to splash on the mat beneath me and run down between my bottom cheeks.

'Miss Gabrielle!' she exclaimed.

Her mouth had come open in annoyance but I just kept on peeing, letting it trickle down over my skin to form a little pool underneath me. My bottom-hole wanted to open too, letting everything out into a big, sticky mess between my thighs, but I held it back, contenting myself with peeing in front of her. She watched, kneeling up with her hands on her hips, until I had finished.

'So, we want to be messy, do we?' she snapped. 'Well, young lady, you may like to know that I wasn't going to spank you, but now I am. How do you like that?'

'No, please, sorry, nurse,' I managed.

'Too late for apologies,' she answered me. 'Right, let's clean you up, then over my knee you go.'

I gave a weak nod, my stomach already fluttering at the thought. She was going to spank my bottom, and she was right to as well. She was always right, whatever she decided. That didn't stop me shivering as she pushed a towel under my bottom to soak up the worst of the pee and went for a bucket. I'd half expected her to make me clean it up, even push my face in it to remind me not to be a dirty girl. She didn't, contenting herself with making me sniff the wet towel before dropping it in the bucket.

After spreading out a new plastic sheet, she had me crawl on to it and roll up. My bottom was wiped and powdered amply, with my legs held apart as my sex was done, then high to make sure my whole bottom received an even coating. With my legs held up I was given a few pats. I thought the spanking was going to start, only for her to stop.

'There we are, nice and dry,' she said, 'which is just as well, as it has to be smacked. Now, a little cream to stop you getting sore. Stay like that. Hold your legs.'

I took hold of my legs under the knees, keeping myself exposed, spread wide and high, as she twisted off the lid of the cream pot and stuck her finger in. It came up thick with cream, far more than she needed, and I sighed as it was pressed to my sex.

'Now, now, let's not get dirty,' she chided, rubbing the cream over my sex and the smooth, shaved skin of my pussy mound. 'I know you like your little dirty games, but that is not the time.'

'Yes, nurse,' I answered, shaking my head in a desperate effort to rid myself of the overwhelming feeling of arousal inside me.

She was stroking my sex, rubbing cream on to me, between my lips, bringing me up towards an orgasm which was going to be inevitable unless she stopped. She did, an instant before it happened, and transferred her attention to my bottom-hole, dabbing on a little cream and slipping the top joint of her finger inside. I clenched to stop myself just doing it in her hand, which I was sure would have earned me the cane, justly. She seemed not to notice and sat back to rub the excess cream into her hands.

'Right, up,' she ordered, rising. 'The sooner we get started, the sooner it will all be over. Come on.'

I obeyed, rising as she did, shaking hard, to stand with my hands crossed over my newly creamed pubic mound as she made herself comfortable on the bed, her knees stuck out to let me get into the proper position. Looking up at me, she patted her lap.

'Come on, I said, let's have that little bottom up.'

Again she patted her lap. I went down slowly, laying myself across her knees, my toes on the ground, my bottom lifted for her convenience. She took me by the wrist, pulling my arm up into the small of my back, gently, but firmly enough to leave me trapped and ready for spanking.

I shut my eyes as her hand settled on my powdery bottom, wondering if she really would be gentle, or if she felt I should genuinely be punished. Her hand lifted; her fingers came down on my bottom, a pat, another, and I knew.

She was so good, gentle and patient, patting my bottom, lightly at first, little more than a caress, until I had begun to sigh with sheer pleasure. My legs came wide, showing off my pussy and bottom-hole in abject surrender to her. Only then did she start to smack harder, fractionally, making my skin sting a little with each slap. I began to warm, my bottom seeming to swell as I was dealt with, my cheeks smacked evenly, all over.

Soon I'd begun to push it up for more, revelling in my spanking in a way I'd seen other girls do but had never thought I would. Poppy gave a little chuckle at the sight and began to work on the insides of my cheeks, slapping her fingertips into my crease, close to my anus. I spread wider, opening myself to her completely, and in response she began to spank my pussy.

It was gentle, but enough to sting and make me gasp as my pussy-mound and lips were smacked. I was sure I could feel myself swelling and was imagining the red of my sex and bottom, open and ready, smacked up to heat and colour as I was punished, naked, blatantly exposed, while the woman spanking me was fully, perfectly dressed.

I think I would have come, because the smacks on my pussy sent the most glorious shocks out from my clitoris, and my head was singing with the sheer joy of what was being done to me. As before, Poppy seemed to gauge my reactions, stopping just before I reached the point of no return and going back to my bottom.

It was harder now, firm swats to make my cheeks bounce and quiver. I didn't care. I was ready, hot and open over her lap, my bottom glowing, my sex agape and running juice. She could see, I knew, and I wasn't surprised when the spanking stopped abruptly and a finger was inserted into my vagina, well up, to wriggle around, inspecting the state of my sex.

'Dirty girl,' she said, and wiped her finger in the crease of my bottom.

Again she began to spank, harder still, until at last I began to gasp and kick my legs in reaction. It was right though, my bottom a hot, fat ball behind me, throbbing and swollen. I knew I'd be red, and could picture myself, my naked body spread out over Poppy's lap, my bottom jumping to the smacks, my skin an angry red, my pussy blatantly wet, my bottom-hole spread out for all to see . . .

I needed to come, while she did it, while I was spanked, beaten, hard, for being a dirty little girl, for peeing myself as I lay nude on the mat. My free hand went back, pushing under my belly, and I was doing it, masturbating as I was beaten, rubbing at my open, sopping pussy as my bottom-cheeks bounced nude to my nurse's slaps.

'Dirty girl!' Poppy repeated. 'So it's like that, is it, you dirty, filthy little slut.'

Her grip tightened, twisting my arm hard up my back. I cried out and again as she finally put the full force of her arm into my beating, smacking her hand down on to my bottom with all her force. I didn't care, I was going to come. My fingers were rubbing frantically at my clitoris; my pussy was pulsing, my anus tightening to pull in the huge load inside as she beat me, harder and harder.

I was thrashing on her lap, my legs kicking, my bottom wiggling frantically and dancing to the slaps, my breasts shaking beneath me, my hair flying around my head. As I started to come I screamed and called out Poppy's name, telling her to spank me harder, to really punish me. She obliged, laying into my poor, bouncing bottom with all her strength, stern and silent as she gave me what I deserved, a good, firm whacking for punishment, because it needed to be done, regardless of what it did to me.

She only stopped when I went limp and even then she held on to me, keeping me in place across her lap. I lay there, my breath coming in ragged pants. My bottom was absolutely burning and I knew that for all my ecstasy I'd been properly spanked, and that I'd probably be carrying bruises in the morning.

Normally, I'd have been in tears, and filled with self-pity and misery at the way I'd been treated. Instead, I was elated, contrite, yet thoroughly happy. Finally I understood what a spanking could do for me, so long as I was handled properly, by somebody who really knew how to punish a girl for sex, by my Poppy.

She had begun to stroke my bottom gently, soothing me and, I was sure, for her own pleasure. I stuck it up obligingly, letting her explore and enjoying the sensation of being comforted after my punishment. After a while she leaned forwards to pick up the cream, still holding me firmly in place as she retrieved it and dabbed out a couple of large blobs on to the crests of my bottom. As she began to cream my smacked cheeks I cocked myself wide and high, lifting myself for her, so that she could get at every crevice of my hot behind and my aching pussy. In response she took a little of the cream and dabbed it on to my bottom-hole, teasing my ring for a moment before returning to creaming my cheeks with slow, circular motions.

With my orgasm over, my need for the toilet had returned stronger than ever. I felt fit to burst, my rectum really straining, but I couldn't bear to break the moment, and for all our intimacy, I didn't feel I should just do it up between my cheeks as I lay over her lap, to say nothing of the mess. So I held tight, letting her cream me, sure that she must be aware of the way my bottom-hole was pouting out, and that she would know what to do.

Only when my whole bottom was a glossy red ball of creamy, smacked flesh did she stop. I thought she was going to let me down, maybe have me lick her at last, only for her fingers to go down between my cheeks again, stroking the bar of flesh between my two holes, then my anus, tickling, until my ring began to twitch.

I could feel myself opening to her, my bottom-hole spreading like a flower, eager to be penetrated. Her

231

tickling grew firmer, concentrating on the hole, easing me slowly open, until I was sure it was just going to happen, whether I liked it or not. I tightened my ring, desperate to control myself, but she gave a little tut of disapproval.

'Let me see,' she said.

My mouth came open in a low moan, but I relaxed and her finger slid up into my bottom.

'I see,' she said, as she pulled out her finger. 'You should have told me you were ready before I changed you. I suppose I ought to get you in a nappy, but it seems a shame to waste one. Look, what would you like to do, would you like to just let it all out?'

I couldn't even answer, the constriction in my throat too tight to allow me to speak. All I managed was a choking sound. Poppy said nothing, but leaned forwards again, to reach a towel from my rack.

'Up,' she said as she sat back.

I lifted myself off her leg. I was shaking uncontrollably as she slid the towel under my tummy and tugged it into place. My bottom-hole was straining, and I knew it was going to happen anyway soon and that I wanted to, but I was still fighting with an urge not to do anything so utterly indecent, something I'd thought I'd got over a long time before.

'There we are,' she said as I settled back on to her lap. 'You can do it now, as soon as you're ready.'

My bottom was the highest part of my body, lifted across her lap, with my legs well spread to show off my straining hole. I could feel my ring pouting up, creamy and loose, completely ready, with only my inhibitions stopping me. Not that it mattered. I was too loose to stop it, my bottom-hole opening, and then I was showing her and it was too late anyway.

I moaned aloud, burying my face in my hands as I felt my anus open and the thick, hard mass within push out. Poppy could see, my nurse, watching the most intimate thing I could possibly do as I lay naked across her lap, my anus gaping to let out my mess between my bottom-cheeks, right in front of her.

'There, there, just do it, let it come,' she said, and began to stroke my hair.

I just burst into tears, overcome by emotion, and with that the last of my resistance went. I let go completely, sobbing as my bottom-hole everted and let it all out. I felt something firm and hot fall against my pussy, and more pushing out between my bottom-cheeks. The tears were running down my cheeks as it came, more and more, all the while with Poppy stroking my hair to soothe me. Soon it had begun to pile up over my anus, heavy and fat, filling the shallow valley of my bottom and lying against my open pussy.

Poppy never said a word, but just watched as I soiled myself, allowing me to do it with absolute understanding. With a huge pile already sitting on my bottom, my anus closed, only to open again as I pushed, deliberately now, squeezing out more. The load on my bottom shifted to the new pressure, and began to edge slowly down over my pussy. Some broke and rolled down between my thighs. Poppy immediately lifted the towel, squashing the mess to my shaved pubic mound as more fell down on to my pussy.

'We'd better do you up, I think,' she said.

I nodded gratefully as she turned the towel up over my bottom, pressing my dirt to my skin and up between my buttocks. Taking the corners, she tied the towel off at my hips, making an impromptu nappy for me. It was tight, and I could feel my load bulging against my flesh, hot and squashy around my bottom and up over my pussy. There was a little more to come, and I squeezed it out, feeling the towel bulge out behind me as it came, to leave me empty, with everything in my nappy.

'There, now down you go,' Poppy said, and patted me on my bulge.

Her voice was thick and deep, and I knew exactly what she meant. I moved down from her lap, sniffing back my tears to look up into her eyes as she opened her legs in front of me. She was smiling, nervous and excited, one corner of her mouth twitching as she returned my gaze.

I kneeled down, my bottom pushed out, the weight of what was in my nappy hanging beneath me, keeping me acutely conscious of it. Poppy's knees had gone wide, her dress rucking up, to show off the tops of her stockings and the bare flesh of her thighs above them, then the white of her panty crotch. She lifted her bottom, to tug her dress up and pull the top of her panties out from under her girdle. They came down, pushed over her thighs to her ankles to present me with her bare pussy, open and wet beneath a thick tangle of curls.

'Lick me, Gabrielle,' she ordered. 'Lick your nurse while you think about what's in your nappy.'

She had edged forwards as she spoke, spreading her knees wider still. I moved close, catching the scent of her sex, and buried my face in her pussy, licking eagerly at her clitoris. Her hand found my head, stroking me and pulling me in as she gave a sigh of pure satisfaction.

I'd come twice, but I was licking her, licking her with my load hanging heavy in my nappy, a load she'd just watched come out. I wiggled my bottom, feeling the mess move beneath me, and I knew I had to do it. As I began to lick more urgently at Poppy's sex, my hand was sneaking down the front of my nappy to find my pussy, dirty and ready, my vagina clogged with mess, my crease wet with my juices.

'You're doing it, aren't you?' Poppy gasped.

I nodded into my mouthful of pussy, admitting my filthy secret.

'You little slut,' she sighed. 'You dirty, filthy little slut. Do it then, and while you frig in your own dirt, you can taste mine.'

Her legs came up as she spoke, opening her bottom and pushing it into my face. Without an instant's hesitation I pushed my tongue into her anus, licking eagerly at the little hole, to taste the earthy, acrid tang, mixed with the taste of sex where her juice had run down.

'That's right, taste me,' she moaned. 'Lick me clean while I frig.'

Her fingers came down to rub at her sex. I kept licking her bottom, my tongue pushing deep to get her taste, her anus opening, wet and hot and slimy. I wanted to come as she did and began to rub myself harder, smearing slimy mess over my pussy as I frigged and wriggling my bottom to make my load swing in my nappy and squash up between my cheeks.

It was going to happen at any moment. Poppy was rubbing hard, her bottom-hole agape, my mouth open over her slippery ring, my tongue deep in her. She was gasping, her sex contracting in my face, her anus tightening on my tongue, my head spinning with her taste and scent.

'I'm coming,' she moaned. 'I'm coming, Gabrielle. Get your tongue in, deep in. Do it, you dirty slut, taste me, lick me . . . yes, I'm coming . . . like that, yes, up my bumhole . . . like that, in, right up my bum . . . I'm so open, I should do it . . . I should, right in your dirty mouth!'

She screamed, coming, even as my own orgasm hit me. I felt her bottom-hole close tight on my tongue, pushing it out, and I was gasping, my mouth wide, dizzy with pleasure as I clawed at my own sex, screaming in unison with Poppy as we came together in blinding, perfect ecstasy.

In the morning I felt not only completely happy and in love with Poppy, but more than confident enough to face the crisis I had expected to come all week. I assumed that at some point Anna Vale was going to discover where Poppy was and, to judge by what I had seen of her character, she was unlikely to take it lying down.

The crisis never came. What did come was a call from Natasha asking what was going on, and to explain why Penny Birch had sent her a message threatening her with dire retribution in return for having stood down Anna Vale's demands for my address. We explained, at once delighting Natasha and making her jealous, so that we ended up promising that she could come and play the next day.

Despite my confidence, the knowledge that I would not have to face up to Anna Vale was a great relief. It also put Poppy into a mood of manic gaiety, which I suspect was partly to hide her guilt. Fortunately I had no appointments, as I certainly wouldn't have been able to concentrate. Instead I spent most of the day as a grown-up baby girl, being nursed and changed and suckled, until I was in a haze of sleepy pleasure. I was spanked again too, as skilfully as before, and finally given an enema, which turned the conversation to Natasha once we had come down from our orgasms.

After everything she had done to me, including subjecting me to Monty Hartle, it seemed only fair that if she was going to come and play then she should be in the submissive role. Poppy agreed, and after a few minutes of discussing elaborate and sadistic tortures she came up with something that would not only suit Natasha perfectly, but give Monty something to think about into the bargain.

Saturday morning was spent shopping, after which we called Natasha. We were perfectly honest about it, sending her a text demanding her presence and telling her to expect trouble. Half-an-hour later she rang my buzzer. We let her up and she came in, smiling, to bounce down on the couch.

236

'So I've finally got to Miss Goody-Two-Shoes Gabrielle, have I?' She laughed. 'Great! Come on then, I'm all yours!'

'I am glad to hear it,' I told her. 'Very well, as you are so keen, we shall begin. Get the equipment, Poppy. Natasha, strip to your panties.'

Poppy ran into the kitchen, laughing. Natasha obeyed immediately and eagerly, quickly undressing down to a pair of tight white cotton panties, the sort Percy made her wear. Ready, she stood, stretching to show off her breasts, then turning to give us a wiggle of her bottom.

'In the bedroom,' I told her.

'What are you going to do, make me do it in my panties?' she asked happily, trotting into the bedroom without the slightest hesitation.

'That might come into it,' I admitted. 'For now, lie down on the sheet.'

I had one of my plastic play sheets ready on the floor and she lay down on it, cocking her knees high to show off the crotch of her panties and folding her hands behind her head. Poppy came in holding a basket, which she put down beside Gabrielle and skipped out again.

'What are those? Knickers?' Natasha queried, peering at the pile of assorted female undergarments in the basket.

'Monty Hartle's panty collection,' I told her. 'Now, kneel up.'

She nodded, turning to climb into a kneeling position, her bottom raised, her tight seat taut across her buttocks. I gave her a gentle pat and she looked back, her eyes showing a touch of apprehension and a great deal of pleasure. Poppy came back, this time holding a bucket with a large stick in it.

'What are you going to do to me?' Natasha asked.

'Quiet,' I said, smacking her again. 'No questions and no whining – just obey orders.'

'Yes, miss,' she answered.

We left her kneeling and watching us as Poppy went to fetch the last of our equipment, a large bag, which she flopped down beside the bucket.

'Plaster of Paris?' Natasha said, reading the legend on the side of the bag. 'Oh, you're not!'

'Be quiet!' I told her. 'You are getting yourself into trouble.'

'Yes, but . . .'

'Do you want to be tied? And given a good spanking first? We will.'

'I'll be good, I promise . . . just . . . you're not going to do my pussy, are you, not without shaving me first?'

'Not your pussy, no, or your breasts, we promise.'

'OK.'

She'd begun to shake a little, and I realised we were getting to her. I couldn't help but grin as Poppy and I set to work.

Natasha watched as we made the mixture, her eyes wide as I stirred the powder in to make a thick, even paste. The moment it was ready we started to use it, dipping a pair of panties each until the plaster was well soaked in, and spreading them out on Natasha's back. With the next two pairs we took her arms, pulling them up to her sides and wrapping each in the soggy panties. More went on her back and around her arms, wound into place even as the plaster began to set. We sped up, frantically slapping plaster-soaked panties on to her body, around her waist and over her arms, to trap them at her sides. Soon her whole waist was circled, with her arms pinned tight, rendering her helpless. We kept going, cocooning her middle in plaster, until we were sure she had no possibility of escape, and only then sitting back. Her whole middle was encased in plaster from just beneath her breasts where they hung, squashed out on the plastic sheet, to immediately above the waistband of her panties. At either hip her hands stuck out of the plaster, her fingers wriggling helplessly as she tried to pull free.

'Can you get up?' I asked.

She moved, kneeling up and trying to rise, only to topple sideways, off balance. Poppy laughed at the sight and reached out to take hold of Natasha's bottom, fondling casually.

'You can crawl around,' I told her. 'We will help if we need you to stand. How does it feel?'

'Tight,' she said, 'warm, too.'

'That is because it is an exothermic reaction,' I told her. 'Now, let me see. What did you do to me? You stuck needles in my bottom, did you not? And you gave me an enema with chocolate cake mixture.'

She moaned, hanging her head.

'So it seems only fair you should get the same treatment, does it not?'

'Not the needles, no, please! I hate injections!'

'You were quite happy giving them to me.'

'Yes, but I . . .'

'Be quiet. So, first . . .'

'Hang on, I need to pee. Could you help me please?'

'No. Do it in your panties.'

'Gabrielle! Must I?'

'Yes, you must,' Poppy answered her, 'and we want to see. Roll over and stick your bum up.'

'And if I don't?'

'Then we plaster your legs together and wait until it happens naturally.'

Natasha sighed, pushing out one knee to lift herself back into a kneeling position, before falling slowly forwards to leave her bottom high in the air, her knees wide. The position stretched the seat of her panties taut across her bottom and pulled the crotch against her sex to show off the outline of her lips, plump and full beneath the cotton, a delightful view. She was breathing hard, and I could see her tummy moving just below the edge of the plaster.

'Come on, Tasha, potty-pants time!' Poppy urged.

Natasha sighed again, and an instant later it started to come, a spot of wet growing on the crotch of her panties at the very centre of her sex, spreading before it burst from the material in a little fountain of yellow fluid which pattered down on to the mat.

'Adorable!' Poppy laughed. 'Just look at her!'

The pee had started to come faster, squirting out through Natasha's panties to form a puddle between her knees and soaking into her crotch so that her pussy showed through the wet material, pink and ready. It was soaking down over her pubic mound, too, her bush showing as a dark patch under the wet cotton, and up over her bottom, slowly, to cling to her cheeks.

Giggling, Poppy moved closer to lay a gentle pat on Natasha's wet bottom, then another, harder. Pee spattered out over the mat as Poppy began to spank to a firm, slow rhythm, setting Natasha gasping and squealing as she was punished. The pee was still coming, too, but as Natasha moved the trickle stopped spraying out backwards and began to run down her leg instead, in pulses, as each spank made a little more squirt out.

'Come on, Gabby,' Poppy urged, 'she needs punishing, don't you, Tasha?'

Natasha's answer was a muted sob. I moved close to touch the soggy panty seat stuck out so temptingly in front of me. Her pee had stopped but her panties were sodden from under her crotch to halfway up her bottom, the wet material plastered tight to her flesh and see-through, showing every detail of her sex and a good deal of her bottom.

Poppy was still spanking away merrily, making Natasha's bottom dance and spattering pee everywhere, including over her own front. She didn't seem to care, laughing in time to Natasha's moans and little, pained gasps.

'You spank,' I instructed. 'I am going to masturbate her.'

'Lucky bitch!' Poppy laughed, and planted a yet harder smack across Natasha's bottom.

Natasha's gasped at the impact, then again as I took hold of her wet panties and tugged them firmly up into the crease of her bottom, spilling out her fleshy cheeks to either side, wet and glossy with her pee and rosy pink from spanking.

'That's right, good and tight, right up her pussy!' Poppy said. 'Oh, you do look a sight, Tasha, with your big, fat bum all rosy and wet with pee and your little panties up your crease!'

'My bum is not fat!' Natasha complained.

'Great!' Poppy laughed. 'She's in plaster; she's pissed her knickers and she's getting a spanking, and she's more worried about having a fat bum! It is fat, isn't it, Gabby? It's certainly wobbly.'

As she spoke she had put her hand to Natasha's bottom, making the cheeks squash out, then smacking again, and laughing as they bounced.

'Fat!' Poppy declared. 'Big and fat, a big, fat wobbly bottom!'

'It's not as big as yours,' Natasha answered.

Poppy's response was a furious salvo of slaps, full across Natasha's cheeks to set her squealing and kicking her legs. I held on tight, hauling the damp panties well up, to force her bottom high and keep it still for punishment. As I did so the wet material pulled tight in between her sex-lips, spilling them out, bare and wet. I cupped her sex, feeling the damp flesh and the pee-soaked cotton. She was warm and I was sure she was ready. Pushing my fingers into her crease, I began to rub at her sex through the wet panty cotton. She moaned in response.

'That's right, Miss Pissy-Panties,' Poppy called, 'come with your wet knicks up your pussy and your big fat bottom stuck in the air! Come while I spank you!'

Natasha moaned again and Poppy began to spank harder still, really laying in to make the now red buttocks dance and quiver. I started to rub faster, cupping her whole sex, with just one finger pushed tight into her crotch. She began to grunt to the smacks, her bottom-cheeks clenching and her thigh muscles tightening.

'She's going to come,' Poppy said. 'She's really going to come. That's right, Miss Pissy-Panties, let it happen, show us what a slut you are. Imagine it, wetting your knickers in front of us and getting off on it, you dirty little slut, you . . .'

She stopped as Natasha cried out in ecstasy. I felt her pussy twitch under my hand, tightening, and she was coming, gasping and panting out her ecstasy, her feet in her pee-puddle, her fingers clutching at air, her buttocks in frantic contraction even as they danced to Poppy's furious slaps.

We kept at her until she started to go limp, when Poppy stopped and I let go of her panties. She slumped slowly down, her knees going wide, into the puddle of her own pee which had spread out beneath her, but too far gone to care.

'That was fun,' Poppy declared happily. 'Fun, but hardly a punishment.'

'True,' I agreed.

'I got put in a pillory once,' Poppy said, 'at this place in Wiltshire. They pelted me with rotten fruit, mud, even horse shit. I've wanted to do it to someone else ever since.'

'No, please,' Natasha managed.

'Yes, I think so,' I told her, 'after all, you thought it would be funny to put tomato and eggs in my hair, didn't you?'

'Yes, but I didn't do it!'

'I'll get the eggs and tomatoes,' Poppy said, climbing to her feet.

'Thank you,' I told her, 'and there is that big pot of natural yoghurt open as well. We can spare that.'

Natasha gave a hollow groan as Poppy skipped out of the room. I quickly cleared part of one wall and spread out another play sheet, the biggest I had. She lay still, unresisting, as I did my best to mop up her pee and pulled off her soggy panties, leaving her nude but for the cast encasing her middle and trapping her arms. Before I was finished Poppy came back with my large mixing bowl. Natasha looked at the contents with an expression of utter disgust. Poppy kicked her bottom.

'Get over there, kneeling up!' she ordered.

'Yes, miss,' Natasha sighed, pulling herself to her knee.

'Stay on the sheets,' I added. 'You're covered in pee, you disgusting girl!'

She gave me the most wonderful look, full of accusation and self-pity, but waited as I moved the sheet to let her crawl over on her knees.

'Which way?' she asked miserably as she reached the wall. 'My bum?'

'No, your front, 'I told her, 'but don't worry, we will see that your bottom gets a fair share. So kneel right up, facing us, knees nice and wide, chest out.'

She obeyed, crawling slowly round to get into position, kneeling with her legs open to show her sex, with her pubic hair plastered to her skin. Sat straight, she pushed out her breasts and looked up, her eyes wide with uncertainty. I picked up an egg. Poppy chose a tomato. Natasha gave a sob and ducked her head down to hide her face.

I threw the egg. It caught her beautifully, right on the top of her head, bursting in her hair to spatter her with the contents and bits of eggshell. Poppy laughed and threw her tomato, which hit Natasha's shoulder, to splash juice and pips out in a star shape, dirtying her face and chest. I tried another egg, which burst on her plaster cast, spattering her chest and legs, even as one from Poppy exploded on the crown of her head. My next egg caught her chest and I switched to tomatoes, laughing as hard as Poppy as the soft red fruit burst over Natasha's skin, soiling her utterly as she gasped and jerked to the impacts and mess ran down her skin.

By the time five of the six eggs and the entire bag of tomatoes had gone she was filthy, her hair matted, sitting in a pool of mess, with even her pubic hair clogged with tomato pips and bits of red pulp. Poppy was going to throw the final egg, but I stopped her, sure there was a better place for it. Putting my finger to my lips, I nodded to Natasha's open thighs. Poppy grinned back.

As the bombardment stopped, Natasha looked up, her face a pale oval in a frame of wet curls. Her hair was a mess, running filthy with egg and tomato, and plastered with bits of shell and skin. In comparison her face was clean, except for a single trickle of juice and pips running down over her forehead. Her chest was anything but clean, her breasts both thoroughly soiled, splashed with food, which was running slowly down over them. A burst egg covered one nipple, with bits of shell sticking to the erect teat and a piece of yolk hanging down from the tip. The other had got off relatively lightly, so I scooped up a handful of mixed tomato pulp and egg from between her legs and smeared it over the dangling globe, rubbing it well into her nipple. Poppy moved up beside me, the yoghurt pot in her hand. Natasha looked at it and bit her lip.

'In her face,' I suggested.

'My thoughts exactly,' Poppy answered, scooping out a handful of the thick yoghurt.

Natasha groaned, and shut her eyes and mouth an instant before the handful was slapped into her face. Poppy was laughing as she rubbed it in, making sure nothing was spared. When she stopped, Natasha came up gasping to display her filthy face, with both eyes closed by mess and bits of yoghurt hanging from her nose and chin. I added a handful of tomato and egg from the mat for good measure, pressing some into her open mouth to leaving her spitting bits of shell and tomato peel.

'Bottom!' Poppy declared happily, scooping up yet more mess to reach around behind Natasha and slap it to the out-thrust globes of her behind.

I added my own handful, Natasha grunting in shock as it was smeared up between her cheeks, and gasping as my finger found her anus and slipped inside, well lubricated with egg yolk. For a moment I fingered her until the noises she was making began to change from disgust to pleasure, when I stopped. Poppy giggled, and held up the egg.

'No, please, not that,' Natasha moaned, shaking her head as Poppy's arm went down.

Natasha's face was a sight to see as the egg was put to her sex. Her mouth hung slack at first, surrendered to the inevitable with no more than a trace of disgust. As the egg was put to her hole, the look of disgust abruptly deepened, only to be replaced by shock as her vagina began to fill, then far, far stronger disgust as the egg burst in her hole, to spatter its contents over her sex and on to the mat beneath her.

Most of the egg actually stayed in her, the shell anyway, with white dripping out, and a beard of mess hanging from her sex-lips. Poppy laughed so hard at the sight that she fell over backwards, clutching herself as she rolled on the floor, unable to look at the filthy Natasha without breaking into new hysterics.

I was little better, my face fixed in a grin which simply would not go away as I watched the muck drip slowly down Natasha's body and on to the floor. It was erotic too, unquestionably, for all the perversity of becoming excited over the sight of a beautiful girl soiled and humiliated. Finally Poppy managed to get herself under control and sat up, grinning broadly as she admired the mess we had made of Natasha.

'Does that pay for the needles?' Poppy asked me.

'Possibly,' I admitted. 'I am not sure.'

'I don't think it does at all,' Poppy answered. 'You were in a real state. This is just a bit of fun really, by comparison.'

'No, it is not!' Natasha answered firmly. 'I'm filthy, and my pussy's full of egg and my bumhole feels all slimy, and I can't even move!'

'Oh, dear, poor thing!' Poppy laughed. 'OK, we'll count it a half.'

'No!' Natasha protested. 'It's a whole! And you made me pee my knickers, and you spanked me. That should be all!'

'Hardly all,' I answered her. 'Still, for now, we will wash you. Help me carry her to the bathroom, Poppy, in the sheet.'

We took hold of the sheet, lifting it by the corners, to half carry, half drag Natasha into the bathroom and heave her into the shower. I was about to turn the tap on when Poppy stopped me.

'There's more than one way to wash a dirty girl,' she said. 'Come on, strip off, let's piss on her.'

She began to strip immediately, peeling off as fast as she could. I joined her, while Natasha squatted miserably in the shower, her eyes wide, peering from a mask of mess. Nude, Poppy climbed in to straddle Natasha's head, her sex pushed out.

'Open wide,' Poppy ordered.

To my surprise, Natasha obeyed, her mouth coming open, her pretty lips well parted, right in front of Poppy's sex.

'Good girl,' Poppy said, 'you see, she likes a little pee pee in her mouth, and she's going to get it.'

Poppy made a little noise in the back of her throat, and I saw the muscles of her tummy tense. I pushed in behind her, close, even as pee spurted from Poppy's sex full into Natasha's open mouth, filling it and bubbling from the sides to run down over her chin and splash on her bare breasts, washing the filthy mixture of yoghurt, egg and tomato down in a stream of yellowish slurry.

'Swallow, bitch!' Poppy ordered.

Immediately Natasha swallowed, closing her mouth so that Poppy's stream exploded full in her face, splashing her lips and cheeks, before she managed to open up again.

'Yes, she's drinking it!' Poppy laughed. 'She's drinking my pee, Gabby! Go on, Tasha, more!'

Natasha obeyed, or tried to, choking the instant she tried to swallow her mouthful of piddle, to send her into a coughing fit, pee bursting out of her mouth and nose, to splash in Poppy's pubic hair and over her belly. Poppy just laughed, and directed her stream a little lower. With urine now splashing over her breasts, Natasha struggled to get her breath back, gasping and coughing, with pee still running out from the sides of her mouth. Plenty had come out of her nose too, leaving a long streamer of mucus hanging from the tip, which broke to fall on to one breast, just as Poppy's stream died away, so that it stayed there, hanging from the tip of Natasha's nipple.

Poppy gave a little wiggle to shake the last few drops of pee out over Natasha's breasts and squeezed herself into the corner of the shower, making room for me. I took hold of Natasha's hair to pull back her head, and her mouth came wide in expectation. I moved close, pressing my sex to her face to rub her nose on myself for a moment before I let my bladder go, full into her mouth.

It felt glorious, my pee gushing into her open mouth and back against my sex, hot and wet. I looked down, watching as she struggled to drink what she could, with piddle splashing out from around her open lips, to cascade down over her breasts. She was already in a pool of it on the plastic sheet, broad and yellow, full of

247

mess, with her bare bottom sat right in it. More was coming too, right into her mouth, and she was trying to kiss my sex and drink it at the same time, lost to her need for submission.

When my pee died away she didn't stop licking. I stayed in place, holding her head as she lapped at my pussy, soiled and filthy beneath me, my plaything, eager to please despite what I'd done, despite the bellyful of urine we'd given her.

Poppy came to me as Natasha licked, to kiss me and stroke my breasts. I responded, hugging her and slipping a hand down to the moist crevice of her sex, enjoying each other, making love as Natasha grovelled, nude and filthy at our feet.

I came first, full in Natasha's face, with Poppy's mouth open to mine. Natasha wasted no time, utterly subservient to us as she moved straight to Poppy's sex to bury her face in among the wet black curls the moment it was presented to her. Moments later, Poppy had also come, and we were hugging and giggling together, still standing over the thoroughly punished Natasha.

'Do I get to come, please?' she asked from beneath us.

'Don't be a slut,' Poppy answered. 'You get to come when we say so, not before. Isn't that right, Gabrielle?'

'Absolutely,' I agreed. 'Now be quiet, Natasha.'

We showered and washed Natasha down as best we could, including her cast. Towels and powder finished the job, along with a well-creamed bottom-hole for Natasha. Poppy and I dressed once more, leaving Natasha naked. She took it patiently until she was clean, dry and sat on my couch, waiting helplessly for us to release her, or continue her torment.

'Am I ... are you finished with me?' she asked doubtfully as I sat down across from her.

'No,' I told her, 'that pays for the needle and for the enema, as you gave us such nice orgasms, but that is not all. Now, what else did you do? Oh, yes, you gave me to Monty Hartle so that he could abuse me and make me his sex toy, did you not?'

'No!' she answered. 'I didn't! That's not fair!'

'No?' I asked. 'Are you sure?'

'Yes ...' she began and stopped, looking at Poppy, who had raised a finger and was wagging it meaningfully.

'OK, I did,' she admitted. 'Sorry.'

'Thank you,' I said. 'You also lied to me.'

'Yes,' she said miserably. 'What are you going to do to me?'

'We are going to make the punishment fit the crime. Now that Poppy and I are together I can not really be expected to provide for Monty's perverse urges. So the job is yours, starting tonight.'

'Tonight? No, please, Gabrielle – not Monty, anything but Monty!'

'Monty,' I said firmly. 'He will be expecting us. In fact, we had better hurry.'

She was looking genuinely scared but she gave no protest, really too high on her own submission to object. We put her in her coat and boots, naked underneath, and helped her down the stairs and out into the street. She had parked quite close and it was dark and cold, so we managed to get to her car without attracting attention and bundled her into the boot, to her renewed protests.

Poppy drove, south through London, to the street in Croydon where Monty lived. He was waiting, beaming all over his fat face as we opened the door and pushed Natasha inside. He was ready too, with a brand new spanking video running, a stack of pizzas in the kitchen and two six packs of beer by his chair. Everything was arranged and we made ourselves comfortable in his living room, eating pizza and drinking beer as we watched the video, with Natasha arranged over the table, her bare bottom stuck out towards us. She had guessed what was going to happen to her, perhaps as early as when we'd lubricated her anus, and said nothing, just squirmed in her cast, with her creamy little hole pulsing and twitching between her cheeks.

Monty was sat back, at ease, watching the pony-tailed blonde on the TV as she was made to repeatedly pull her panties up and down by the dirty old man who was supposedly her uncle. He had pulled out his cock and nodded to me before reaching for a slice of pizza. I gave Poppy a questioning look, but she just shrugged and sat back to watch as I got down on all fours to take Monty's cock in my mouth as he pulled up his belly for me. He was soon hard, stiffening in my mouth to the sound of the blonde's breathless squeals as she was spanked.

Ready, he pushed the last of his pizza slice into his mouth and got down on his knees, pressing his cock up between Natasha's buttocks. She moaned as she felt it press to her flesh, and gave a broken sob as he took it in hand, pushing lower, to the slick, ready hole of her anus. Poppy and I watched, fascinated, as her bumhole stretched slowly open around the head of his penis, accommodating him really quite easily, or at least a lot more easily than I had done.

She was groaning as his cock was forced slowly up into her rectum, bit by bit, until it was right up and all we could see was her bottom, sweetly curved beneath his great, pasty gut. Her mouth was wide, gasping for air as he began to bugger her, moving in her anus with his eyes fixed on the TV, watching the unfortunate blonde girl who was now standing in the corner, her panties around her thighs, her hot bottom presented to the room.

'Fucking nice,' Monty groaned. 'Go on, lick her cunt, Gabby.'

'Please,' Natasha moaned. 'Please, Gabrielle.'

I could hardly refuse, and got down underneath them to find Monty's hard balls pushing up against Natasha's sex and his cock jammed to the hilt in her anus. Her ring was pulling in and out as he buggered her, straining around his fat shaft, the same way mine had strained as I lost my anal virginity to him. I lifted my head to kiss her pussy, his balls pressing to my face as he pushed himself up her bottom.

He was really getting quite urgent as I started to lick Natasha, making it hard to do my job properly. I tried anyway, lapping at her clitoris and holding on to her open thighs, with my face pressed to the soft, furry mound of her sex.

'Watch this,' Monty grated from above us, 'this is good, where the uncle greases up the girl's bumhole and fingers her up it, just watch.'

Natasha gave a broken sob in response. I could understand her feelings, utter humiliation, as she was being buggered and the man up her bottom got off on a completely different girl, and a video at that. It was typical Monty, though, and as I heard the squashy sound of the girl's bottom-hole being lubricated and a fresh sob, he suddenly stiffened.

'Yeah, in her mouth!' he grunted. 'Oh, fuck, that's good!'

He jammed himself into Natasha to the hilt, squashing his balls in my face. I was trying to lick, but she hadn't come and was sobbing with reaction as he pulled slowly back, his slimy erection pulling from her hole to fall against my cheek.

'Suck on this,' he ordered, and before I could speak I had been taken by the hair and his cock stuffed in my mouth, fresh from Natasha's bottom-hole. She was dribbling come too on to my face as Monty pushed his cock down, deep in my mouth, filling my senses with the taste of his come and Natasha's bottom.

He made me suck him clean but pulled out in the end to leave me gasping, my mouth wide, with sperm and Natasha's juices smeared over my face. She was moaning, though, and pushing her bottom down, to squat on my face. I gave in, licking at her as she started to rub herself on me, my tongue in her pussy, then on her bottom-hole as she moved. I heard Poppy's little gasp of shock as she watched me lick up the sperm as it oozed from Natasha's anus, or I thought it was shock, until I felt her come down on me, and her face pressed in beside mine. Her tongue came out, lapping at the filthy mess, until it was running out over her lips.

We kissed, sharing the mess of sperm, juice and saliva, only to have Natasha grind her bottom into our faces, demanding attention. She got it, Poppy's tongue up her bottom, mine on her clitoris, as we licked her, our mouths full of male come and pussy juice, lapping frantically at her underside, our faces smeared in it, her bottom wiggling frantically against us.

I heard her moan and she was coming, crying out in raw ecstasy as we burrowed our tongues into her body, filthy and uninhibited, completely lost in the pleasure of her sex. All I could do was lick, letting her come in my face, over and over, until at last her contractions subsided and stopped and I felt it was fair to pull away. Poppy did so too, grinning down at me as she rocked back on her haunches, her face sticky with come. So was mine, and we shared an extremely slimy kiss when I had managed to sit up.

'Dirty bitches,' Monty commented as we broke apart. 'You two going to do it?'

I gave Poppy a glance. She smiled and shrugged, her hands going straight to her blouse.

'Nice tits,' Monty said as Poppy's blouse came open. 'Do you fuck then, with guys?'

'Sometimes,' Poppy admitted, 'when I'm told to.'

Monty swallowed hard, his eyes glued to her. The video had finished, and we had his sole attention as we undressed, stripping nude on the floor. Even Natasha was watching, having managed to roll off the table and prop herself against a chair.

I was about to give a floor show to Monty with my new girlfriend, and I could feel a slight sense of having been abused as Poppy folded me in her arms. No one else seemed to care, and as she began to kiss me I gave up any thought of holding back. We went down together, cuddling and groping on the floor, at first as much for Monty's benefit as our own, then with greater enthusiasm as we began to get carried away.

Poppy was full of passion, kissing and stroking and licking without the slightest inhibition. I responded, my pleasure growing, but always with the slight sense of regret in the back of my mind. Monty was wanking as he watched, and I was performing for him and showing off my girlfriend, both naked, our every intimate secret on view. He had spanked me again and again, come in my face repeatedly, buggered me, and here I was, showing off for him – and, worse, showing off my girlfriend. We'd ruined his panty collection, maybe, but it was a fraction of what he deserved.

I was going to come anyway, abused or not, with Poppy on top of me, her pussy in my face and hers in mine. With her glorious bottom in front of me and her tongue on my clitoris, it was simply too much, and with a last stab of regret I let myself go, crying out my ecstasy an instant before she too came, full in my face. We pulled apart slowly, to collapse back on the floor. Monty was red-faced, his cock half-stiff, the skin oily and damp, a piece of pizza in his free hand.

'Fuck!' he swore. 'I was getting there. How about a lap dance? You know, with your arse right in my face.'

For a moment I looked at him, incredulous. I could just see it, me gyrating in front of him, making myself his sex toy, as always, and with him wanking one-handed and eating pizza with the other.

'Give me a minute,' I answered him.

'Nice,' he said, and relaxed, still stroking his cock, but with most of his attention on eating.

253

I took a slice of pizza and one of the cans of cheap bitter beer he'd bought for us. Monty carried on masturbating as I ate, his eyes moving constantly, to Natasha's body, to Poppy's, to mine, and back. Poppy had curled up on a chair, her legs up, her pussy peeping out from between her thighs, either indifferent to him or enjoying making a show of herself. Natasha was even less concerned, sitting with her back to the chair and her legs up, everything on full show as she tried to pick at her plaster corset.

'How they'd do that thing, Tasha?' Monty asked.

'You will find out when you help her to get it off,' I answered quickly. 'Are you ready?'

'Yeah, if you are.'

'I am.'

I swallowed the last of my beer, trying to ignore the horrible metallic taste as it went down my throat. It was liquid, which was what mattered. Monty turned his attention to me as I stood, his piggy eyes moving up my body as I came to stand in front of him. He reached out, to push a button on his stereo. Music blared out, a heavy rock tune, impossibly fast. He thought about it for a moment, then turned it off.

'Plenty of arse,' he instructed, 'that's the sexiest thing about you, your arse.'

I nodded and began to dance, slowly, moving my hips to an imaginary beat and sliding my fingers slowly up my body, to caress my belly, then my breasts. He began to wank faster, his eyes fixed on me, never wavering as he reached out for a fresh slice of pizza. I turned, presenting him with my bottom, wiggling as I bent, to show him the rear view of my pussy and my bottom-hole. Bracing my hands on my knees, I began to sway, my bare bottom pushed out, just inches from his cock. I reached back to spread my cheeks, stretching my anus in blatant display, the way he liked me to.

'Nice,' he said. 'You're better than the girls down the Midnight, you know. They never spread their arseholes like that. You ought to do it pro, Gabby.'

'They don't touch, either, I expect,' I said, and wiggled my bottom down into his lap, rubbing myself against his cock.'

'Fuck me!' he grunted. 'That is good. Sit on my cock, yeah, maybe I can get it up your arse.'

'Not tonight,' I answered, 'just the dance, from me. You can bugger Natasha again later if you need to.'

He laughed. I turned again, wriggling down in front of him, my breasts in my hands. I wanted to take my time, to tease him, until his cock was fully hard and until I was ready. He was stiffening, and it wasn't going to be too long in any case. So I began to move faster and to make my moves more sensuous, and sexier, stroking my nipples until they were hard, pushing my naked breasts into his face so that he could suck on them, fingering my pussy to let him taste my juice, and again and again bending to give him long, lingering views of my bottom-hole.

By the time I was ready he was rock hard, his erection a solid bar of meat in his hand, his face red and sweating. He'd come right forward in the chair to let me grind my bottom into his lap, rubbing on his cock and moving away only when he had actually pushed the head into my wet hole.

'Come on, Gabby,' he whined. 'At least let me fuck you; you're sopping!'

'I know,' I answered, turning again to straddle his legs, my pussy directly over his cock. 'Go on, pop it in then.'

He pushed his cock down, brushing my clitoris before the head found my vagina and pushed inside. I squirmed down on to his lap, filling myself, and wiggling my bottom on his balls, before rising, to move back.

'You fucking little prick-tease!' he panted. 'Come on, Gabby, up your arse, you know you want it.'

I nodded blearily.

'OK,' I said, 'you win. I will squat on you. Just put it in my pussy first, and let me open myself slowly, yes?'

'Anything you like, you little fuck-dolly,' he answered.

He was grinning and holding his cock up like a pole, ready for me to lower myself on to him, taking the full, fat bulk of his erection up my bottom. I came close, still dancing, to climb up on to the chair, my feet pushing in at either side of his great thighs. I was ready, and as he looked up, his eyes fixed to my sex, I let go, my pee exploding out over him, full in his face.

Poppy burst out laughing as Monty yelled out in shock, throwing up his arms, but too late. He'd been about to take a mouthful of pizza, and my stream had gone right in his mouth, choking him, to leave him coughing and spluttering helplessly as my urine splashed over him, in his face and hair, down his front, over his straining erection and his trousers, the chair, the carpet, and splashing to all sides to wet his stereo, the pizza he'd been eating and even the wall.

I couldn't stop laughing as I pissed on him. It was so funny, just watching him flail his arms wildly in a vain effort to protect himself and only make a bigger mess. I didn't care. I was nude; my clothes were well out of the way, and it wasn't my flat.

'Bitch!' he finally managed, spitting out a mouthful of pee and pizza dough. 'Fucking hell, Gabby!'

'That's one to remember me by,' I said cheerfully, and jumped down. 'Come on, Poppy, time to go.'

'Hey, hang on . . .' Monty started.

'Tut, tut, no whining,' I told him. 'You've got Natasha for the weekend, and you did deserve that. So have fun tidying up, and no tantrums, because I still have to write that report, remember? Good boy.'

He'd sunk back in his chair, a whole range of emotions working over his face as the pee dripped slowly down it. There was nothing he could do, and he knew it. So Poppy and I cleaned ourselves up, dressed and went, leaving Monty frantically trying to sponge down his chair while Natasha sat and laughed at him. I knew she'd end up having it taken out on her bottom – but so did she and, when it came down to it, she took only what she wanted to.

Outside, we were laughing so hard we had to cling on to each other for support. Not wishing to be too mean to Natasha, we left the car at Monty's and took the train back. We were in thoroughly high spirits and cuddling a lot, which drew a fair number of odd looks from the sort of people who still can't handle the thought of two women together. At Victoria Station we bought some smoked salmon bagels, and walked back eating them, hand in hand. I was already imagining the session of nursing I undoubtedly had coming, and was eager to get in to the flat. Unfortunately there was somebody waiting by my door – Jo Warren.

'Hi, Gabrielle,' she greeted me, nodding to Poppy. 'Sorry to come over like this, but I am so stressed out. I need to try your Practical Regression Therapy.'

NEXUS NEW BOOKS

To be published in November

PLAYTHINGS OF THE PRIVATE HOUSE
Esme Ombreux

When Olena, nubile and much-appreciated guest at the secretive flagellant community that is the Private House, is kinapped, Supreme Mistress Jem Darke and her lover Julia, chief of the guards, are unusually at a loss as to what to do. But Talia, the fey, submissive but resourceful leader of the forest people, who live a bucolic but perverted life on the House's large estate, has evidence that leads to Madame la Patronne, Jem's rival in the arts of dominance. Jem, Julia, Talia and her lover Anne agree a plan of pursuit. Their actions lead them straight into deep sexual waters: how far will they be required to submit to Madame la Patronne, whose imperious sexuality knows no limits. And even if their tormented odyssey brings them to Oleana, will she even want to return?

ISBN 0 352 33761 3

CRUEL TRIUMPH
William Doughty

Alice is Steve's demon dominatrix, and red-hot lover and friend. After a few years of trust, commitment and fantastic sex, the couple are invited to a very special party at the sumptuous home of the successful, dominant and *very* perverted Kurt. Alice's interest is piqued, and Steve learns the hard way that he does not know the extremes of Alice's sexuality quite as well as he thinks he does. Just how far does Alice's new-found taste for submission extend beyond the realms of SM fantasy into reality? And will Steve lose Alice to the assertive Kurt, or will he find the strength within himnself to give Alice what she *really* wants.

ISBN 0 352 33759 1

THE HOUSE AT MALDONA
Yolanda Celbridge

There's a hidden world deep in the heart of southern Spain where the bizarre rituals of the Inquisition have survived to this day. A strange, some would say perverse, society of women has formed the House of Maldona. Like the Knights Templar of old, their lives are governed by a strict set of rules and a hierarchy based on discipline. When Jane, an adventurous young Chelsea girl, travels to Spain to look for her friends, she finds instead the welcoming arms of Maldona's lesbian elite. Becoming involved in their strange games and ceremonies, she is to discover shocking things about herself and her ancestors.

ISBN 0 352 33740 0

If you would like more information about Nexus titles, please visit our website at www.nexus-books.co.uk, or send a stamped addressed envelope to:

Nexus, Thames Wharf Studios,
Rainville Road, London W6 9HA

NEXUS BACKLIST

This information is correct at time of printing. For up-to-date information, please visit our website at www.nexus-books.co.uk

All books are priced at £5.99 unless another price is given.

Nexus books with a contemporary setting

ACCIDENTS WILL HAPPEN	Lucy Golden ISBN 0 352 33596 3	☐
ANGEL	Lindsay Gordon ISBN 0 352 33590 4	☐
BARE BEHIND £6.99	Penny Birch ISBN 0 352 33721 4	☐
BEAST	Wendy Swanscombe ISBN 0 352 33649 8	☐
THE BLACK FLAME	Lisette Ashton ISBN 0 352 33668 4	☐
BROUGHT TO HEEL	Arabella Knight ISBN 0 352 33508 4	☐
CAGED!	Yolanda Celbridge ISBN 0 352 33650 1	☐
CANDY IN CAPTIVITY	Arabella Knight ISBN 0 352 33495 9	☐
CAPTIVES OF THE PRIVATE HOUSE	Esme Ombreux ISBN 0 352 33619 6	☐
CHERI CHASTISED £6.99	Yolanda Celbridge ISBN 0 352 33707 9	☐
DANCE OF SUBMISSION	Lisette Ashton ISBN 0 352 33450 9	☐
DIRTY LAUNDRY £6.99	Penny Birch ISBN 0 352 33680 3	☐
DISCIPLINED SKIN	Wendy Swanscombe ISBN 0 352 33541 6	☐

DISPLAYS OF EXPERIENCE	Lucy Golden	☐
	ISBN 0 352 33505 X	
DISPLAYS OF PENITENTS	Lucy Golden	☐
£6.99	ISBN 0 352 33646 3	
DRAWN TO DISCIPLINE	Tara Black	☐
	ISBN 0 352 33626 9	
EDEN UNVEILED	Maria del Rey	☐
	ISBN 0 352 32542 4	
AN EDUCATION IN THE	Esme Ombreux	☐
PRIVATE HOUSE	ISBN 0 352 33525 4	
EMMA'S SECRET DOMINATION	Hilary James	☐
	ISBN 0 352 33226 3	
GISELLE	Jean Aveline	☐
	ISBN 0 352 33440 1	
GROOMING LUCY	Yvonne Marshall	☐
	ISBN 0 352 33529 7	
HEART OF DESIRE	Maria del Rey	☐
	ISBN 0 352 32900 9	
HIS MISTRESS'S VOICE	G. C. Scott	☐
	ISBN 0 352 33425 8	
IN FOR A PENNY	Penny Birch	☐
	ISBN 0 352 33449 5	
INTIMATE INSTRUCTION	Arabella Knight	☐
	ISBN 0 352 33618 8	
THE LAST STRAW	Christina Shelly	☐
	ISBN 0 352 33643 9	
NURSES ENSLAVED	Yolanda Celbridge	☐
	ISBN 0 352 33601 3	
THE ORDER	Nadine Somers	☐
	ISBN 0 352 33460 6	
THE PALACE OF EROS	Delver Maddingley	☐
£4.99	ISBN 0 352 32921 1	
PALE PLEASURES	Wendy Swanscombe	☐
£6.99	ISBN 0 352 33702 8	
PEACHES AND CREAM	Aishling Morgan	☐
£6.99	ISBN 0 352 33672 2	

PEEPING AT PAMELA	Yolanda Celbridge ISBN 0 352 33538 6	☐
PENNY PIECES	Penny Birch ISBN 0 352 33631 5	☐
PET TRAINING IN THE PRIVATE HOUSE	Esme Ombreux ISBN 0 352 33655 2	☐
REGIME £6.99	Penny Birch ISBN 0 352 33666 8	☐
RITUAL STRIPES £6.99	Tara Black ISBN 0 352 33701 X	☐
SEE-THROUGH	Lindsay Gordon ISBN 0 352 33656 0	☐
SILKEN SLAVERY	Christina Shelly ISBN 0 352 33708 7	☐
SKIN SLAVE	Yolanda Celbridge ISBN 0 352 33507 6	☐
SLAVE ACTS £6.99	Jennifer Jane Pope ISBN 0 352 33665 X	☐
THE SLAVE AUCTION	Lisette Ashton ISBN 0 352 33481 9	☐
SLAVE GENESIS	Jennifer Jane Pope ISBN 0 352 33503 3	☐
SLAVE REVELATIONS	Jennifer Jane Pope ISBN 0 352 33627 7	☐
SLAVE SENTENCE	Lisette Ashton ISBN 0 352 33494 0	☐
SOLDIER GIRLS	Yolanda Celbridge ISBN 0 352 33586 6	☐
THE SUBMISSION GALLERY	Lindsay Gordon ISBN 0 352 33370 7	☐
SURRENDER	Laura Bowen ISBN 0 352 33524 6	☐
THE TAMING OF TRUDI £6.99	Yolanda Celbridge ISBN 0 352 33673 0	☐
TEASING CHARLOTTE £6.99	Yvonne Marshall ISBN 0 352 33681 1	☐
TEMPER TANTRUMS	Penny Birch ISBN 0 352 33647 1	☐

THE TORTURE CHAMBER	Lisette Ashton	☐
	ISBN 0 352 33530 0	
UNIFORM DOLL	Penny Birch	☐
£6.99	ISBN 0 352 33698 6	
WHIP HAND	G. C. Scott	☐
£6.99	ISBN 0 352 33694 3	
THE YOUNG WIFE	Stephanie Calvin	☐
	ISBN 0 352 33502 5	

Nexus books with Ancient and Fantasy settings

CAPTIVE	Aishling Morgan	☐
	ISBN 0 352 33585 8	
DEEP BLUE	Aishling Morgan	☐
	ISBN 0 352 33600 5	
DUNGEONS OF LIDIR	Aran Ashe	☐
	ISBN 0 352 33506 8	
INNOCENT	Aishling Morgan	☐
£6.99	ISBN 0 352 33699 4	
MAIDEN	Aishling Morgan	☐
	ISBN 0 352 33466 5	
NYMPHS OF DIONYSUS	Susan Tinoff	☐
£4.99	ISBN 0 352 33150 X	
PLEASURE TOY	Aishling Morgan	☐
	ISBN 0 352 33634 X	
SLAVE MINES OF TORMUNIL	Aran Ashe	☐
£6.99	ISBN 0 352 33695 1	
THE SLAVE OF LIDIR	Aran Ashe	☐
	ISBN 0 352 33504 1	
TIGER, TIGER	Aishling Morgan	☐
	ISBN 0 352 33455 X	

Period

CONFESSION OF AN ENGLISH SLAVE	Yolanda Celbridge	☐
	ISBN 0 352 33433 9	
THE MASTER OF CASTLELEIGH	Jacqueline Bellevois	☐
	ISBN 0 352 32644 7	
PURITY	Aishling Morgan	☐
	ISBN 0 352 33510 6	
VELVET SKIN	Aishling Morgan	☐
	ISBN 0 352 33660 9	

Samplers and collections

NEW EROTICA 5	Various ISBN 0 352 33540 8	☐
EROTICON 1	Various ISBN 0 352 33593 9	☐
EROTICON 2	Various ISBN 0 352 33594 7	☐
EROTICON 3	Various ISBN 0 352 33597 1	☐
EROTICON 4	Various ISBN 0 352 33602 1	☐
THE NEXUS LETTERS	Various ISBN 0 352 33621 8	☐
SATURNALIA £7.99	ed. Paul Scott ISBN 0 352 33717 6	☐
MY SECRET GARDEN SHED £7.99	ed. Paul Scott ISBN 0 352 33725 7	☐

Nexus Classics

A new imprint dedicated to putting the finest works of erotic fiction back in print.

AMANDA IN THE PRIVATE HOUSE £6.99	Esme Ombreux ISBN 0 352 33705 2	☐
BAD PENNY	Penny Birch ISBN 0 352 33661 7	☐
BRAT £6.99	Penny Birch ISBN 0 352 33674 9	☐
DARK DELIGHTS £6.99	Maria del Rey ISBN 0 352 33667 6	☐
DARK DESIRES	Maria del Rey ISBN 0 352 33648 X	☐
DISPLAYS OF INNOCENTS £6.99	Lucy Golden ISBN 0 352 33679 X	☐
DISCIPLINE OF THE PRIVATE HOUSE £6.99	Esme Ombreux ISBN 0 352 33459 2	☐
EDEN UNVEILED	Maria del Rey ISBN 0 352 33542 4	☐

HIS MISTRESS'S VOICE	G. C. Scott ISBN 0 352 33425 8	☐
THE INDIGNITIES OF ISABELLE £6.99	Penny Birch writing as Cruella ISBN 0 352 33696 X	☐
LETTERS TO CHLOE	Stefan Gerrard ISBN 0 352 33632 3	☐
MEMOIRS OF A CORNISH GOVERNESS £6.99	Yolanda Celbridge ISBN 0 352 33722 2	☐
ONE WEEK IN THE PRIVATE HOUSE £6.99	Esme Ombreux ISBN 0 352 33706 0	☐
PARADISE BAY	Maria del Rey ISBN 0 352 33645 5	☐
PENNY IN HARNESS	Penny Birch ISBN 0 352 33651 X	☐
THE PLEASURE PRINCIPLE	Maria del Rey ISBN 0 352 33482 7	☐
PLEASURE ISLAND	Aran Ashe ISBN 0 352 33628 5	☐
SISTERS OF SEVERCY	Jean Aveline ISBN 0 352 33620 X	☐
A TASTE OF AMBER	Penny Birch ISBN 0 352 33654 4	☐

------ ✄ -----------------------------

Please send me the books I have ticked above.

Name   ....

Address   ....

            ....

            ....

            .... Post code....................

Send to: **Cash Sales, Nexus Books, Thames Wharf Studios, Rainville Road, London W6 9HA**

US customers: for prices and details of how to order books for delivery by mail, call 1-800-343-4499.

Please enclose a cheque or postal order, made payable to **Nexus Books Ltd**, to the value of the books you have ordered plus postage and packing costs as follows:

UK and BFPO – £1.00 for the first book, 50p for each subsequent book.

Overseas (including Republic of Ireland) – £2.00 for the first book, £1.00 for each subsequent book.

If you would prefer to pay by VISA, ACCESS/MASTERCARD, AMEX, DINERS CLUB or SWITCH, please write your card number and expiry date here:

....

Please allow up to 28 days for delivery.

Signature ....

Our privacy policy.

We will not disclose information you supply us to any other parties. We will not disclose any information which identifies you personally to any person without your express consent.

From time to time we may send out information about Nexus books and special offers. Please tick here if you do *not* wish to receive Nexus information. ☐

------ ✄ -----------------------------